LEIF

VIKING GLORY

CELESTE BARCLAY

All rights reserved.

No part of this publication may be sold, copied, distributed, reproduced or transmitted in any form or by any means, mechanical or digital, including photocopying and recording or by any information storage and retrieval system without the prior written permission of both the publisher, Oliver Heber Books and the author, Celeste Barclay, except in the case of brief quotations embodied in critical articles and reviews.

PUBLISHER'S NOTE: This is a work of fiction. Names, characters, places, and incidents either are the product of the author's imagination or used fictitiously. Any resemblance to actual persons, living or dead, business establishments, events, or locales is entirely coincidental.

Copyright © by Celeste Barclay.

0 9 8 7 6 5 4 3 2 1

Published by Oliver Heber Books

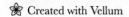 Created with Vellum

Thank you to all my readers who continue to encourage my imagination and creativity. You make me confident enough to keep writing and sharing.

Happy reading, y'all.

Celeste

VIKING GLORY

Leif
Freya
Tyra & Bjorn
Strian
Lena & Ivar

LEIF'S FAMILY TREE

ONE

Leif looked around his chambers within his father's longhouse and breathed a sigh of relief. He noticed the large fur rugs spread throughout the chamber. His two favorites placed strategically before the fire and the bedside he preferred. He looked at his shield that hung on the wall near the door in a symbolic position but waiting at the ready. The chests that held his clothes and some of his finer acquisitions from voyages near and far sat beside his bed and along the far wall. And in the center was his most favorite possession. His oversized bed was one of the few that could accommodate his long and broad frame. He shook his head at his longing to climb under the pile of furs and onto the stuffed mattress that beckoned him. He took in the chair placed before the fire where he longed to sit now with a cup of warm mead. It had been two months since he slept in his own bed, and he looked forward to nothing more than pulling the furs over his head and sleeping until he could no longer ignore his hunger. Alas, he would not be crawling into his bed again for several more hours. A feast awaited him to celebrate his and his crew's return from their latest expedition to explore the isle of Britannia. He bathed and wore fresh clothes, so he had no excuse for lingering other than a bone weariness that set in during the last storm at sea. He was eager to spend time at home no matter how much he loved sailing. Their last expedition had been profitable with several raids of monasteries that yielded jewels and both silver and gold, but he was ready for respite.

Leif left his chambers and knocked on the door next to his. He heard movement on the other side, but it was only moments before his sister, Freya, opened her door. She, too, looked tired but clean. A few pieces of jewelry she confiscated from the holy houses that allegedly swore to a life of poverty and deprivation adorned her trim frame.

"That armband suits you well. It compliments your muscles." Leif smirked and dodged a strike from one of those muscular arms.

Only a year younger than he, his sister was a well-known and feared shieldmaiden. Her lithe form was strong and agile making her a ferocious and competent opponent to any man. Freya's beauty was stunning, but Leif had taken every opportunity since they were children to tease her about her unusual strength, even among the female warriors.

"At least one of us inherited our father's prowess. Such a shame it wasn't you."

Leif laughed as he wrapped his arm around his sister's shoulders and escorted her outside. Once they stepped beyond the door, he dropped his arm before she could shrug it off. He was close to his sister, and he counted her as his closest confidante besides their cousin, Bjorn, but he knew of how self-conscious she was about proving herself to everyone in their village. As the daughter of the jarl, her tribe expected her to make a good wife to another jarl, but they also expected her to defend her people. Freya and Leif were their parents' only surviving children. She strove to be the best inside and outside of the longhouse. Freya worked twice as hard as most so she could master the skills of running a household while also mastering the skills of a fighter. She didn't like to look as though her father or brother coddled her, even though she adored their protectiveness as much as their confidence in her.

"Are you looking forward to the feast?" Freya asked.

"I am looking forward to my bed more."

"And who will warm it tonight? Who will catch your eye?"

"Actually, tonight I would prefer to retire alone. I crave sleep more than I crave a woman."

"That would be a first," Freya snorted.

"Who do you have your eye on?"

"I, too, look forward to sleeping alone. But nobody expects anything different from me."

"You're just more discreet."

"I just have fewer options."

Leif shrugged knowing that was the truth. Few men attempted to look at his sister, let alone touch her. There had been a few, but Freya saw the wisdom in keeping her attachments short and uncomplicated for one day she would leave to make her home among another village with another jarl. She understood no husband would want a wife who was too knowledgeable about bed sport. For a bride in a political match, there was a stark difference between knowing enough to satisfy her new husband and knowing enough to make him suspicious of her fidelity and loyalty. Leif counted himself lucky in that area since people only expected him to enjoy himself before and after his marriage.

Freya entered the great hall ahead of Leif and moved to her spot at the head table, sitting next to their mother. Leif looked around and waved to several men who hailed him and attempted to place a mead horn into his hand. He drank sparingly as always. It was a rare occasion now when he let himself get so intoxicated that he was not in complete control of his faculties. He learned how dangerous that was as a young man. Too much alcohol led him to bed the wrong woman whose husband did not like to share, and he came close to losing his life for a night he couldn't even remember.

Leif sat to his father's right with his mother and sister to his father's left. His cousin, Bjorn, already sat to his right.

"You came," Bjorn observed.

"You know, like I do, none of us could miss this. Look at the men. They're enjoying the feast and revelry. We couldn't disappoint everyone by not appearing."

"I don't know how they cannot crave peace and quiet as much as we do after such a long time spent together."

"I am beginning to think you, Freya, and I are the strange ones."

"Perhaps. But that doesn't mean I don't still want to retire early with a willing woman and then lose myself to sleep for a full moon."

"If that's the case, no one will fault you for retiring early. You know neither Freya nor I will leave with someone, so we're stuck here until the end. Even after Mother and Father retire."

Leif sighed and forced himself not to swipe his hand across his face. He looked around the crowded hall and envied the others their merriment and light heartedness. The voyage was a financial success but with more setbacks than usual. Weather delayed them in both directions and fighting with another band of Norsemen had cost them many men before they even landed in Scotland. Responsibility of captaining the ships lay at the hands of Leif, Bjorn, Freya, and their two other closest friends, Tyra and Strian. The five warriors grew up together in the Trondelag and captained their ships after being sent off on expeditions without their fathers. Tyra was the daughter of his father's cousin, and Strian was the son of his father's previous warrior captain.

Leif looked around and found Tyra and Strian sitting with their families at the table closest to the jarl's. They looked as exhausted as he did, but they both seemed to enjoy the festivities. They had the responsibility of their own ships and men, but the overall expedition rested on his shoulders, and he only shared the burden with Freya and Bjorn.

"You need a woman between your sheets and between your legs," Bjorn teased.

"That may well be, but I need sleep far more."

"Old man. You must work out your cock to keep it in shape, or it'll shrivel up like an old man's sword arm."

"If that were the case, your cock should be the strongest in the village. Yet that isn't what I hear from many of the women." Leif laughed as Bjorn looked ready to smash in his teeth.

"Perhaps they only say that to make you feel better."

Leif laughed even harder, but it was cut short when the door to the hall swung open and a contingent of warriors, who did not belong to his father, strode in. Leif recognized Rangvald Thorsson as the bear of a man who led the pack. They approached, and his father stood when their unexpected guests arrived at the head table.

"What brings you here, Rangvald? It's good to see you, old friend, but we weren't expecting you," boomed Ivar Sorenson. Leif glanced at his father to see if he might determine his real reaction to the neighboring jarl's arrival. His father seemed relaxed for once, unlike his usual tense and wary disposition.

"Would that I brought good news and a desire to make merry as I see your people are now."

Leif noticed the blood splatter and mud that crusted Rangvald's boots and the bottom of his leather trousers. Ivar nodded and laid his hand on Leif's shoulder.

"Perhaps we should retire to my chambers for this conversation," Ivar suggested. Leif rose to follow his father along with Bjorn. His father shook his head as Freya moved to join them. Anger then resignation flashed in her eyes. "It's not like that, Daughter. I need you to watch his men. See how they behave, their mood, and report back. They won't suspect anything if it's you who mingles rather than your brother." Ivar murmured for only their ears.

Freya nodded and looked mollified even if Leif knew she still wasn't pleased about being excluded. He looked over his shoulder to see his sister move toward the men with a mead pitcher. Her graceful movements and beauty caught their attention, and Leif wanted to stay behind to protect her.

"Strian will watch her," Bjorn reminded him. Ensconced in Leif's father's war room, the men wasted no time in discussing Rangvald's arrival.

"Hakin Hakinsson has been testing our borders again. We caught some of his men on both your land and mine. They've been menacing the shepherds and stealing livestock. It's more than just a war band attempting to harass us. He means to invade our lands. His reach doesn't match his ambition, but he thinks it does. Hakin would end the truce and take his chances against both of us. He believes we won't seek one another's support."

"He believes the old rumors we harbor rancor for one another after I didn't marry your sister." It was a statement not a question. It was well-known in the Trondelag that Ivar's father betrothed him to Rangvald's sister, Inga, from childhood. They even attempted a trial marriage but were ill suited to each other, and Ivar was already in love with Leif's mother, Lena. Inga, tired of living as a second-place choice, returned home within a moon. Rumors spread that Rangvald held a grudge, but it was not the case. Rangvald had tried to convince his father not to send Inga as Lena was no secret to anyone. However, Rangvald and Ivar allowed the rumors to continue as it served a purpose. It allowed them to each collect information from other jarls and villages that otherwise would not share if it was common knowledge that they were allies.

Now, Ivar looked at Rangvald and stroked his beard, twirling the beaded ends between his fingers. He studied the man and took in the same blood and mud that Leif noticed. "You would have us make our alliance public."

"I see no other way. If we fight on our own, we waste time and resources. Hakin won't fight on two fronts. He will attack one of us and then move to the other. We have a choice. We can either meet him as a unified army or one of us faces him head on while the other attacks from the rear, trapping them in the middle. Either way, we won't fare well if we try to go it alone. We can win, of that I am sure, but losing men and resources is unnecessary if we fight together."

"I would have to say I agree. How many men can you bring? I have about two hundred here I can send and still keep a hundred to protect the village."

"I have the same."

"And Hakin?"

"He would match us. He didn't leave as many men at home."

"Father, why not lead Hakin to our land, but rather than meet him, we go to his home and attack there?" Leif interrupted. "We wipe out his home, his food stores, his people, and then he won't have the means to fight us. We then trap him between our armies. Without a place to retreat and no means to move forward, we can end this once and for all."

"And what of our people? Do they face him while we make our way to his home? Why not go to his home after we defeat him?" Ivar reasoned.

"Evacuate our people and lead him to an isolated area. We cannot guarantee how many men we'll have after the battle. We use our full force now to leave nothing for him to return to in case he is victorious." Leif darted his eyes among the men gathered. Bjorn nodded while Rangvald and Ivar appeared throughtful.

Ivar and Rangvald exchanged a look before Ivar nodded his head. "And just where would you have us lead him?"

"We push him back into the mountain pass near Stjordal. We can trap him there."

Rangvald held up his hand to interrupt father and son as they negotiated. "Your son is right. If he travels further south than Stjordal, he will reach our main settlements in Maere and Egge. We would do well to stop him now. If we send men with longboats north, we can attack his home while he is away. Then those men will attack from the rear."

"And whose men would that be?" Ivar asked.

"Does it matter?" Rangvald replied.

"No. But we can load the fresh supplies here into our boats. You don't have much, I am sure, after your journey here. I will send Leif with the others to Steinkjer, and once the settlement is nothing but ash, he will meet us near Stjordal. How long do you think we have?"

"A week maybe. That would be at the most. I don't believe he knows I sailed here," Rangvald explained. "I must return to my home and prepare my people."

"Leif returned only this morning. Their boats need repairing tonight and into the early morning. The men need a night's sleep rather than a night of feasting. I don't look forward to disappointing them, but there is no other choice if they're to prepare for sailing in the morning." Ivar looked at his son and nephew. "Gather Freya, Strian, and Tyra. We must plan."

Ivar and Rangvald moved back to the main hall to announce the change in plans while Leif and Bjorn signaled for the others to join them. Leif watched as Bjorn's face grew red and a scowl deeper than usual settled between his brows. Leif followed Bjorn's gaze but could find nothing unusual. Freya and Tyra were among Rangvald's men. Freya stood behind one as she poured mead, and Tyra sat on one man's lap and seemed to be listening intently to his tale.

"What's the matter?"

"Where is Strian? He's supposed to be watching Tyra and Freya?"

"He is. Look to the left of the room. He is watching them and everything that goes on around them."

"But he isn't close enough if one of those men decides he'd like to explore."

"Bjorn, no man would touch Freya. Everyone knows she is the jarl's daughter, and I doubt any man is foolish enough to think they could take from Tyra anything she doesn't offer. She's likely to cut off their hand before asking questions."

Bjorn grunted, but his face relaxed. Leif signaled for the other three to join him and Bjorn. They moved back into the jarl's war room to discuss the new developments. "What did you learn?" Leif asked his sister.

"Hakin is making moves toward the border of our lands. He's already been spotted stealing livestock. He's even set a few fields ablaze after stealing from the harvest."

"Rangvald's men are eager for the fight. Their blood is up, and they believe they can already smell victory," Tyra added.

Bjorn worked his jaw and forced himself not to snap at Tyra's recklessness if she knew the men were already excitable. Tyra's parents died in a fire when the group was still young. He, Leif, and Strian had sworn a blood oath to protect her as though she was their own sister. She lived with an aunt and uncle along with their children, but Bjorn still felt compelled to keep a close eye on her.

"They are eager to fight and believe this should be an easy win," Tyra continued.

"It is a foolish man who goes into battle assuming he will win," Strian commented. "Those aren't the men I want to depend upon."

"I agree, but the alliance stands, and it will serve us well. Father has agreed that we should attack Hakin's holding while he is away. Burn it to the ground if we can. Then we join Rangvald but from the rear. We will trap Hakin between our armies near Stjordal," Leif explained.

"You would push him inland away from his boats, and ours, and then box him into one of the mountain passes." Freya nodded her head. "We must sail to Steinkjer if this is the goal. I assume we will leave in the morning. If time wasn't a concern, Rangvald wouldn't have come. He would have sent a messenger instead. He came in person to convey the urgency."

"You're right. He believes there's less than a week until Hakin will be close enough to engage. We need to evacuate our people to the coast in case Hakin breaks free, but we'll leave a hundred men behind and two long boats in case they must escape. We sail at first light," Bjorn shared.

"Will our boats be ready in time? Mine took serious damage during the last storm. The entire hull needs refitting but there are several patches needed at least." Strian looked doubtful.

"Mine too, Strian. The shipbuilders will work all night to ensure we're ready. We need to oversee the loading of supplies and prepare the men for the journey," Bjorn answered.

"I don't envy you being there when the men learn their feasting is over," Freya linked arms with Tyra and skirted the large table that held maps and other scrolls. "We have our own ships to tend to."

"Sister—" but it did no good. Freya and Tyra were already through the doorway. Leif bit back a curse, but he appreciated his sister's wisdom to have the two women away from the men when their father shared the news that none would retire for their own private feast. "Perhaps my father will have already told them."

"Afraid to tell the men that if they haven't already swyved a woman, they're out of luck now?" Strian inquired.

"Afraid? No. Dreading it? Yes."

Strian clapped Leif on the back with a chuckle. "The joys of being a jarl."

Leif just nodded.

TWO

The entire settlement worked throughout the night to prepare for the warriors' departure. There was little sleep for anyone. Just before dawn, the sailors were all sent to their homes for a few hours of rest. None of the captains wanted disaster to strike from a crew too tired to man their places. Leif dragged himself from his bed after far too little time under his furs. Once again, he glanced around his chamber and longed for time to sleep.

I shall sleep when I am dead, I suppose.

It was little consolation, but he would have to make do. He gathered his belongings and waited for his sister to emerge from her chambers. She carried even less than he did. He always marveled at how she traveled with less than any man he knew but still had clean clothes. It was as though her sack was bottomless, yet it was smaller than his.

"I could have done with another day of sleep," Freya grumbled. "I should like to run Hakin through myself for stealing my time of rest."

"Only if I don't get to him first."

They arrived at the docks as the village gathered to send off the men and women who would defend their land. Leif and Freya hugged their mother goodbye while their father embraced Freya and clapped Leif on the back. Warriors were already boarding boats, and sailors stowed supplies in the holds along with several horses. Rangvald's men were busy preparing their own ships for departure.

"Who's that?" Tyra asked as she joined her fellow captains and jarl. She pointed to a longboat that was just appearing around a bend in the fjord.

Freya shielded her eyes and squinted to make out the sails. "Looks to be another of Rangvald's ships."

"Rangvald!" Ivar called to his fellow jarl. "You seem to have visitors."

Rangvald and his other captains joined them. "That is Erik's ship. He's supposed to be guarding the homestead."

"I wondered where your son was."

"He hadn't returned from his last fishing voyage before we left. I gave instructions he was to remain at home in my place. Something must have brought him here."

Crews continued to ready the boats while Rangvald, Ivar, and the others waited for the new boat to dock.

"Erik Rangvaldson, we didn't expect you," Ivar boomed when a large blond man came into view at the bow.

"I look for my father," an equally deep voice replied. "I see I have found him." The man jumped from the ship before it docked and waded to shore.

"Son, you're supposed to be at home."

"Sigrid's been taken," Erik stated in place of a greeting.

"What? How?"

"She was in the woods collecting plants and casting runes to prepare us for the coming battle when a band of men rode off with her. One of the shepherd boys saw it happen and ran back to the village. I didn't arrive until the next day. Men were already out scouting, but they lost the trail when rain washed away any markers. All they knew was the men were taking her north."

"Back to Steinkjer. Why not to Hakin himself?" Freya asked as she sized up the man before her.

Erik returned her frank assessment with clear appreciation before turning back to his father. "We don't think he stole her, so she could assist him but to keep her from assisting us."

"She's your seer?" Freya wondered.

"Yes, and my niece. Sigrid Torbensdóttir," Rangvald answered.

"Why did you sail here and not after her?" Freya questioned Erik.

"Freya!" Leif growled.

"It is a reasonable question. If she is of value to Rangvald's people, why not follow her to her obvious destination? Coming here only wastes time."

"Freya, enough," Ivar interjected.

"It's fine. She's right to ask such questions. I didn't have the men to follow her, and as you can see, my longboat's meant for fishing not for war. My war ship is here, captained by my first mate. When I left with a few men to fish, I didn't expect to need to rescue my cousin. If I sailed north with this boat, the chances of success would be slim. This boat wouldn't withstand the water near Steinkjer. You can see that. We would lose both Sigrid and my men."

Freya looked past Erik's shoulder before looking at him and nodding. A faint smile graced Erik's lips at her approval before he turned serious and addressed his father.

"I would have my ship back and send Harold with the fishing boat back to guard the village. I will go for Sigrid now."

"That makes little sense. We plan to sail for Steinkjer ourselves. We will recover your seer and destroy Hakin's holding," Leif looked to Ivar and Rangvald.

"He is right, Ivar. While I would rather have my son fetch her, it's not a good use of our men to send him along with your fighters. I need Erik and his men alongside me when we face Hakin head on. That means returning home first to gather our army."

"I believe you have much to catch me up on, Father." Erik looked around the gathered warriors.

"You are right. You shall sail back with me as I share our plans." Rangvald wrapped his thick arm around his son's shoulders and pulled him in for a quick embrace before both men turned toward their boats, but not before Erik cast Freya another grin. She returned it before scowling. They could hear Erik's laughter as the two men walked away.

"Don't," Freya hissed to Tyra, who only shrugged and smiled. The two women moved toward their boats, leaving the men to stare after them.

"Keep an eye on your sister and Rangvald's son." Ivar muttered to Leif before he and Lena left the three remaining captains to board their ships. Leif oversaw the final preparations for their ships. Rangvald and his crew set sail, and Ivar's ships awaited their turn to launch. Ivar approached, waving his son over. "Leif, I would have one more word with you."

Something in his voice made Leif wary, and a prickle of warning ran down his back. He looked at the man he admired above all others but did not resemble in the least. While Freya was a near replica of their mother, Leif bore a resemblance to his mother but not his father. His father's copper hair stood out along with his barrel chest and booming voice. Leif's sun-bleached hair was white in summer, and his broad back tapered to a narrow vee at his hips. The two looked so little alike that rumors circulated for years about his parentage, but anyone who met the two realized that nature had a wicked sense of humor. Mannerisms he could never have learned made it clear Leif was his father's son. As a babe, Leif's temper and scowls matched his father's when he was hungry or overtired. Ivar's men noticed that when sleeping under the stars, both slept in the same position with one leg bent and the other crossed over it at the ankle. They walked and sat the same way, shared a sharp wit, and turnips made them both violently ill.

"Yes, Father."

"This seer, Sigrid, is known to be shy but a great beauty. You are to bring her to her uncle. Untouched." Ivar gave him a pointed look. "I haven't arranged a marriage for you, but we're already allied with Rangvald, so we don't need a marriage to his people. I haven't forced the issue, but I believe I will make inquiries when you return. You and your sister both are long overdue to find mates rather than bedwarmers."

"Father, why the warning? You've never issued one before."

"You'll understand when you meet the woman. She isn't yours to have. Complete the mission, then join us with Rangvald. I shall travel overland to meet his army. I would see for myself the damage Hakin has caused."

"Father—"

"Enough," Ivar barked loudly enough for others to turn their head.

Leif straightened to his full height as he scanned those who watched them. "As you wish. But know that I will not wed an unwilling bride nor one I cannot like."

"Fair enough. I wed your mother because I have loved her since we were children. I would wish the same for you."

"And if it isn't with a bride of your choosing?"

"We shall solve that problem if it should arise. May the gods be with you."

"For Odin."

"For Odin."

The two men embraced again before Leif boarded his ship. As the five longboats pulled away from the docks, Leif thought over what his father said. He didn't understand why his father warned him away from this woman, but his father's comments gave him a moment of pause when he remembered that the seer, Sigrid, was shy. Leif looked to the ships that followed him and saw Freya's white-blonde head moving about her ship and then Tyra's darker one at the helm of her own boat. He thanked Odin for sending the two women along with him. Leif suspected they would be of great help in convincing the young woman to come along with strangers.

The two-day voyage north was smooth with wind at their backs the entire way. They found a narrow fjord to drop anchor just south of Hakin's settlement at Steinkjer. They continued on foot as they approached the large village. There was clear prosperity and a comfortable lifestyle. There were also few guards left behind because Hakin assumed no one would dare attack him. His assumptions would be his downfall.

"We wait until nightfall when we can encircle the village. Tyra and Freya, your crews will round up the women and children. Bring them outside the walls and away from where we'll set the fires. Strian, you and Bjorn will move to the longhouses while I find the armory. Take any able-bodied man willing to surrender. We will divide the thralls among all of our boats to keep them from banding together."

"You would leave the women and children here? Alone?"

"Freya, we do not wage war against women and children."

"Did I ever say we should? You arrogant arse. You are the one who would by leaving them with no protection or means to hunt and farm. Your war would be one of starvation. They come on my ship as my thralls."

"Father didn't say we're to bring anyone other than the seer back."

"Then you will be the one who kills them and gives them mercy."

"Mercy?" Mercy was a foreign idea to most Vikings. Death in battle was the finest form of glory for a warrior, but mercy was a sign of weakness. Freya knew this just like the others, and she backed her brother into a corner. "Freya, you push the bounds of brotherly love and patience."

"That may be, but would you rather have me starve than live the life of one of our thralls if I were in their situation?"

"And you question me about mercy?" Leif surveyed his sister, knowing what they all did. Killing them on their own land would be better than being enslaved for the rest of their lives. Death would be a reprieve, be mercy, for them.

"This isn't mercy. It is practical. We can always use more servants and farm workers. Our people continue to multiply, and this means we have need of more workers to support our farms and households."

Brother and sister exchanged a hard look while the others waited. They were used to these standoffs, and as often as Leif won, Freya won twice as often.

"They are your problem then. You must get them to your ship and deal with them until we return home. Tyra's ship will take the male thralls and already is near bursting with supplies." Leif crossed his arms.

"I would expect nothing else." Freya's smile could only be described as smug.

"It is a good thing she's your sister and not your wife. You'd never have use of your own balls again if she were," Strian laughed.

"It's just as well she fights like a berserker and has a mind more cunning than any man we know," Leif mused.

"Where do you think they have her held?" Bjorn brought them back to the task at hand.

"With Hakin not here, I would imagine in the kitchens," Freya answered.

"Then Strian and I will find her and bring her back to the meeting point," Bjorn suggested.

"Remember, she's shy. Don't scare the shite out of her," Freya warned.

The group disbanded as each captain found his or her crew and moved into position. Just after dusk, they launched their attack. With few to defend the settlement, the battle was over before it began. They rounded up the surviving men, women, and children, but there was one person missing. No one could find the seer.

"Where in Odin's name could she be? She wasn't in a longhouse, the armory, or in other storage buildings." Strian wiped blood from his sword as he looked around. Leif shook his head and wiped sweat from his forehead before another drop could sting his eyes.

Tyra stepped away from the group and stared into the tree line. She thought she saw a faint light bobbing in the distance. She took off at a run, calling back over her shoulder, "I know where she is, but she won't be there long. At least, not alive."

Nothing more was said when the others spotted the same light she had. The men overtook Tyra and Freya, but they were not far behind. They entered the woods just in time to see a man in a dark robe rear his arm back in preparation to draw his knife blade across a young woman's throat. Someone had stretched the woman across an altar naked. She held so still the slender figure was difficult to discern in the dark. Freya pulled her bow from her shoulder and nocked an arrow as she drew back the string. The arrow flew with pinpoint accuracy and buried itself between the man's shoulders.

Leif moved forward, but Tyra blocked him. "No. Let me and Freya go first."

Leif tried to step around her, but Tyra would not budge. The woman was not as muscularly built as his sister, but it was to her advantage. Men always underestimated her strength, and she capitalized on that along with her agility to gain the upper hand as she did now. Tyra pushed her weight into Leif's chest and nearly unbalanced him. "I'm sure she's terrified. The woman doesn't need three blood-soaked giants surrounding her when she's naked and tied to an altar. Stay here."

Leif looked down at her as Bjorn and Strian came to stand beside him.

"She's right," Strian whispered. "Let the woman have her dignity. Let Freya and Tyra release her and cover her up before she meets us. There's no doubt she has seen us already."

Leif and Bjorn nodded. Freya and Tyra crept to the altar and found a beaten woman. Freya slipped the leather vest off her shoulders leaving a linen tunic underneath. Tyra cut a large swath from the bottom of her own tunic. Freya and Tyra worked to cut the woman's bindings and to help her off the altar. Her legs gave out, but Freya and Tyra caught her before she could collapse.

"Take my vest and use the fabric from Tyra's tunic to wrap yourself in a skirt. It will be enough to cover you until we can get you back to our ships," Freya explained.

The young woman didn't need to be told twice as she cast looks toward the three hulking forms that watched them. It was too dark for her to make out their faces, so she knew she had a modicum of privacy as she put on the improvised clothing.

"Who are you? How did you know I was here?"

"I'm Freya Ivarsdóttir, and this is Tyra Sveinsdóttir. Your jarl, Rangvald Thorsson, sent us to find you, Sigrid, while we attacked Hakin's home."

"You're a jarl's daughter?" Sigrid wobbled as she attempted a bow, but her legs still weren't steady enough.

"Yes. My brother, our cousin, and friends led the raid." Freya gestured with her head to the men who stood behind her. "We can explain once we're aboard my boat. We cannot linger any longer."

Leif's patience was finished. He watched as the younger woman tottered, looking close to collapsing twice. He marched forward once he saw the women were only talking. "Can you not natter later? We must be on our way." Leif drew up short when the young woman's face came into view from the torches near the altar. He sucked in a breath as he took in her tousled hair and battered face.

"Who did this?" he seethed. Sigrid gasped as she looked at

Leif for the first time. She shook her head and tried to back up.

"You," Sigrid whispered. "It's you."

"Do you know me?" The woman's reaction perplexed Leif. "Have we already met?"

Sigrid shook her head again, but her eyes were large in her sallow and tired face. "He is dead."

"Who is?" Leif wondered, confused by the change in subject, his curiosity piqued by her earlier comment.

"You asked who beat me. The man is dead." Sigrid pointed to the ground. "One of you put an arrow in his back."

"Then we must be on our way." Leif turned away but heard the gasp and then the scuffle as Freya and Tyra caught the woman when her knees refused to bear her weight anymore. Leif stepped forward and swept her into his arms. He felt her go rigid for a moment before she looked into his stormy gray eyes. Something passed between them before she rested her head against his shoulder and closed her own misty silver eyes. Leif caught a wisp of floral scent from her blonde hair that rested against his shoulder. His heart sped and heat rushed to his groin. The feel of her in his arms was better than any other woman had ever felt. He had barely touched her. She sighed but kept her eyes closed.

"You came."

"Did you know I was supposed to?"

"Yes." Sigrid's eyes flew open, and she attempted to sit up but almost fell out of Leif's arms. "My staff. I cannot leave without it. I must have it."

"You are the seer then."

"Yes." Sigrid continued to wriggle to get down. Her bottom brushed across the head of his already hard length, and he bit back a groan as he shifted her higher against his chest. "We shall bring your staff. We won't leave it behind."

Leif's words mollified her. She nodded as she watched him

before closing her eyes once again. "How'd you know someone would come?" Leif asked.

"Not someone. *You*."

"What do you mean?"

"Rangvald would have sent someone, most likely my cousin, but I knew I would meet you soon."

"How could you know that?" Leif wondered. Sigrid gave a wry laugh and raised one eyebrow even though both of her eyes remained closed. "You saw us meeting."

"I have."

"Have not had? You've seen it more than once?"

They reached the larger group of warriors and captives before they could say more.

"I'm Sigrid," she whispered to Leif.

"I know. I am Leif," he whispered back.

"I know." Her smile made Leif's heart skip. "Perhaps you should put me down now."

Leif shook his head, but at her confused look, he explained aloud to everyone, "This woman, Sigrid, is the woman we searched for. She is Rangvald Thorsson's seer and is under my protection." Sigrid stared up at him. He had all but declared her his woman. He explained for only her ears, "The men's lust will still run hot after the battle even if it was short and not very hard. I would have none of them think you are available to them. You are under my protection until we can return you to your jarl."

"Perhaps you could put me down now, so I look more like the seer I am and less like the concubine they now think I am," Sigrid stated abruptly.

"What? No." Leif looked around and saw the smirks from the men and the knowing looks from the women. He saw jealousy flash in the eyes of both men and women. He wasn't sure if his announcement had provided her the protection he intended.

"Leif, she'll travel with me. You may have intended well, but she's right. They will think you have claimed her for yourself to warm your bed. Father will be furious if such rumors reach him. I heard him before we left." Freya said no more, but her meaning was clear to Leif. She wasn't warning him away from Sigrid as much as she was warning him of their father. He nodded and watched as Freya escorted her guest aboard ship. As she reached the top of the rope ladder, she looked over her shoulder at Leif and nodded once.

"I heard you tell my brother you knew he would come. That you saw the two of you meeting." Freya didn't mince words.

"You have superb ears."

"For my brother's protection, I have the best."

"You believe he is the one in need of protection?"

"You are a seer. You cast runes to learn of our fates. You commune with the spirits in their world."

"Does that make me a danger?"

"It could." Freya crossed her arms as she examined the woman in the light from the torches hung on the mast's pegs. "You have the power to alter his fate."

"I do not. I may be a seer, but I cannot alter what the gods already have planned for us. I might see parts of that fate, and I may ask the gods to change their plans, but I am not the one to make those decisions. I'm not one of them, but a woman just as you are."

Freya looked long and hard at Sigrid. They were close in age. "How old are you?"

"I am two-and-twenty. My mother trained me from when I was a young girl, but I have been on my own for close to half my life. You?"

"Four-and-twenty. My brother is a year older. You're Rangvald's niece, so how could you be alone?"

"My mother was his sister, but she chose a cottage away from the village. She preferred us to have our space, so we might work in peace. There are those who believe we're little more than practitioners of the dark arts. They may look to us in times of fortune and celebrate our gifts, but when the fates no longer smile upon them, they force us to shoulder the blame for the unpredictability of our gods."

"Your uncle didn't lend you his protection?"

"Of course, he did, but my mother still preferred to stay away. Out of sight, out of mind. I followed her lead once she was gone."

"That didn't serve you well this time. They still stole you away." A look crossed Sigrid's face that made Freya squint as she stepped closer. "What are you not saying?"

Sigrid did not respond. Freya leaned so far forward that their noses almost touched, but Sigrid didn't flinch. She remained tight lipped and kept looking Freya in the eye. She'd seen more than enough in her lifetime, even in the past week, to not be cowed by anyone.

"I suggest you explain yourself because I hold little trust or patience for those who I believe are lying," Freya warned

"I have said nothing false."

"No, you may not have. But your omissions are lies of their own."

"What you believe to be omissions, I believe to be keeping my own council. We don't know each other. We would be fools to trust each other completely."

"You seemed to trust my brother completely and rather easily."

"So it seemed."

The two women stared at one another not making any headway until one of Freya's men came to her about setting their course. "This isn't nearly done."

"I didn't suspect it was."

"Freund! Find our guest food and a blanket," Freya called out to a boy of ten or twelve who scurried to follow his captain's orders.

Sigrid moved to the rail. She looked out over the waves as they sailed from the fjord into open water. She let the wind sweep over her and lift the hair from her warm face. She wrapped the blanket given to her around her shoulders as she watched a school of fish swim alongside the boat just under the surface, illuminated by the lanterns scattered about the deck. Sigrid breathed in the crisp and tangy saltwater air and let her eyes slide shut. Her mind summoned the sight of Leif but not as she had seen him that night.

Sigrid saw various versions from over the years. She saw Leif on the eve of his first battle when he was not much older than the boy, Freund. She saw him at a feast to celebrate the All Father during a fall harvest. His image in battle always disconcerted her the most. A blend of emotions that ranged from awe to fear to pride to relief surged through her during these visions of violence. All her mind's conjuring left her unsettled and in need of solitude that would be unavailable for the indefinite future. She watched the horizon despite the darkness, anchoring herself against the rolling of the boat. She sighed at last and moved away to find a spot out of the wind next to several large barrels. Sigrid pulled the blanket around herself once again with her staff tucked into the crook of her crossed arms. Sleep, something that had been elusive and dangerous for the last two days, claimed her.

THREE

The sun rose over the same horizon Sigrid gazed at in the dark when her eyes cracked open. She rubbed the sleep from them as she straightened her aching back and stretched her stiff limbs. She came to her feet and scanned the area around her. Sigrid saw land to the port side and a hazy mass to the starboard. She watched as the crew rowed hard now that they faced a headwind. Sigrid heard Freya calling orders as she stood at the helm. Freya looked like a goddess with her white-blonde hair braided with beads woven through them and dangling from the ends. Sigrid could see the sword strapped to her back and the knives that poked from her belt. She glanced at Freya's boots, sure that she saw at least two in each shoe. The woman wore more weapons than any man Sigrid ever met. Even her cousin, Erik, wore fewer, and he was the captain of his father's warriors. Freya must have sensed someone watching her because she locked gazes with Sigrid and offered her a small smile with a nod of her head.

It would seem we have come to a truce. We shall see how long it lasts. I would rather be with her than against her.

Freya spoke in hushed tones to a man Sigrid saw the night before and handed the wheel over to him before making her way toward Sigrid. She walked with the easy gait of someone who spent as much time on the water as on land. Her hips rolled as her knees remained soft. She looked to glide along the boards of the deck.

"Did you sleep well enough?"

"I did, thank you. It has been several days since I let myself close my eyes for more than a moment at a time. I suppose I needed the rest."

"You didn't mention how you came to be tied to the altar."

"No, I didn't." Sigrid watched Freya with caution. She saw Freya in her visions almost as often as she saw Leif. The woman was admirable in her dedication to her family and tribe. Sigrid had seen her serving in her parents' longhouse as many times as in battle. She had said more than one prayer to ask the gods to watch over the young woman. So far fate had been on both of their sides. She also knew Freya trusted few and liked even fewer. Devotion to her family ran deep, and she would react to any threat to them. Real or perceived.

"Five men came to my small hut while my uncle Rangvald was on his way to your settlement. Erik hadn't returned yet from his fishing voyage. The men surrounded me in the woods. We traveled over land and took a small skiff the last part of the way. Hakin's homestead was vacant, as you saw, but their own seer was there. He is the one you killed. They didn't want me for any other reason than to keep me from aiding Rangvald or your army. He was prepared to kill me on the chance I might offer you guidance in battle that would turn the tide away from Hakin."

"And you didn't fight back? You let them take you?"

"I may not be a shieldmaiden like you are, but make no mistake, I wasn't going anywhere I didn't need to go."

"Need to go?"

"I went with the men because the fates decided I should go to Hakin's home. To see and hear that which no one thought I'd be able to share. The gods intended for your brother to come to my aid, and I knew you would be with him."

"Why would the fates tell you such a thing?"

"Do you recall two winters ago when you were on the Orkney isles? You faced another band of Norsemen who didn't care for your arrival. It was a vicious battle that left you with a practically severed arm and a punctured lung."

Freya went rigid, and Sigrid felt the rage flowing from her. "How could you have known that? We remained there for a moon longer than planned because of my injuries. We were almost trapped for the winter because I was too weak to move."

"And your brother refused to give you up."

"I begged him to end it then and there. To let me die rather than linger on. It's clear he refused." Freya glared at her. "How could you know that? Only Leif, Tyra, Bjorn, and Strian know just how injured I was. We kept it from the men and said I was fevered. Then we claimed we needed to collect more supplies before we could leave."

"First, credit your men with more sense and loyalty. They all knew how injured you were. They never argued and agreed with Leif's demand you all remain there. Did you never wonder why not one man ever complained? Not a one of them grumbled about not going home or moving on for more treasures? Second, I saw it all. I've seen every battle Leif, and thus you, have fought since his first. Your first battle came two years after his despite how you argued and persisted that your father should allow you to join Leif, Bjorn, and Strian sooner. You would have died had you joined Leif on that ill-fated first voyage. He still bares scars he's shown no one. Scars no one but he can see."

"You've seen all of that? The runes showed you our fate?"

"They did that more than once, but it wasn't the runes that let me watch you and your brother as if I was with you."

"Divinations? Spirit walking?" Freya wondered. Sigrid nodded as she looked about to make sure no one was listening too intently to their conversation. She trusted Freya and Leif, but she knew better than to trust anyone else. She already knew Tyra, Bjorn, and Strian didn't hold the same faith in seers as Freya and Leif did. "You fear how others will react if they learn of your gift."

"Gift. Curse. Depends on the day."

"What did you learn while a captive at Hakin's?"

Sigrid opened her mouth but bit her lip. "I don't wish to keep anything from you, Freya. I haven't any reason to. What I have to say, I must do before Leif too. You both must know together before the others can. I must tell you before Tyra, Bjorn, and Strian learn of it. Freya, it isn't good."

The two women looked at one another and an understanding passed between them. Freya wasn't sure what to make of Sigrid's story. Humility forced her to admit there was much of life and the world she didn't understand. There was much the gods never meant the average person to know. It was such knowledge they gifted seers with, and in this moment, looking at Sigrid, she didn't envy her.

"Fine. You must be hungry and in need of relief. Go below deck to my cabin. You can use a pot there then have the cook give you something warm. Freund!"

The boy came running at his captain's bidding. Sigrid had to stifle her laugh as she saw the look of adoration and puppy love on the boy's young face. "Thank you," she said to both before Freund gestured for her to follow him. By the time Sigrid came back above deck a half an hour later, Freya's and Leif's longboats were tied abreast, and Leif stood on the deck speaking to his sister. She approached with hesitation when Freya waved her over.

"Good morning," Leif offered her a warm smile, and Sigrid's mouth went dry. She knew what the fates had in store for her, but it didn't make this conversation any easier. She took in his long hair braided back from his face with the sides sheared close to the skin. His beard was much shorter than most men she knew, but it suited him well. She realized that she preferred him cleaner shaven than the times she had seen him with a full beard. Leif's face was far too handsome to hide behind a layer of fur. He set his strong jaw as he watched her wary approach. His gray eyes twinkled this morning with a light of persistent mischief that had been there since he was a boy. She couldn't help but smile back, but it dissolved when she remembered what she had to share.

"Good morning," Sigrid looked to Freya.

"I have shared none of what you told me. I thought it was best to let you tell your own story."

While Sigrid appreciated Freya's respect, she dreaded having to tell Leif that she had been a virtual voyeur in his life since the time they were both young.

"Sigrid, you don't look so happy to see me," Leif mused. She swallowed again, then peered at him. His warm smile would change soon enough. "Do you fear telling me you're a seer? Erik and Rangvald already told us."

"I already knew you knew of it. It's why you thought you came for me."

Leif's brow furrowed. "What other reason is there?"

"Before I can explain, you must know how I knew what I'm about to share. Leif, I knew you would come for me because I saw it before they even took me."

"That must have been a relief for you then. You knew someone would rescue you."

"I let them take me because it had to be you and Freya who came for me. I've had visions of you and Freya since I was a child. I saw you at your first battle, at Freya's first one, the first time you—" a furious blush crept over her face, and Leif's eyebrows shot up to his hairline. "You must believe that was *not* something I *ever* wanted to see. It was what happened afterward with the woman's husband that the gods warned me about. I cast runes and prayed to the gods to remember your fate wasn't to die that night."

"What else have you seen?"

"Nothing else of that nature, thank the All Father. But I

have seen much of your lives both during battle and while at home. I must tell you both something now, and you must decide what to do with it. You won't believe me at first, but I have no reason to lie. I could have no way of knowing unless I had seen it while I walked with the spirits."

Leif watched the young woman struggle with her emotions as she looked between the two. He saw her eyes mist as she blinked away the moisture. Leif wanted nothing more than to wrap her in his arms and reassure her she didn't need to share whatever troubled her so much, but he knew that if it caused her this much turmoil, it was something he had to know. He caught himself as he reached out his hand to her arm, but at her watery smile, he didn't hesitate again. Leif placed his hand on her forearm and felt the tremble. She swallowed before taking a deep breath.

"Strian's uncle. It's Strian's uncle who has caused all of this. The man knows no bounds to his ambition, but he knows how to manipulate others. The man killed his own brother to become your father's captain of warriors. He's also the man who's been feeding secrets to Hakin."

"What?" Freya gasped.

"That cannot be," Leif muttered. "Everyone knows of his loyalty to my father since they were boys."

Sigrid shook her head. "No, he hasn't been. Far from it. He loves your mother, or at least believes he does. When it was time for your father to marry my Aunt Inga, he thought he could finally make Lena his. He never accepted that your father would have kept her as his mistress before ever giving her up and most definitely not to another man. Instead, he bedded my Aunt Inga who married Hakin's younger brother, Grímr. They come together every chance they have, which hasn't been often these last few years, but it's Einar's children she bore, not her husband's. Inga loves Einar, but he's obsessed with your mother. Einar would see your father and both of you destroyed before he dies. Einar still believes he can have Lena. He would leave his wife and Inga to have your mother."

"How do you know all of this," Leif whispered hoarsely.

"Strian's father is not at rest yet. Eindride's spirit lingers and has been my guide since Einar killed him."

"Why haven't you made any effort to tell us? To inform us? You must know our people are allies. You never saw fit to make this known." Leif couldn't believe what he was certain was the truth, but he wished could be lies.

"I couldn't."

"Why," Leif demanded. His voice was rising with each question, and his hand that offered support a moment ago was now a vice around her wrist. Sigrid looked down at her wrist and then up to Freya, but her face showed no compassion for Sigrid's position. Sigrid twisted her arm, and Leif released her. He stared at his hand as if he hadn't even realized he held her arm pinned in place.

"Eindride refused to let me. He made it clear we can't trust Einar. He feared for Strian's life if someone made his shame known. Eindride is convinced Einar will kill Strian before he allows himself to submit to your father's justice. However, it has become desperate now. In the past, the information Einar shared was harmless. Little more than crops and numbers of livestock. He shared information about your voyages, but Hakin took little interest in it until this last one. The Norsemen you battled on the way to Scotland were Hakin's. They were trying to sink your ships to leave your father unprotected as Hakin moves south to attack."

"That doesn't explain why you let them take you."

"Einar was one of the men who had me taken. He traveled with Hakin's men for the first night before he doubled back to return before your father could realize he left. He is there now and will ride out with your father if they haven't already left. I know their plan. Einar assumed I'd be dead by now with no one to tell what he and the other men discussed."

"And what was it you learned?" Freya spoke up.

"Einar intends to poison your father a little at a time. He wants to weaken your father before his men, then deny him Valhalla by killing him in his sleep rather than allowing him to die in battle."

"He has so little honor as that?" Freya scoffed, "I find that hard to believe."

"The man has no honor at all. None. Einar will try to rape Tyra before you return home. He will bring Strian to the brink of death before Bjorn kills him for his attack on Tyra. Einar and Hakin agreed he will have Leif's jarldom once your father dies. Hakin would kill you and Leif. Then his own younger brother, Inga's husband, will take Rangvald's place after they kill him and Erik."

"That's a great many people they must ensure are dead to make their plan work," Freya mused.

"Patience. Look at how long Einar has coveted your mother. When you return, you will find Einar's wife dead with her throat slit buried in a shallow grave in the woods just east of your homestead."

"And you didn't see that in any of your visions before this?" Leif wondered.

"I don't get to pick what the spirits and runes reveal. I cannot control whether fate will show me or when it will happen. Sometimes it's not until after the fact that I learn of what has transpired." Sigrid looked into Leif's eyes as she spoke her last truth. "It is only ever you who I can see before the events, so that means Freya and the others if they will be with you. But it is you the gods have sent me to see."

"What does that mean?"

"Honestly? I don't know for sure. But the gods intend for me to be a part of your life either from a distance or, as it is now, up close."

"Close," Leif murmured.

Freya cleared her throat as she looked between the two. "I believe this is what Father meant when he said you are to keep your distance."

"Your father doesn't believe me to be a suitable companion to his son. I'm not advantageous enough." Sigrid smiled as she saw Leif shift uncomfortably. "That assumes I aspire to the position."

Freya snorted as she dragged Sigrid toward the steps to her cabin. "It is time we get you clothed before my brother loses the little sense you've seen to protect."

Leif watched the two women walk away and knew he was well out of his depths with either of them, but if they paired together, he stood little chance of remaining in control. He looked over to see Tyra watching and grinning from her own deck.

Thor's hammer. I will be lucky to come out alive between Einar and these women. But Father is mistaken if he thinks she's not the right match for me. She will be mine. Of that I can promise him and All Father. Sigrid will be my wife.

FOUR

The attack came in the dead of night, but Leif was prepared. They spotted the three longboats following them since early evening. Tyra and Bjorn sailed ahead knowing the distance and formation kept them hidden from their pursuers. They sailed into a fjord where they would wait until Leif, Strian, and Freya sailed by with their attackers in their wake. Leif, Freya, and Strian prepared for the men to attempt boarding their ships and had their grappling hooks and arrows at the ready before the strangers pulled alongside them. Freya was the first to board an enemy ship, her sword drawn, slicing as she thrust her shield at any foe foolish enough to underestimate the power she kept barely contained. Strian went next as he boarded the ship that tried to overtake his. Leif lit the fire arrow as the signal for Bjorn and Tyra to emerge from their hiding spot. The attackers lobbed several flaming tar-covered logs onto the longboats causing damage to the decks. One boat rammed the side of Tyra's longboat, causing several boards to crack and splinter. But they battered none of the ships enough to make them unseaworthy during the battle. Tyra and Bjorn's engagement meant the five to three battle was only a brief training exercise for Leif and his crews.

Leif jumped to Freya's boat and elbowed his way to his sister who stood speaking to Bjorn near the rails of their boats. "Where is Sigrid?"

"I am glad to see you safe as well, Brother."

"I can see you are well enough, but I don't know that about Sigrid."

"She's in my cabin with the door bolted and barred from the inside."

Leif nodded and looked to Bjorn. "Fire their ships. Take any survivors as thralls. We can sell or ransom them. I don't care, but I recognized more than one of Hakin's men. This was his doing." Leif charged below stairs and pounded on Freya's cabin door. "Sigrid, it's me. Leif. The battle is over. Open the door, please."

Leif forced himself to take several deep breaths lest he maul the woman when she let him in. He heard objects being moved away from the door before she lifted the bar and the bolt slid back to its home. She pulled the door open and peered out. Leif saw the knife in her hand. She dropped it when she knew he was alone and threw open the door wide then stepped back. His intention not to maul her fell away the moment he could reach her. He pulled her into his arms, and he felt her come willingly. She wrapped her arms around his neck as he lifted her off her feet. Their mouths came together with a hunger born of fear and longing. The kiss wasn't gentle but fed a simmer that had started for Sigrid long before it did for Leif.

"I knew today wasn't the day you would die, but it didn't make it any easier to wait."

"Knowing Freya would have told you to bar yourself here didn't make it any easier to wait to find you."

Leif brushed his lips across her mouth with more finesse than their first kiss. He waited to see if she would change her mind, but her body pressed against his. His tongue whispered against the seam of her mouth before he flicked the tip to express his desire. She gasped and opened to him. His tongue wasn't in the same hurry as the rest of him seemed to be. He swept her mouth as he explored every nook and cranny. She sucked, eliciting a groan as he kicked the door shut and spun them, so her back rested against the wood. His hands slid to cup her backside as he lifted her higher. She wrapped her legs around his waist as she wound her fingers through his hair. His hands massaged the swell of her bottom. He groaned again as his cock twitched when his fingers sank into the firm yet supple flesh covered only by a light linen tunic.

Sigrid didn't recognize the whimper coming from what felt like a soul deep need. The kiss remained slow even as the passion fired again between them. Neither was in a rush to end the kiss or to even further their embrace. Leif knew she was an innocent from her tentative acceptance of his tongue's invasion, but he reveled in her willingness to match his desire and need with her own fire. He had never been with a virgin before, and he intended to make his first time with his future bride be in his bed and not aboard his sister's ship. It certainly wouldn't be up against the wall of her cabin. He slid his lips along her cheek until he could alternate gliding his tongue and nipping his way down her neck to her collar bone. There, he peppered her flesh with the lightest kisses that seemed to just graze her skin.

Rather than soothe her need and bring their tryst to an end, it seemed to spur Sigrid on further. She pulled his hair, and when he raised his head, she dove in for another searing kiss. It was her tongue that explored now, and Leif was unwilling to stop her. She tangled her tongue with his as she shared her need with his own. It was only when they were both out of breath that they pulled apart.

Leif ran the pad of his thumb over her chafed skin, red from his beard rubbing against it. When it brushed her lips, she nipped, then sucked the tip into her mouth. Leif's cock leaked within his leather pants. He knew he would embarrass himself soon if he didn't set her away from him, but he didn't have the resolve needed. Not yet, at least. He walked them to the only chair in the cabin and sat down. Leif groaned yet again when the heat from her bare sheath rubbed against his engorged cock as she straddled him. He could feel it through his pants. Leif lifted her and arranged her to sit on his lap with both feet on one side.

"Sigrid, this isn't why I came down here." She bit her lip before nodding her head. "I'm sorry I got carried away."

"Leif, I didn't nod my head because I agree you shouldn't have done it. Just the opposite. I nodded my head because that was what the gods wanted. It was what I wanted."

"You don't know what you mean. I know you're a virgin. You don't understand what I was prepared to do. How far I would have gone if I hadn't come to my senses."

"And you're not listening. I may be a maiden, but I know what occurs between a man and woman. Remember, I have seen you." They both blushed before Sigrid shook her head and continued. "I knew you'd come for me. I've known your path, and I've seen you for years because the gods have linked our fates together."

Leif drew in a breath as he tried to take in what she hinted. "Are you saying the gods intend for you to become my people's seer?"

"In a way," Sigrid hedged.

"In what way?"

"The gods don't intend for me to live alone in a hut outside your settlement as I've done at my own."

"Do they intend you to be mine?"

"As much as you are mine."

"You are sure of this." Leif heard the certainty in Sigrid's voice, but he wasn't as convinced yet.

"I've had many visions and divinations since I came into my gift. Just as many have been about other people as they have been of you. But my first vision, the one that came when I was only a girl of nine winters was of us with our children in our own longhouse. This vision came years before I knew how a man and woman beget children. It came before I knew who you were. You were just a blond godlike figure who I sat beside and slept next to. This vision has only become stronger and clearer with age. It's the one vision of the far future that's never changed. Others have morphed or shifted with the tide of fate and the actions of man, but that vision never wavers."

"You knew the first night, and you said nothing."

"What was I supposed to say when you and your friends found me naked and tied to an altar? Was I supposed to call out, 'Leif, we haven't met yet, but we will wed. Don't mind that your cousin and best friend can see your future wife without a stitch on.' Is that how you'd have liked your introduction and my introduction to your family to have gone?"

Leif's expression told her everything she needed to know. It was a mixture of horror and embarrassment with a strong dose of confusion.

"I didn't think that was the case. And I wasn't feeling up to making such an important revelation after spending the better part of two days tied up and exposed to the elements."

"That man had you bound for two days? You waited through that without trying to escape?"

Sigrid sighed as if she were explaining something to a young child, and as if her patience were wearing thin. "I've already told you the gods determined you and I were to meet. They showed this would come to pass. I admit I didn't know someone would bind me and prepare me for sacrifice. I only knew fate planned for you to rescue me. It wasn't my place, or even my right, to go against what the gods have in store for any of us. I can only be a conduit to their ideas, but I can't foresee or influence their motivations. Even when I cast runes, I only get glimpses into the plans fate has. People can still change those when they act of their own free will."

"You had that much faith in me? That I would arrive in time and that I would know where to find you?"

"I have faith in both you and the gods. They sent you here to find me. You're a man of honor and determination, so I knew you wouldn't leave without searching for me. I have faith the gods will provide. They may be fickle in nature, but that isn't always the case. Leif, too many of my visions came true over the past thirteen years for me not to have faith in my gift and the gods."

"What visions do you have for this battle? You told me you've seen us together with our children, but you didn't tell me if you have any reason to believe that might not be what fate will allow. What should I know going into this now that I've learned of Einar's duplicity?"

"I've seen the battle begin, and I've seen Einar ride to Hakin's side, but the gods haven't revealed more yet. When we go ashore, I can cast the runes to try for more guidance. There is no guarantee I will learn enough to give you the upper hand, even though I believe that's why the gods had you rescue me. People can change the future by the choices they make in the present. Not everyone obeys fate's plans."

"All right. There's something I would have us go back to. You've seen we are to wed, but is that what you want?"

Sigrid was slow to answer. She accepted her destiny years ago, and her visions of Leif had her falling in love with him before she grew into a woman. Sigrid knew this situation was new to him, and she had no desire to scare him away. Sigrid wouldn't force a marriage onto him if he didn't want it. She could only show him what she knew from past prophecies. It would be his choice to accept or rebel.

"Should I take your silence for what it seems? You don't wish to wed me but will do so because you believe this is your fate."

"That isn't the case at all. You must remember I have an advantage, and it's not one I want to abuse. I have known you since I was nine even if we'd never met before. It feels like I've grown up with you. I've not only seen the events of your life, but I've often felt them too. It's not a question of whether I wish to wed, but more of whether you would want to wed me knowing I'm already well acquainted with you when you know nothing of me. Will you wed me because that's what fate has foretold?"

"I would have us become better acquainted. There's something that draws me to you. I feel it, and I believe it's the will of the gods and something unique to you. I don't know how to describe it, and I don't yet understand it, but neither do I want to ignore it. However, this development will infuriate my father. His warning to stay away from you was explicit."

Sigrid sighed and tried to slide from his lap to gain even an ounce of space between them, but Leif boxed her in with his arms wrapped around her hips. She knew that if she forced the matter, he would release her, but the intensity of his gaze locked her back into place.

"Your father wants a more advantageous match for you and for your tribe. He's already aware of our fate. He merely believes he can change it."

"How does he know? How is that possible?"

"Before we were born, your father met my mother, Signy. It was when Rangvald came to retrieve Inga. My mother went with him. She reassured everyone the future was playing out just as it was supposed to when people feared your father's insistence on marrying your mother would bring the gods' wrath. It was the meddling and ambition of man that created the problem, not the gods. She told your father he would one day have a son who would marry her daughter, and the tribes would ally forever. That it would bind our people better than a mere friendship. Your father wasn't quick to agree. It seems thirty years of contemplation has changed nothing. He would still ally with another tribe to secure your position in the Trondelag."

Leif mulled over what Sigrid shared. The wealth of information in a matter of only minutes overwhelmed him. As much as he tried to concentrate on the implications of Einar's betrayal and how Einar's duplicity influenced this feud with Hakin, all he could think about was the relationship Sigrid described between them. She was right about being in a better position to know what she wanted than he was. He was most frustrated that he didn't know as much about her as she did him. He found himself jealous that fate granted Sigrid the opportunity to get to know him when fate never gave him even a hint she existed.

Leif realized he coveted knowing his partner as well as Sigrid did. Leif wanted to learn everything about her. His cock twitched as he admitted he had an all-consuming carnal desire to know her, but a burning sensation took residence in his chest as he realized how much he wanted to know the most mundane things that would be a husband's—or even a friend's—right to know. He felt a driving need to discover such things as her favorite color, favorite food, greatest fear, and fondest memory. He wished to know the intricacies of her soul as she knew his.

The more he considered how he wanted to discover who Sigrid was, the stronger the wave of guilt became for not thinking about the impending battle. He recognized he should focus on the strategic implications of what Sigrid shared. He knew he should consider the logistics of waging a battle that had two fronts. That he should try to picture his enemy's reactions and maneuvers during the fight.

A soft hand cupped his cheek as Sigrid pressed a gentle kiss to his forehead. Leif looked into her silver eyes and saw compassion and understanding. "You have much to think about that doesn't involve me. I'm not going anywhere. For the meantime, I'll advise you as best I can with what the spirits share with me. There will be plenty of time to consider the rest after we know our people are free of harassment and assault."

Leif's arms tightened around Sigrid as they drew her into the shelter of his broad chest. "I envy how well you already understand me. I would someday understand you in the same way."

Sigrid placed her hand over his heart and absorbed the steady rhythm that calmed her own racing pulse. "You will, but we have a long road ahead of us. It won't be easy, and I won't bind you to a future you may decide you don't want."

"Even if you have seen our future together?"

"It is what fate holds right now, but it can change just as the weather does. The actions of man don't always fall in line with what the gods will."

Leif kissed the top of her head as they sat together. They both sensed the rightness of their embrace. It was no longer contact born of physical hunger but a bond of companionship. Time seemed to slide away while both were lost in their own thoughts until a strong knock pounded the door.

Sigrid scrambled from Leif's lap, and he crossed the room to open the door. Freya stood on the other side of the threshold with her hands on her hips as she peered around Leif. She took in Sigrid's tired expression, but her clothes and her hair were unmussed. Satisfied that Sigrid's maidenhead was still intact, Freya's gaze shifted back to her brother.

"In case you have forgotten, you have your own ship to captain. You cannot spend the rest of the night swooning over your newfound love. I would like to catch a few winks, and Sigrid looks like she's about to drop. Go to your own boat and your own cabin, Brother." Freya moved aside and gestured for Leif to leave. Instead, he turned back to Sigrid and walked to her.

Leif rested his hands on her waist as he looked down. He realized she was shorter than most of the women he knew. While her frame was solid, and he had felt her strength during their embrace, she was far smaller and delicate than he was. It stamped a brand of protectiveness upon his heart in that moment. He would allow no more harm to come to her, and he would punish any man who thought to abuse what was his.

"Sleep well, little one. We will talk more tomorrow."

"I would like that very much," Sigrid whispered as she stood on her toes to kiss his cheek.

Freya cleared her throat none too softly.

"I know, Sister. I am on my way out."

"You and my brother were closed in here for quite some time, but you don't look like a woman ravished."

"That would be because I am not a ravished woman."

"My brother didn't steal any kisses?" Freya looked at Sigrid in disbelief.

"I didn't say that." Sigrid shrugged one shoulder as she pulled the spare blanket from the end of the bed. "We kissed, but we also talked. The kisses were nice, but the conversation was necessary."

"Nice," Freya erupted in laughter. "I look forward to informing him that his kisses are just 'nice.'"

"You will do no such thing! You know they were more than that, but do you want to hear the details of your brother's intimate forays?"

Freya sobered as she shook her head, a look of mild disgust crossing her face as her top lip curled. "Most definitely not." The women moved about the cabin in companionable silence until Sigrid moved to curl into the chair. "What are you doing? You can't sleep there."

"Would you rather I go above deck?" Sigrid realized she presumed she could sleep within the shelter of the cabin, but she never received the invitation.

"Of course not. Nor do I intend for you to sleep in a chair. I was remiss in not sending you to my cabin last night. This bunk is wide enough for both of us. You will sleep in a proper bed."

"I don't want to inconvenience you." Sigrid hesitated to accept Freya's invitation since she wasn't sure if it was genuine or mere etiquette.

"You're as good as my sister now that my brother has met you. I would see you safe and comfortable, not for his sake but for your own. I rather like you, and I hope we might become friends if we are to be family."

Sigrid's eyes opened wide, and she was sure she looked gormless as she gawked at the other young woman.

"You seem shocked that I would accept what you've told us. If you were after the wealth and status of the future jarl's wife, you would've sought him out rather than waited for him to come. If fate didn't predestine it, then my brother never would have a reason to meet you. No one would have taken you, or at the least, there wouldn't be a reason to send my brother. And I cannot imagine a woman willing to be a sacrifice for an enemy. You weren't on that altar because you believe the gods wanted you as a gift. So, in my estimation, you're truthful about your intentions. I would rather be friends with my brother's wife than adversaries. I'm close to Leif, as you know, and I want no one to come between us. Besides, I like you in your own right."

Freya shrugged and then gestured for Sigrid to climb into bed. "I shall sleep on the outside in case anything should happen. I might need to protect you or make my way to the deck without tripping over you."

Sigrid nodded as she moved to her side of the bunk. It was only moments later that both women sank into a deep sleep not to stir until the early rays streamed in from the window.

FIVE

With the morning light, the captains could assess the damage done to their ships. While none were in danger of sinking, the smoldering remains of the tar projectiles launched from the enemy's catapults left the decks of Strian's and Bjorn's boats compromised and at risk for caving in. The gash along the side of Tyra's hull was well above the water level for where they now sailed; however, the added weight of treasure and supplies confiscated before they burned their opponents' ships was weighing down Tyra's boat. If it settled much lower, it was at risk to take on water. The five-boat flotilla anchored as close to the shore as they could, and the five captains along with their first mates and Sigrid waded ashore to discuss their plans.

"We must go over land. I will leave men behind to fix the side of my boat. When they're finished, they can move onto the decks of Strian's and Bjorn's boats. You know my crew has the best carpenters and shipbuilders of the bunch."

"Tyra, you're right. We can't risk further damage, or it being swamped. We'll take the horses off and continue. It'll slow us, but we are close enough to the inlet where we would have anchored to not be more than a few hours behind. But that means riding hard. Geirr, stay here with Sigrid." Leif turned to Sigrid and spoke, "I don't want you getting soaked again. And there's no need for you to return to the boats. I'll bring your staff, and you'll ride with me. Geirr is my first mate, and I trust him while we return to the ship."

Sigrid nodded. She wished she could be of help, but she knew there was little she could do that the crew wouldn't already have begun or could accomplish without her. It was best if she remained out of the way, and with only the thin linen tunic and the vest Freya lent her, she would remain chilled if she went back into the water. Leif stole a quick kiss before turning away. At Bjorn's snigger, Leif shot him a warning look that wiped the smile from his face. The crews moved to unload and bring the horses ashore. They snorted and tossed their manes, not at all pleased by the frigid waters that reached their knees. Once supplies, saddles, and horses were on the pebble beach, the five captains issued their final orders for the men who would stay behind to repair the ships and guard the workers. They knew they were to follow as soon as was feasible. There were enough men to sail the boats further down the coastline and meet the riders later.

"You ride with me." Leif's tone imparted it wasn't a suggestion or a request.

"Wouldn't it be better for the horse if I rode with Freya or Tyra? Our combined weight would be little more than yours without me."

Leif lifted Sigrid and placed her on his saddle. While his movements were gentle, they still shocked Sigrid, who was unaccustomed to being manhandled. She bit her tongue until Leif sat behind her, wrapped them into the warmth of his fur cloak, and kneed his horse into a trot.

"You may know now that we are to wed, but that doesn't make you my keeper. I'm not yours to order about nor am I a sack of grain to haul over a saddle."

"But you are mine to protect, and I can do that best when you ride with me. Whether we are to marry or not, my father and Rangvald tasked me with finding you and bringing you back."

"Does that mean you don't trust your friends to keep me safe?"

"That isn't at all what I said, and you know that." Leif gave her a flinty stare as she looked back over her shoulder.

She wasn't to be outdone. Her brows lowered, and her lips thinned as she stared at the man seated behind her. She didn't want to argue the first time they had an opportunity to spend extended time together, but she also wasn't going to give him the impression that she would accept being treated like chattel. However, her glower only made his lips twitch. "You find humor in treating me little better than a possession. You find my frustration entertaining."

"I didn't say either of those things. But I find your face to be beautiful, even when you are in a fit of pique, and I believe I shall enjoy seeing your temper as long as we can make up afterward."

Sigrid's nose flared as her lips went from a flat, thin line to pursed, and her jaw set in a hard line. "Do you believe a wife is to be seen and not heard, just as a child would be?"

"I never implied that either. I didn't think to ask if you wanted to ride with me because I thought you would prefer it that way. It's proven to be an opportunity to talk, hasn't it? I also won't have any of the men doubt you are under my protection."

"About that. You have made it known I am your woman, but since none of them know the real situation, I sound like little more than your bedmate. If we marry, I'd rather not appear to be a concubine who pleased you enough to wed. I'm sure your other women wouldn't appreciate that."

"Other women? I thought you'd know I keep no concubines or bed slaves."

"I do, but I also know you don't spend many nights sleeping alone when you are home. There are those who would claim you as their own."

"Does that bother you? Knowing I've been with other women."

Sigrid looked forward for a moment and studied the landscape that fell away as the horses cantered across the lowlands. "It's not so much that it bothers me to know there are others. I just haven't enjoyed being granted those visions. None so clear as your first time, but I've still known."

Leif was silent for so long Sigrid wasn't sure if the conversation was over. She hadn't intended to sound possessive or peevish, but it was the truth. She wasn't prepared to let him know that she had seen far more than she admitted. Seeing him bed other women as clearly as if she were there was never enjoyable. She understood she couldn't control what the spirits showed her, and the visions linked to what happened before or after he bedded a woman, but it wasn't her favorite experience by far.

"I can't imagine what that must be like. To believe you are to marry someone but to watch them bed another. I wouldn't be so calm if the situation were reversed. I find the notion of another man touching you, and me having to know and watch, infuriating. I don't know that I could do it. And not for so many years. I feel as though I owe you an apology."

"You don't. What you have done up to this point has been your own path to walk. I have just been an observer."

"Do you fear I will continue on with the way I've been?"

Sigrid could only shrug. She wasn't about to admit that was her greatest fear. Thinking about sharing Leif once they pledged themselves to one another had burned a hole through her heart more than once. Leif turned her head so he could look at her.

"Do you fear that?" Her nod would have been imperceptible if he weren't holding her chin. "Have your visions shown me bedding other women once we are together?"

"No," she whispered. "Other than the instance with our children, I have seen little of what our lives would be after we wed. I have seen shadows of events yet to come, but nothing about our married life."

"Don't you think that's odd? You've seen everything up to that point."

"And so, I fear there is a reason the spirits don't allow me to see more."

"You must know then I've told more than one woman I'll never have a concubine. I've had no desire for a relationship with another woman, even if only for the relief of having a regular partner to bed. Something has always held me back from making that commitment. It never felt right." Leif tried to gauge her reaction to what he said. He knew she saw events in his life, but he didn't know in how much detail she knew his thoughts and feelings.

"I dreamed of us last night, Sigrid. It was unlike any dream I've ever had. Nothing has ever been so real or clear. It was of us. I saw us as a married couple, and I am positive I had no other woman whose bed I visited. In fact, we shared the chamber I now claim until I could build you your own longhouse for us to live in. I saw other women from my past, but I acknowledged them with little more than a glance. My father has never strayed from my mother, and while many men take mistresses and bed slaves, I have no interest in such ties. I'd rather have one woman I can commit to with all I am than manage the competition and maneuvering of many. The right woman will always be more than satisfying for a man's needs."

Sigrid looked at him. Leif's brow furrowed, but he could tell she was considering his words, and when she nodded her head, Leif breathed again. "I believe you. I believe your intentions, but you are a man who has given into his temptations before."

"There was nothing at stake."

"Fair enough."

"Sigrid, if I fail you as a husband, you need only make your wishes to leave known. I will return you to Rangvald."

Sigrid's eyes opened wide in surprise. She never considered Leif to be a man who would give up anything he claimed as his own. "Have I been that selfish in your visions that you believe I'd want you to live in misery for the sake of my desire or pride?"

"No, you haven't. But I can't think of too many men, ones who'll one day be a jarl, who would admit defeat and allow their woman to leave them."

"There's something about you. A light, a fire, I could never see extinguished, not by me." Sigrid smiled and shifted in his arms. Leif swallowed a groan as her backside rubbed against his already hard and aching cock. She aroused him the moment he saw her, then made him hard once she perched before him. It was the sweetest, and most painful, torture he had ever experienced. She looked at him again, only to shift once more. "If you'd like to remain a maiden and not have me take you into those trees, please for the love of the gods, sit still."

Sigrid's smile told him she knew what she was doing. "Why should I be the only one to suffer in silence?"

Leif instinctively tightened his hold and allowed his thumb to brush along the underside of her breast. When Sigrid leaned further back against his chest, he twisted his hand to hold the underside in the palm of his hand. This time he allowed her to hear his soft groan. The air that escaped his lips tickled her ear making her heart race. Sigrid covered his hand and pressed him into her aching flesh as she arched her back to tilt her hips toward his rod. Her breast overflowed his hand, and he spread his fingers wide to enjoy its fullness.

"You're temptation incarnate, Sigrid."

"You're one to talk. I've never felt my body respond this way. It doesn't even feel like my own anymore. I admit to desiring you for years now, but to be in your arms makes me yearn for more."

"And I've only known you a day, but I've never wanted a

woman more. I want all of you, not just your body but to know who you are."

"What would you know?"

"Your childhood. How you learned of your gift?"

"My childhood was just as any child's, I suppose. While my mother and I lived in our hut, I spent much of my time in the village when I was young. I played with Erik and his brothers and sisters. I learned to wield a knife and even a short sword, but it wasn't long after that, that my visions began. I was nine when I had my first, but I thought it was a dream."

"Was that your vision of us?"

"Yes. I didn't know who you were, so I didn't think much of it. Rangvald's wife had just given birth a few weeks earlier, and I had spent a lot of time with the babe. I figured that was the reason for the dream. A young girl fantasizing about her future. However, by the time I was ten winters, the visions were more frequent and much more distinct. Along with them, I felt a sense of warning that had nothing to do with where I was or what I was doing. My mother suspected my gift was making itself known. Once I confessed to seeing events that weren't real, or at least I thought they weren't real, my mother explained what it meant. I knew she was my uncle's seer, but I didn't understand what that meant until my own visions took hold. After that, my mother kept me away from the village most of the time. I could visit with Erik and my other cousins, but my time spent with the other children of the village was over."

"That must have been very hard at such a young age."

Sigrid shrugged as she looked out at the land they traversed. "It was, and it wasn't. I missed playing, but the visions left me shaken when they showed battles and death. They were unpredictable then, or at least I didn't understand the warning signs."

"And what are those? I would know, so I am prepared and can protect you." Leif's hand that had held her breast spread protectively over her belly. It held her against him but was also a clear sign he believed she and any babe she would carry were his. She had waited so long for this that she closed her eyes and released a shuddering breath. Tears pricked the back of her eyes.

"Does it upset you to speak of this? We don't have to," Leif whispered.

Sigrid shook her head and took a deep breath. "I don't mind speaking of my visions."

"Then why the sudden tension?"

Sigrid shrugged, then looked back over her shoulder. Leif read her emotions as if he had always known her. He felt he understood her like he did his sister after spending his lifetime with Freya.

"You've feared I would reject you. You breathe easy because I would keep you as my own. You haven't trusted in the gods with your whole heart or your whole mind."

She nodded as her eyes watered, but she blinked away her tears before they could fall. "It's not always easy to trust the gods when their will seems to so oppose your own feelings."

"I believe the gods are telling me you are to be my wife, but more than just that, you're to be my partner. That is what I feel. I don't understand how I can be so sure of something I hadn't thought of even two days ago. But I am."

"That's what fate does."

"Then I accept my fate."

Sigrid smiled before looking out at the land again. "You asked me how I know one of my visions is coming. It differs, but there are a few patterns they follow. Sometimes my vision narrows with the edges turning to black. It is as if I can't see anything but what is in front of me. Other times my fingers will tingle as if they have fallen asleep, and the blood is just coming back into them. A heat travels up my arms and settles into my chest. These two signs don't bother me much, and I wait for them to come. Most often, the feeling will stay with me until I am asleep, or I spirit walk. However, when imminent danger is present, and more so when it involves you, a ringing starts in my ears, my head feels as though it is being squeezed by a vice, and my heart hurts so much I fear I can't catch my breath. Those visions come fast and furious. They overpower me, and I can do little more than sit or lie down until they pass. After they end, I can't move. It's as if I'm paralyzed. It can be anywhere from a few minutes to a few hours before I feel like I own my body again."

"Do these severe visions happen often?"

Sigrid swung her leg over the saddle so she sat sideways and could look at Leif without twisting her neck.

"They only occur when you're in grave danger during battle. Except for twice, they're always about you, and I can only see you. I can't see anything else happening around you. That's what makes it the most frightening. I can't tell what else is going on, and that makes it most disconcerting. The only two times it wasn't about you was when you feared Freya would lose her arm. I couldn't move for an entire day after that one, and the other time was when Erik went hunting and wolves surrounded him. I saw it in time and recovered enough to warn Uncle Rangvald. My uncle and his men arrived just as the beasts attacked Erik. One scratched him, and one bit his side, crushing a rib. Erik suffered a horrible fever and came close to dying. He would have if I wasn't granted the vision."

"I've been in many battles. Does that mean you experience these overpowering episodes often?"

Sigrid nodded. "I didn't have one last night because it was a minor fight. I'm not so affected when the attack doesn't put you in grave danger. I see it but only after my hands tingle and my vision tunnels."

"But the other ones. How many have you had?" Leif asked. Sigrid swallowed. She didn't want to tell him for fear he would feel guilty now he knew how these affected her. "Sigrid, don't hide this from me. I told you, I need to know this, so I can protect you."

Sigrid laughed. "You can't protect me from those. They come only when you're in battle and grave danger. You wouldn't be with me then. It is inconsequential how many I've had."

"That's not how I feel. I'd be sure you aren't alone then when I travel."

"You must remember that I've lived much of my life alone, and I enjoy the solitude. My mother died when I was thirteen winters, and I lived alone after that."

"What? Your uncle didn't care for you? How could he abandon you like that?"

"He did no such thing. He made sure I had all I needed, and he posted guards near my hut until I was eighteen winters. After that, I refused his coddling. But he's always ensured that I have food and supplies. Uncle Rangvald respected my choice."

"Rangvald neglected you," Leif grumbled. This last insight hadn't distracted him. "You still haven't told me how many times you've suffered this, this—. I don't even know what to call it. Sigrid, you will tell me. I did this to you. I would know what harm I've done."

"You didn't do this. You have too much pride by half. It was the gods who granted me this, so it is they who did this."

"Don't mince words. You know what I mean."

"Twenty-five," she relented.

"Twenty-five times!"

"Shh, you shall draw attention to us."

"I've been the reason for your near paralysis twenty-five times, and you expect me not to react?"

"This is why I didn't want to tell you."

Leif's jaw set, and he stared out over Sigrid's head as he pulled her tight against his chest again. She swung her leg back over the saddle to face forward, and they traveled on in silence. The only acknowledgement was Leif's hand that stroked over her ribs and belly, periodically sliding over her breasts. Sigrid's responding shiver kept Leif's hand moving.

SIX

"We rest here," Leif called out. He knew Sigrid would be sore after riding for so long. He also could tell she was becoming restless as her head turned, and she scanned the landscape more. Leif pulled his horse to a stop near a small stream. He dismounted then lifted Sigrid from the horse. He slid her down his body, and her breath hitched as her mound contacted his still rock-hard rod. Her eyes drifted closed for a moment as she grasped the front of his vest. Leif held her steady as her legs became accustomed to holding her weight. When her eyes opened, Leif frowned. There was something different about her. He placed his hand on her forehead, but she wasn't feverish, even with the glassiness of her eyes.

"I am not ill."

"Then what—? You've had a vision. While we rode, you had a vision and said nothing." He pulled her along to gain the privacy of the nearby woods.

"Leif, I'm not yet used to sharing my visions with others when they're not ones that need immediate action or I summon on purpose. The vision was of us stopping here, and we—" Sigrid's cheeks flushed, and she could not look above Leif's chest.

"What, Sigrid? What did you see?"

She swayed into his body and pressed against him. "I saw us slip into the woods after I cast the runes. You—you touch me in a way that," she looked up at him, "brings me pleasure unlike anything I imagined. Never in my visions did I experience what the women in your bed did. Until this one."

"You said before, more than once, that you've never seen clearly what happens. It would seem you haven't been honest."

"It's uncomfortable to admit that I've seen as much as I have, and those aren't the visions I enjoyed or care to relive," Sigrid huffed.

Leif nodded before cupping her jaw. "What did you see for us?" His voice was deeper and huskier than usual. He tilted her head up and grazed his thumb under her chin and along her throat as his fingers tangled in her hair.

"I saw you, your mouth on my breasts." Sigrid was breathless as she described the vision that had made her ache for the last hour of their ride. She attempted to hide her movements as she allowed her mound to rub against the rise of the saddle, allowing the pressure to bring her release more than once. "Your fingers inside me."

Leif groaned. He snatched her hand and dragged her through the tree line. "We shall find her some privacy." Leif did not look around as he called back over his shoulder. He didn't want to see the knowing looks he knew were on every man's face. Tyra stepped forward, but Leif's scowl warned her away. Sigrid nodded and smiled as she trotted to keep up. Once they were alone within the trees, Leif found the one with the broadest trunk and pulled them around it.

They came together in a tangle of arms and hands. Leif pulled her linen tunic to her waist and lifted her, so she could wrap her legs around his waist. She pulled at the ties to her vest and slid the tunic Freya lent her down one shoulder. Leif held her in place with one arm as his hand plucked her breasts free of their covering. He took in the sight of their generous size, much fuller than he would have expected on a woman so petite, but ones he had already held in his large hands. However, seeing them bare was an experience he was unprepared for. They sat high and firm with berry-colored nipples pointing toward him. Arousal and the cool air had already turned them to darts, and his mouth feasted upon them. His tongue swirled around one before sucking on it as if he was a starving babe. He took as much of her breast into his mouth as he could, and her mewling cries spurred him on.

Leif's free hand kneaded and squeezed her other breast. He shifted the arm that supported her, and he pressed one hip forward for her to perch on, against which she ground her aching mound. He slid a finger into her and felt the dew from her sheath dripping to his knuckles. Her hips sped while her hands tugged on his shirt as she tried to ride higher and closer to his straining cock. Her need fired him to slip a second finger into her entrance. As wild as their desire was, both knew this wasn't enough. Leif lowered them to the ground, and he freed his mouth long enough to look over her shoulder for danger. He whipped his cloak from his shoulders and awkwardly spread it out before pressing Sigrid to the ground. Her legs remained locked around his waist as he thrust over her.

"I would have you right now, Leif."

He groaned at her words but stilled when he felt her reaching to untie the fall of his pants. He caught her fingers before she did more than untie the bow. "If you free me, I will be inside you, spilling my seed."

"That's what I want. I want you."

Leif ground his teeth as he tried to overlook her innocent plea. "You didn't say we joined our bodies when you described this. Did you see us come together?"

Sigrid shook her head. "I only saw your mouth on my breasts and your fingers as they were a moment ago."

"Then perhaps we're not meant to go that far this time."

Once again, Sigrid nodded. "Don't think it's a lack of desire that makes me hold back."

"I understand. You're believing and trusting my visions. If fate meant for us to make love here, then I would have seen it."

Leif swallowed as he thought about the phrase make love. He had never once used it to describe his sexual encounters. He had used plenty of other words, most unsuitable for her virginal ears, but he knew he had loved none of his bed partners, so the term would have been misplaced. But now, with Sigrid in his arms, he knew the word described what he wanted between them. He wanted to experience the emotion that went with coupling when it was two souls merging rather than an urgent search for release.

He looked around to be sure no one could see them. They were still close enough to the others for their safety but tucked out of sight. He lowered his mouth to hers again, but this time they shared a languid kiss. His fingers sought her entrance and pushed the tunic higher before they slid home again. He moved his mouth to recapture her breast while his thumb roamed until it found the hidden pearl that would bring her first release by his hand. He slid a second finger into her sheath as he caressed the satiny flesh of her core.

Sigrid tangled her fingers into his hair as her other hand slid over his chest. She couldn't wedge her hand between them to cup his cock, but she was more than satisfied to feel it rocking against her, so she settled for grasping his tight backside. It was so different from her own. One cheek fit within her hand, and it felt just as rock hard as the length that rubbed against her.

"I am close, Leif. Don't stop," Sigrid felt the telltale tightness low in her belly. She unhooked her legs, so she could press her feet against the ground to lever her hips against his thrusting fingers and his cock that ground against her mons.

Leif feared being too rough until something registered in his head. She knew what her release felt like. A feeling that almost mirrored rage took over him as he became determined to give her the strongest, most all-encompassing climax she had ever experienced. He would wipe every other memory from her mind.

Sigrid exploded around him in a wave of pleasure so intense her toes curled, and her fingers became talons. Her moan was long and loud as the sensations carried on and on. When Leif tried to pull away, she clamped her knees around his hips and tried to reach between them, but Leif nudged her hand away.

"Not yet," she panted. Sigrid shifted and the new position brought on a second wave. She sought his mouth and for a minute thought he was trying to pull away before he relented. She opened to his thrusting tongue and sucked, eliciting a groan from Leif before he ripped himself away from her and rolled onto his back.

Sigrid lay panting and chilled now Leif's heat no longer surrounded her. She felt his shifting emotions, but her own pleasure engulfed her, and she couldn't register the change. Now she turned to look at Leif, who stared at the leaves overhead.

"You didn't seem to enjoy that as I did, but you wouldn't let me help you."

Leif looked over to Sigrid and saw her wounded expression. He pulled her to him and held her flushed body. She settled, but he felt a new tension radiating from her. It was the same as he felt. It wasn't just pent-up physical frustration. His was a jealousy that blinded him.

"Who was he? Or who were they?"

"Who were what? I don't understand what you're asking me."

"Who's touched you before?"

Sigrid tried to sit up, but his hold on her only allowed her to prop up on an elbow. "No one's touched me before you. I told you I live a solitary life. You know I'm a maiden, so I don't understand what you're asking."

"You said you were close. How could you have known what you were close to unless you've laid with another man? Perhaps not taken his cock into you but let him touch you."

Sigrid pushed against him until she could sit up. "Your tone tells me you think I'm no more than a whore. How could you think that about me? And even if I wasn't an innocent, you never knew you had a claim to me before we met. None of my visions showed me remaining pure for you. I could've done what any woman my age does. You expect me to accept all the times I've had to see you pleasure and be pleasured by other women, but the mere thought of another man touching me has you angry. That is absurd."

Sigrid tried to stand, but Leif's arms brought her back down to lie across his chest.

"It may well be absurd. I don't deny that, but I also don't deny that thinking about you being with another man infuriates me to where I can't see anything else. Who were they?" He ground out the final question.

"Let go. I can't think clearly when I'm touching you like this. I can't think anything more than how I have ached for you for years. How I've found my release as I watched you, imagined you, needed you but could never have you," she finished with a sob. "You don't like the idea, but you don't understand what it was like to see it all. To have fallen in love with you while you have loved every other woman you have crossed paths with."

Sigrid snapped her mouth shut as she realized what she admitted. She scrambled to her feet and pulled her clothes back into place as she scurried back to the tree line. Leif's hand wrapped around her arm just above the elbow and pulled her to a stop. He saw the humiliation she felt and felt wretched for being the cause.

"It seems jealousy is far too natural for both of us," he murmured. He took a deep breath before continuing. "I wish I could undo the past. I wish my father had accepted your mother's vision, so they could have set a betrothal. We could have wed years ago and saved you the heartache of what you've seen. I find I'm even more jealous now I know it wasn't another man who taught you about pleasure but your own hand. That you know you don't need me. I wish I were those fingers introducing you to the sensations I wish I'd been the one creating." Leif stopped to caress her cheek, avoiding her bruises, and cupped her face within his hands. "I wish I wasn't jealous that you've had time to fall in love when it was stolen from me. Stolen all because my father was too stubborn and ambitious."

Sigrid watched as his gray eyes switched from a translucence created by their physical exertion to a dark gray like billowing storm clouds.

"Neither of us can alter that which has happened. I can't unsee what I have. You can't bring back the part of my innocence I lost from curiosity and impatience. And neither of us can change your father's choices. Choices born out of not only ambition, but a love that leads him to believe he's doing what's best for you."

"I don't know how well I can set all parts of the past aside, but I assure you I will always be faithful to you, and I will wed you regardless of what my father wishes." Sigrid nodded, but Leif saw a sadness that lived deeper than just regret for missed opportunities. "You fear I won't come to love you. You believe I desire you, but you're not convinced I'll love you as you love me. Or worse, that if I do, it'll be because of fate and not you."

Sigrid did not answer, but the twitch of her jaw told Leif his assessment was correct.

"Sigrid, I don't have the power to see the future as you do. But I know what I feel now. I won't deny I lust over you. We both know I do, however, it's more than that. Perhaps I've always been meant to love you, but that can only happen if I'm drawn to who you are. And I am. I see fire and strength in you. You're resourceful and independent to live on your own for so long. Your loyalty to your tribe and to me gives me faith for our future. Your sharp tongue challenges me and makes me curious for what you'll say next. The calm you bring is a balm to my warrior soul. I've already learned and observed these things about you, so I believe it'd be impossible for me not to come to love you. I'm more than halfway there already."

He pressed a kiss to the tip of her nose, her forehead, and each cheek before starting the most tender kiss he had ever shared. He had never imagined a kiss that could exchange so much feeling beyond desire.

"It won't just be the visions you've seen that make me fight for your hand. It's already what I feel for you that won't allow me to let you go."

Sigrid smiled, and Leif took her hand to lead her back to the others.

SEVEN

Sigrid moved to the fire while the rest of the party gathered more wood, tended the horses, hunted, or stood guard. There were knowing looks when they returned, but Sigrid's release of Leif's hand and purposeful walk to the fire circle made a few question whether as much happened as they imagined. Those still in the campsite watched as she gathered her staff and sat crossed legged before the fire. She stared into the flames intently for several minutes before she twisted the rounded top of her staff. It came apart, and she dumped a small sack into her lap before returning the top. She shook the sack while she closed her eyes. Without looking, she opened the bag and emptied it in front of her legs. Her lips murmured words no one could make out before she tilted her head back and glanced at the sky. She shifted to kneel and looked at the small items she dropped.

Most recognized what she was doing and gave her ample space, fearful of what they didn't know or understand. Several allowed curiosity to get the better of them as they crept closer. Everyone watched as Sigrid leaned over the assortment of animal bones and small stones etched with different symbols. This set of runes had been in her family since her great-grandmother. Years of use wore them smooth, but deeply engraved, the markings stood the test of time.

Sigrid looked up to search for Leif, and he startled her when she realized he stood just over her shoulder. She had not heard him approach. "Before I explain what I see, I would attempt to speak to Eindride," she whispered. "The state I enter isn't something all people can handle. I can't risk being accused of witchcraft."

Sigrid looked at Leif and hoped he would understand what she didn't want to say.

"You'd have me send away those men who might fear you or speak ill of you."

"I don't want to tell you what to do with your own men, but I must not risk my safety if you would have me continue to be your seer."

"And to be my wife." Sigrid's only response was a thinning of her lips as she continued to look into Leif's eyes. "You're under my protection, and everyone knows that, but I understand that isn't enough to change people's superstitions. I'll speak with the others and have them create a working party."

"Or I can go to the woods. That may be less obvious."

"You can't go alone. Freya and I will accompany you."

Sigrid looked toward the tree line before nodding. "I'll need a small fire, and there are berries that would help. I'll look for those if you could build the fire."

It didn't take long before Freya and Leif perched on a fallen log and watched Sigrid eat a handful of berries. They were ones parents warned all children against because of their power to cause hallucinations and even death. Leif bounced his knee up and down so often Freya clamped her hand over it.

"You're not making this any better," she whispered. "I'm not eager to risk her poisoning herself, but you must trust she knows what she's doing."

Sigrid marked a wide circle around where she sat then looked over at Freya and Leif. "I can feel the effects beginning.

My body may shake, and I will speak but you won't understand. I may even fall to the ground and not move. No matter what happens, you aren't to touch me. Have faith the gods will guide me to the spirits, and the spirits will bring me back."

Sigrid didn't wait for a response from the pair. She turned back to the fire and stared as the flames danced before her. Sigrid looked in the bluest part of the flame, allowing the wavering hues to lull her into a hypnotic state. Slowly, she sang. Her voice started as little more than a light breeze rustling fallen leaves. As her body swayed, her voice became stronger until the melody was clear and sharp. While she didn't have the most musical voice, the song was pleasant to the ears. Leif and Freya both found themselves lulled by the dulcet tones. They watched as the trance consumed Sigrid, and her song ebbed into a babbling with no distinguishable words, but the rise and fall of her cadence sounded like conversation.

Sigrid began the song her mother taught her the first time she attempted to walk with the spirits. Over the years, with more confidence and experience, the song became a part of her. She no longer had to think of the words or tune, rather it flowed forth from her soul. Her body felt light as it floated above the earth, but she didn't move toward the sky or any clouds. Instead, there was a darkness that surrounded her, but she didn't fear it. She found herself walking with purpose toward a new fire. This one burned with flames that leaped toward the heavens.

Around the fire, Sigrid could see men and women preparing for battle as they sacrificed a goat on a makeshift altar. These were people she didn't recognize. She was sure they weren't her uncle's men, and she doubted they were Ivar's. The mead horns passed from hand to hand as the men surged into one another, thrusting their shoulders forth in mock battle. Those surrounding the berserkers pounded their targes with the hilts of their knives. They feasted to prepare for a long fight, but they reveled in the glory of their assumed victory.

"My brother and Hakin are sure the gods have smiled upon them and will grant them the victory they believe they deserve."

Sigrid turned at the voice she recognized. The outline of a man stood beside her. His features were only hints of a man's face. The strength he once possessed still radiated from him along with a discontent born of wandering the spirit world, denied of his right to Valhalla.

"Do you know where they are? Where they plan to fight?"

"Not yet, but we will soon enough."

Sigrid walked toward the gathering unafraid that anyone would see her. Eindride continued alongside her, walking as though he were still a flesh and bone man rather than a spirit caught in limbo. They stood just outside the ring of Norsemen and listened.

"We shall be victorious with heads rolling and blood flowing from our enemies' bodies as we slay those who would thwart our right to rule the Trondelag. Ivar is nothing but a weak old man with a son who would rather sail away to Britannia than rule his own people. Who will Ivar leave his people to? That unnatural beast woman he calls daughter? I think not. I will leave none alive. The man they call Rangvald is nothing more than a pitiful idiot who can't see past the end of his nose. If he could, he would know his sister is our means to victory." Hakin shouted to all surrounding him. He reached for a man's hand, and Sigrid recognized him as Einar. "This man is one of us. I shall reward him for his loyalty with a new woman in his bed and a new land to lead. Without his knowledge, we couldn't outsmart them. At least not so easily."

The crowd roared as they watched the two men boast and gloat. Sigrid looked past them to where another man stood with a woman. The woman's attention was riveted to Einar, and the man's focus was on the woman. It didn't take much for Sigrid to deduce that the woman was Inga, Rangvald's sister and Einar's lover. The man whose gaze bore into her must have been her husband, Grímr.

He knows he's a cuckold. He knows his wife is bedding Einar. My faith isn't in his loyalty to his brother or to Einar. He'll kill both if he's given the chance. The gods tried to warn everyone when he was named the man wearing a face mask. They may have thought the gods meant a warrior's helmet, but I can see the gods meant he'd be two-faced.

"You've deduced what none of the others seem to see, or they aren't willing to see. That's Grímr, Hakin's younger brother and the man saddled with the duplicitous Inga. The woman has born five children, but it requires only one look to know who sired them, and it's not her husband. He can't divorce her or Hakin loses his connection to Einar. Hakin holds no love for Einar and doesn't trust him, but he's willing to lead the man by the nose and allow him to fuck his brother's wife as long as he's the means to destroying Ivar and Rangvald. Grímr has more men supporting him rather than Hakin, and his brother's pride and ego are so great he can't imagine anyone, let alone his little brother, rising against him. Hakin's plan is to tell Einar he'll have Ivar's homestead, but Einar won't live to see the end of this battle. Hakin will give the land to Grímr, and he intends to keep Rangvald's for himself since it's closer. However, Grímr doesn't intend to let either of them return to Steinkjer. He will allow Hakin and those loyal to him to fight and die while Grímr leads the second half of their forces from the rear." Eindride explained what he'd learned during his time as the living dead. He gazed ahead of him, his focus never wavering, even as he spoke to Sigrid.

"Little do any of them know that Rangvald and Ivar intend to trap them between their forces."

"This is true. Let us listen more to where they believe they shall fight."

Both Sigrid and Eindride watched Grímr glare at Inga then Hakin and Einar. Then they wove their way through the gathered crowd until they stood behind Hakin's brother. Sigrid could feel the anger pouring forth as though it was her own emotion. She felt the hatred the man harbored for those who took him for granted and underestimated him time and again. The feeling was so consuming her heart throbbed while her head felt as though a pebble rolled around from side to side. It was the kernel of an idea, one that didn't belong to her, but one she couldn't quite grasp. Her gaze shifted back to Inga when she could no longer bear the animosity that possessed her.

Watching Inga, she felt a longing that resembled love, but Sigrid recognized it as the more insidious covetousness. Inga coveted the attention Einar paid to Hakin. She coveted Einar for the influence and power she believed he would bring her. She coveted revenge on Ivar for repudiating her and Lena for claiming the man who would have made her a *frú*, the jarl's wife and ruling lady of the tribe. Instead, Lena claimed the title of *frú*, and that left Inga with a younger brother for a husband.

Sigrid absorbed the jealousy that poisoned Inga and was sure Inga's heart had shriveled like a fruit left in the sun to dry. The next person she focused on was Einar, so she and Eindride drifted to stand before him, knowing he couldn't see either of them. He crowed at the praise and attention lavished upon him. Einar was little more than Hakin's lap dog, yapping for a treat as the crowd cheered on his antics. Einar pounded his chest and raised his sword above his head.

"Ivar will never know how he lost the battle. He'll never know because I shall take his head from his shoulders before he figures out it was I who sold his secrets. I will have my due, and when I do, no one will suspect who is the greatest spy in our land."

"And no one will dispute who the man is with the least honor," Eindride growled as he stared at a brother he no longer recognized. They were less than two years apart in age, but their parents died of a sickness when they were young boys. Eindride became a mother, father, and brother to Einar.

The depths of ambition created by Einar's greed were so great as to turn him against his brother and make him commit fratricide with little thought to his conscience. Eindride's soul couldn't move past the betrayal that cost him his life.

Sigrid shot Eindride a look of compassion as she felt his brother's greed seep into her. She looked around and saw the wealth the warriors displayed, and she felt compelled to take it all for herself. She had never longed for material wealth before, but Einar's avarice was compelling as Sigrid once again took on the consciousness of those she studied. Shaking her head, she forced herself to think of Leif and what she would do when she returned from her spirit walk. Feeling more grounded, she listened to Hakin.

"We shall lead them on a merry chase until it wears them out. When their supplies run low, and they are far from home, we shall begin our real attack. In the meantime, we will harry them with skirmishes that cost them men and horses. We leave no survivors. Ever."

"So that is the plan. To wear them to the ground and destroy them once they have no means to support their campaign," Eindride's low voice rumbled.

"It would seem so. Will this be enough to offer Ivar and Rangvald?" Sigrid worried the information wasn't specific enough.

"It'll have to do. You can't stay here much longer. You must return to the true land of the living before you end up here with me. Permanently. Tell Leif what you've seen. He'll know what to do with the information. Tell Strian I'm proud of him. Tell him the stag was his."

Sigrid looked at the warriors, both men and women, who continued to drink around their large fire. She watched Grímr, Inga, Einar, and Hakin. A shiver of dread surged through her. She looked to Eindride, but he was already gone. She closed her eyes and cleared her mind, beginning her chant once again. The chant ebbed into her song. Just as she had entered the world of spirits, she drifted back into the world of the living. Her body floated back down until it felt heavy once more. Stillness brought her mind and soul to ease as the sounds of the woods filtered into her mind. She felt her arms then legs come back to life with a tingling sensation she welcomed.

The spirits had released her, and she hadn't poisoned herself. She felt more like herself, as if she awoke from a restful night's sleep. Her eyes fluttered open, and once again, her gaze returned to the flames. She watched them dance as her heartbeat returned to its normal pace. When she felt normal, she looked around for Leif and Freya. Freya sat as she had when Sigrid kneeled to chant. Leif was pacing like a caged wolf. Sigrid could feel the tension pouring off him as he stalked about with his back to her. She rose and nodded to Freya as she approached Leif like she would any wild animal.

Leif fought to contain his anxiety as he waited for Sigrid to return from her spirit walk. He hadn't felt this much anxiety since his early days as a warrior, inexperienced in how to prepare his mind for battle. He witnessed Sigrid's transition from song to chant, curious what she thought and saw while calling to the spirit world. It became obvious when she entered the trance. That was when the intrigue ended, and Leif's misery began.

Sigrid mumbled unintelligible words as her body moved as though she was walking. Her head turned from side to side, but her eyes remained closed. At times, her body twitched or went rigid as though frightened. Leif found it excruciating to wait and not know whether this was part of a normal experience for her. He remembered her warning, but it didn't diminish his worry. The temptation to interrupt was so distracting that Freya ordered him to walk about, at a distance from her, until he could settle. He hadn't done that yet. Leif knew he would fret until the beautiful, sharp-tongued, insightful woman he was growing remarkably fond of returned to him.

Sigrid tapped Leif on the shoulder and jumped back when he swung around ready to attack.

"It's just—" Sigrid didn't complete her thought before Leif engulfed her in his warm embrace. They both sighed in relief at the contact between their bodies. Leif buried his nose in her hair as one arm wrapped around her waist, and the other tangled in her hair. Sigrid burrowed into his chest as she clung to his shirt. When she could relax her fingers, she slid her arms around his waist.

"Thank the gods. Don't ever do that again," Leif murmured.

"Shh, silly man. You know I will, but I will try to avoid you watching."

"If you do, you will not be far from me. I don't want you to ever risk yourself without me near to protect you."

"I was well. I promise."

"You looked anything but well. You terrified me."

"I warned you about it. Why didn't you listen?"

"I did, but that still isn't enough to prepare someone for what we watched."

Sigrid looked back over her shoulder and smiled at Freya, who sat grinning.

"Freya doesn't seem as worked up as you do."

"That's because she doesn't want to bury herself balls deep into you and never let go."

"I should hope not. She doesn't have any balls, I assume. It would make it rather difficult."

Leif growled as he tipped her head back and brought his mouth down to her. His fear she might not be well like she insisted kept him from unleashing the passion that coursed through him. Sigrid's responding thrust of her tongue and insistent demand for entry into his mouth was the invitation Leif needed. Their tongues dueled as they tangled about each other like growing vines. Leif spun them so his back was to his sister before both hands slid down to cup Sigrid's backside. He pulled her tight against his aching rod, and her responding moan was the most satisfying sound he had ever heard. Freya's loud throat clearing did little to diminish their pursuit of pleasure and reassurance.

"Brother, we need to get back before the others send out a search party. And I have no desire to see you bed anyone let alone my new friend."

Leif pulled back as what Freya said registered. He looked at his sister and then at Sigrid. Freya cocked an eyebrow as she held her hands on her hips.

"You heard me just fine. You have the hearing of a dog. And the manners as well from the looks of how you're slobbering over her."

It stunned Leif to hear Freya acknowledge Sigrid as a friend after such a short time. He knew his sudden attachment was unusual, but to hear his sister admit to having a new friend was uncharacteristic. Beside Tyra, Freya had fewer friends than fingers on one hand. She trusted few and relied on even fewer. Leif looked back down at Sigrid and saw her grinning. She released Leif and stepped around him. She grinned at Freya, and they linked arms as they walked back toward camp.

"Coming?" Sigrid called back without looking.

Leif shook his head, but his own silly grin wouldn't leave his face. If Sigrid won over Freya that easily, then there might be a fighting chance to win over his father. Ivar might not relent to Leif's requests, but it was a rarity when the fierce warrior turned down his beloved daughter.

EIGHT

Sigrid looked around the campsite to see whether anyone paid attention to their extended absence. She knew time in the spirit world didn't pass as it did in the human world. She wasn't gone that long despite how Leif whittled, but she was gone just enough to make the other suspicious. No one seemed to pay any attention to her, but she caught wary glances that told her the others suspected why she disappeared with Leif and Freya.

Leif approached and wrapped his arm around her waist, reminding everyone once again of his claim of protection. Sigrid couldn't help but lean into the warmth and support his body offered. Exhaustion swept over her, and she needed food to nourish her after the exertions of her trance. Sigrid felt drained and wished only to sleep, but she knew that wouldn't be an option until she could explain everything to the others, especially Strian.

"Would you have me explain to Strian what I know, or will you do it?"

"We should do it together. We can do so after the others bed down. It isn't unusual for the captains to meet when everyone else retires. Keeping you with me wouldn't be out of the ordinary after they've seen me claim you more than once."

"Claim me? Was I a treasure up for grabs?"

"A treasure for sure, but if anyone grabs you, they will forfeit their life." If Sigrid didn't know Leif as she did, his ferocity would have frightened her. Instead, she embraced his protectiveness as a welcome. She never envisioned their actual meeting, so despite the years, she couldn't have prepared for his reaction to learning what fate desired for them both. Sigrid counted it as a blessing that not only did Leif accept her declaration but drew her close both physically and emotionally. Sigrid knew that was the hand of Freyja guiding them both. The goddess of love and life brought them together and made their meeting one that spoke to their intuition.

They both held a bone deep understanding something intended to bring them together and fighting such an attraction was useless. Rather, it seemed Leif shared her opinion it would be better to make the most of their time instead of fighting against the inevitable. Sigrid welcomed this since she hadn't looked forward to a battle of wills to make Leif see their fate.

Leif moved about the campsite as he checked on his crew. He made sure to double the watch throughout the night. The men and few women sent to hunt returned while he was in the woods, so the evening meal was ready. His belly rumbled as the smell of roasting meat wafted toward him. He counted the crew members from his boat and the others. He knew who was dispatched on watch already, and he tallied that against who he saw now.

After Sigrid's declaration that Einar was betraying his tribe, Leif held everyone to suspicion. The only ones blameless that he knew he could always trust were Freya, Bjorn, Strian, and Tyra. It had always been that way, but more so now he knew the danger they faced. It had shocked him to his core to discover Einar's deception. Leif knew it would devastate his father as well, but it made Leif suspicious of whether any of the others were working with Einar. He didn't want to doubt the warriors he traveled with. Leif needed to trust them when they entered battle as it was the only way to ensure most would return home, but the reality settled into him that not all of them might be there with the truest of intentions.

It rankled, but wisdom prevailed, and Leif accepted the possibility without being rash. He accounted for every member of their party, but he noticed several darting looks toward Sigrid. The lustful ones annoyed him, but it was the suspicious ones that raised his hackles. He knew the suspicion was born of superstition and ignorance, which made them even more dangerous than the men drooling over her. He resolved to have her sleep beside him that night and every other despite her complaints the warriors would assume she was his bedmate. She would be, of a sort. It wouldn't surprise those who traveled with them when he announced his intention to marry her. He would do it now, but he knew he had to wait to gain his father's approval, and he knew that would be an uphill battle. He would have those present recognize his intentions and see her as a helpmate, so they supported her arrival at her new home. It would be the best way to ensure they welcomed her as an outsider.

Leif made his way around the fire and signaled to Bjorn, Tyra, and Strian to meet him away from the others. They each separated themselves and moved toward the tree line. Freya led Sigrid to the group. Leif could see the apprehension in Sigrid's eyes. He knew the following conversation wouldn't be easy on her.

"Sigrid had a vision, and it concerns all of us. We need to hear her out as it will influence the outcome of this fight with Hakin." Leif saw no reason to pussy foot around what he needed to say. He looked at Sigrid and saw his abruptness took her aback. Perhaps she wasn't as well suited to his approach as his warriors were. He held out his hand, and when she placed hers into his much larger one, he drew her in front of him and wrapped his arms around her waist. Sigrid leaned back into the cocoon of his arms and took a deep breath before she began.

"This is a tale that has taken more than a score of years to grow into what I tell you now. I share what I know only because it's for the best that you know what I do." Sigrid looked at the others as they shifted where they stood. "Maybe we should sit."

Leif's grip tightened, but when she moved to sit beside him, he wrapped his arm around her waist. The others joined them on the ground.

"I don't know who's aware that Ivar was once betrothed to Rangvald's younger sister. Ivar only agreed to the marriage because his father insisted, but he was already in love with Lena. Inga was unwilling to live with Ivar's neglect, so Rangvald came to retrieve her. My mother was their sister, too. She came with Rangvald and told him of a vision that involved his son and her daughter." Sigrid tilted her head toward Leif. "My mother's prophecy didn't thrill Ivar. It's why he warned Leif away from me before you left. Anyway, Einar wasn't happy when Inga left because he coveted Lena for himself."

"My uncle?" Strian interjected.

Sigrid turned sorrowful eyes toward Strian and nodded. "He is still in love with Lena despite having a wife and a mistress."

"He doesn't have a mistress."

"Not in your tribe, but he has a woman he beds whenever he can. He has for years. It's my Aunt Inga." Sigrid let that information sink in. Strian looked surprised but not bothered. "Strian, what I say next, I wish I never had to. I don't know how to say this without hurting you, so please know I take no pleasure in this."

Sigrid turned tear-filled eyes toward Strian, whose own eyes widened when he saw how upset Sigrid was becoming.

"Strian, your Uncle Einar killed your father. He did so in Eindride's sleep, depriving him of Valhalla. Your father's soul isn't at rest. But I believe he will be soon."

"What!" Strian jumped to his feet and backed away from the group. "How could you know that? You're lying."

Bjorn tried to pull him back to the circle, but Strian shoved away.

"Strian, I have no reason to lie. I'm not part of your tribe, and this story does my family no favors either. Your uncle wanted to draw closer to your jarl to become closer to your *frú*. He thought he could win Lena over if he proved himself as Ivar's chief warrior. When Lena never paid attention to him, he grew bitter even though he's convinced he still loves her. He has conspired with Hakin for years, slipping small pieces of information about crops and herds but nothing too significant. He also bedded Inga in what he thought was revenge on Ivar, but when Ivar found out years ago, he didn't even flinch. Ivar and Lena believe the affair ended, but Einar is the father of all of Inga's children even though she married Hakin's younger brother."

Sigrid looked around. She wanted to make sure everyone could keep up with the twisted branches of this crooked family tree.

"Strian, your uncle gave Hakin far more important information last winter. It was Hakin's men who attacked on the way to Scotland just as they did on the way here. Hakin promised Einar the jarldom once they kill Ivar. Einar plans to finally claim Lena. When you return, you will find his wife already dead. Hakin has also promised Grímr, his younger brother, that he could have Rangvald's jarldom."

"And you know all of this because the runes told you?" Bjorn's skepticism dripped from his voice.

"I know what I can share of the actual battle from the runes, but what I share now, I know because I have walked with the spirits. I learned what Eindride has shown me, and I learned more today because Eindride took me to Hakin's camp."

"You're nothing more than a witch! My father is in Valhalla, and my uncle would never dishonor our family."

Leif leaped to his feet and lunged at Strian.

"The stag was yours."

Strian froze as Leif's arm swung toward him, but fortunately for Strian, Bjorn was still paying attention and blocked the blow.

"No one knows that. How could you have known?" Strian's stricken face showed everyone the depth of his pain.

"Your father told me not an hour ago. Strian, he's proud of you. I believe he wants you to know that."

"No one knows about the stag," Strian whispered as he looked incredulously at her.

"What are you talking about?" Tyra chimed in as she looked back and forth between Sigrid and Strian.

"When I was eight winters, my father allowed me to go hunting with him and my uncle. We spotted a large stag in the clearing, and we all took the shot. Uncle Einar was adamant he killed the buck, but it was the fletching of my arrow that stuck out of the animal's heart. Einar threatened to take me before the *"thing"* for being dishonorable and trying to claim his prize. My father knew the stag died because of my arrow, but he also knew I wasn't anywhere near old enough to defend myself against my uncle if it came to battle. Everyone knows there's no love lost between my uncle and me, but I never realized he was more dishonorable than taking the credit for felling a deer. Only my father would know that."

Strian stepped closer to Sigrid and tentatively held out his hands to her. Sigrid placed her hands in his without reservation. Leif seethed. He knew most of his anger now stemmed from jealousy rather than Strian's accusations, but he wanted to tear apart any man who touched Sigrid. Sigrid shot him a quelling look before squeezing her eyes shut. Strian jumped and a look of awe crossed his face.

"Thank you," he whispered.

"What did she do?" demanded Bjorn.

Sigrid smiled at Strian, but neither said anything. Sigrid shared Eindride's love and pride for his son through her and into his son's hands. Strian felt his father's presence as if he were the one holding them. Sigrid backed away.

"Grímr is a furious man. Even more dangerous when angry. While pride consumes Hakin and Einar and ambition drives them, spite drives Grímr, which makes him even more unpredictable. Grímr intends to kill both Hakin and Einar. He will banish Inga if he has the chance. He doesn't want to claim Einar's children as his own, but he has had no choice. Once Einar is dead, and he sends Inga away, he will have no other heirs. He sees their usefulness. It won't be enough to defeat just Hakin and Einar. We can't leave Grímr alive."

"Inga is no warrior, but she wasn't at Hakin's homestead. We didn't find her there." Freya mentioned.

"I know. I didn't see her there either. I don't know where she is, but I know she isn't with her husband or the warriors. Otherwise, I'd have observed her with them."

"What did my father show you tonight?" Strian guided them back to the matter that most needed their attention.

"Hakin intends to harry you. He wants to draw Ivar and Rangvald into skirmishes to run down your supplies and thin your forces. He believes he can fool all of you into these smaller fights that way the true battle is just an opportunity to pick off the last of you one by one."

"And Grímr and Einar agree to this method?" Leif wondered.

"They have no reason to disagree. Einar thinks he is a few kills away from being a jarl, and Grímr has no intention of letting either of them walk away from the battlefield. It would be easy enough to kill both Einar and Hakin in battle. Grímr has more men loyal to him than his brother suspects. I believe his brother doesn't suspect at all. And Einar believes your tribe will follow him since he's captain of Ivar's warriors."

"Then he intends to kill me," Leif interjected. "And Freya too."

"Einar told Hakin's people you spend too much time sailing and hold no real claim over your people."

"Einar would need to kill all of us. He thinks that's possible?" Freya quipped.

"I don't know that he thinks beyond what he wishes to see happen. He believes he can control his own fate as much as he can control yours. He thinks it's the gods' will that he be jarl." Sigrid looked at Freya, adding, "He will also try to kill Erik."

Freya drew back not understanding why Sigrid directed the comment at her. She had only seen the man once, and that was just before they left to rescue Sigrid. She looked questioningly at Sigrid, but the other woman already turned to face the others.

"Did you see how we fought?" Bjorn demanded.

"Bjorn," Leif warned.

"What? She has seen this much. I would know what she has to say about what matters. So, we know who our enemies are. We already knew most of that. What we need to know is whether we win and how to win."

"Sigrid is a seer not a warrior. It isn't her duty to make us win. She has no power over how we fight." Leif stepped forward and pushed between them. Sigrid turned to look up at Leif and rested her hands on his forearm. She shook her head, but when he tried to press forward, she shoved against his chest.

"I can defend myself," she hissed.

"You don't have to."

"But I can, and I will." Sigrid turned to look at Bjorn as Leif slipped his arms around her waist and drew her back. His protectiveness grated on her nerves when what they needed to focus on was the upcoming battle. However, a small part of her basked in the feel of Leif's masculine frame encircling her so willingly. "Bjorn is right. You need to know how to win. I can't promise success, but I can tell you what the runes showed me." Bjorn gloated as Leif snarled. "Enough. You are both worse than stray mutts. I'm not a bone for you to snap over."

"But I do plan to lick and taste all of you," Leif leaned over to whisper in her ear. The warmth of his breath tickled her skin, and she couldn't suppress the shudder that slid through her. She broke free of his hold and moved out of his reach. She couldn't concentrate with his presence and wicked suggestions looming over her.

"The runes told me victory would be yours but not without a fight. The only way is for something to make secret desires known and unlikely partnerships come to bear."

"What does that even mean?" Bjorn demanded.

"It means those things coveted can no longer be kept hidden, and it will make partners from unlikely pairs."

"I understood the words you used. I don't understand how that will help, nor do I understand how any of that will happen." Bjorn crossed his arms.

Sigrid shrugged. "It isn't my place to make you believe or even understand. I know you can, and you will, but I can't make you do it."

"You're being cryptic, and we don't have time to muddle through your riddles," Tyra cut in. She looked at Bjorn who nodded. "Just speak plainly, Seer."

Sigrid shook her head and stood with her staff in hand. "You aren't prepared for all fate has shown me. You will know when the gods are ready. Until then, I can tell you someone will deceive and convince Rangvald's forces to alter their positions during the fight. They will suffer heavy losses, but the deception will prove to be to their advantage. Ivar's forces will avoid most of the minor skirmishes because of you five. Loyalties will be questioned among you, but it's uncertainty that drives it, not true mistrust."

"You believe us to be victorious?"

"Yes, Strian. Leif and Freya will survive to lead your tribe one day. Rangvald's people will prosper when Hakin and Grímr fall, and you, Strian, will have vengeance for your father. He will make his way to Valhalla."

Freya stood as the group questioned Sigrid. She was still mulling over Sigrid's comment about Rangvald's son. "Am I to save someone?"

Sigrid turned to look at Freya and smiled. "You are both to be saved."

Before anyone could ask more of her, Sigrid turned toward the camp and walked back.

"Just a moment," Tyra caught up to her. "That's it? You won't tell us more about how to win? Isn't that what you're supposed to see?"

"It might be, but that isn't what the gods have revealed so far. I can no more force the gods to my will than you can. They grant me the knowledge they wish me to have. It would appear the details of this war aren't ones they believe I need. At least not at this point." Sigrid turned to look at Tyra. "I am not trying to be awkward. This gift of sight is sometimes more a curse than anything else. It often leaves me frustrated and frightened when I can't make a difference because I don't always learn all I need to in time. Sometimes it's not until it's too late to change anything. I believe the gods do that to remind me it's not my place to change fate but only to impart it when they choose. I wish I could tell you more. I wish I knew more," she looked back at Leif, "because I would save myself the heartache of not knowing."

NINE

Leif watched as Tyra and Sigrid spoke. He could see something filled both women with tension, but their conversation seemed cordial enough. Leif wanted to pepper Sigrid with questions just as much as the others did, but he knew it would get him nowhere. He knew she already shared what she could. He also knew he should focus on the battle to come and not worry about a stranger's feelings. Except she no longer felt like a stranger. She felt like a revelation that explained what he had felt and sensed all his life. Leif followed the rest of the group back to camp but kept his distance. He went to check on his horse, needing a few moments of solitude to consider everything he saw and heard that evening. He admitted to himself that the sight of Sigrid spirit walking still shook him.

Leif knew it was a sight he would have to get accustomed to if he were to marry her, but it wasn't one he would ever enjoy. Just the opposite. He would rather run into the hills or dive into a frozen fjord than watch the trance she fell into. Leif wanted to push her to reveal more about the battle, but he knew she had no more she could share. He also knew pushing her would only drive a wedge between them. Leif's soul recognized Sigrid would marry him no matter what because she spent her life seeing that vision. However, his soul wanted a mate, not just a woman living out what she believed was an unalterable destiny.

I have never been alone before. I have family all around me who I care about, and I have plenty of women to choose from. I have bedded most, and some of them many times. It's not like there aren't choices when it comes to finding company. But I realize now I'm lonely. Or at least I was. I have had no one to confide in. Not truly. Not about how I feel or what I think when I can't share with anyone else. I am the jarl's son. I don't have the luxury to share everything I think or feel, not even with Freya and Bjorn. I am tired of always holding back a part of me, tired of forcing myself to remain separate from those who can talk and act freely. I have found no one I want to share these things with or who I can trust. At least not until now.

I don't understand how I can be so sure of Sigrid. What did she mean when she said loyalties will be tested? Does she mean I will test her loyalties, or will she test mine? Was that comment even directed at me? I'm always surrounded by people, but I am lonely just as often. I think it'd be easier if I didn't have people surrounding me at every turn. I find I only want Sigrid. I'd walk away from it all if I could take her with me. I understand none of this.

How can I feel so sure of someone I met only a couple of days ago? How can a stranger make me feel calmer and more secure than the people I've spent my entire life with? Why do the gods torment me and make me think about feelings I've ignored for years? Why can't I continue enjoying life and avoid admitting how I really feel?

Because I want her. I want her with more than just my mind and my body. Though the gods know I can't quit thinking about sinking into her and making her mine. I would fill her with my seed and watch her grow round over and over again with our children. I can't cease thinking about how she felt and sounded when I brought her to release. I would do that every night for the rest of our lives. Damn. I'm hard as a fucking poleax now. That wasn't even what I meant to think about. I was trying to keep from thinking about how much I desire her body. But it's more than that. I trust her with everything about me. I trust Freya and the others with my life and my riches, but I trust Sigrid with my secret thoughts. I trust Sigrid with my soul. But how?

Leif drew his dagger as he heard a soft rustle come from behind him.

"Calm yourself, Brother. I don't need to be speared."

"Then you shouldn't sneak up on me."

"I didn't. I made enough noise to wake the dead, but you weren't listening. I could've killed you, and you'd have been dead before you knew you were on your way to Valhalla. Can't you stop thinking about her long enough not to lose your life? I don't choose to go into battle with some love-struck idiot who'd rather be making cow eyes than defending his people."

"Are you questioning my loyalty? Is the prophecy playing out already?"

"You know I'm not. I know you're loyal, but I also know you're distracted. I don't wish to see you dead or lose my life trying to protect yours because you've forgotten your purpose."

"You heard Sigrid. Neither of us is to die, at least not soon. I won't be distracted when it comes time to fight, but I won't be made to feel guilty because I'm confused about what's happening. A few days ago, all I wanted was to sleep in my bed and not deal with the world for at least a moon. But no, I find out we are in danger of having our home and our lives stolen from us. And as though knowing yet another battle is imminent isn't enough to keep my mind busy, I discover the gods have been giving a stranger a view into my life and my bed chamber that no one should have. I didn't ask for any of this. All I asked for was time at home. Now I have neither my bed nor my life to call my own. Do you have any idea what it's like to know some woman I've never met before, didn't even know existed, has watched me for years? She has seen and heard me, known what I've thought and felt, and I had no idea. Do you know how unnerving that is? It's as though I've been spied on for years with no chance to even the field. I hate it. I would undo all of it and never have met her like this. And for reasons I can't even begin to understand, I want nothing more—"

Leif saw Freya's eyes widen, but when he noticed, he also realized it wasn't because of what he said. She was looking past him. "What?" he demanded as he spun around. His eyes landed on Sigrid, who stood between Strian and Tyra. Even Bjorn looked shocked.

Sigrid whistled, and a horse jostled the others before walking to her. "He was mine before they took me. He became yours when you raided Hakin's home." She said nothing else before she swung herself onto the horse's bare back. She spun the horse around and kneed it. "Good fortune to you all. You shall all live to fight another war."

"Sigrid! Sigrid!" Leif turned on the others. "You might have told me you were there. You could have spoken up." Leif pulled his horse free from the others and mounted.

"You seemed to do more than enough talking." Bjorn smirked. "And just when I was getting to like her. Maybe she'll still marry into our family now that her options are open."

"Arse."

Leif pushed his horse into a canter and then a gallop as he followed Sigrid. He followed her into the woods toward the spot they used earlier, but she was nowhere to be seen. Leif scanned the area and saw a flash of motion to his right. He followed the blonde hair that caught the wisps of light filtering through the branches. He puzzled over why she was doubling back around to the other side of the camp.

Sigrid sat with her arms crossed as she waited for Leif to catch up. "You assumed I was running away rather than trying to get some distance from you."

"You rode off. It's not like you stomped away."

"Because I'm not a toddler. I do not stomp nor am I stupid enough to run away. I need space from you, but I have no intention of traveling alone when I don't know where I am. I also know there's an army looking to pick a fight. I don't want to meet up with them."

"Then why take your horse?"

"Because I'm also not stupid enough to leave camp with no way to escape if something happens."

"You didn't hear what I was about to say."

"No, I didn't. I just heard what you actually *did* say."

"And it didn't sound good."

Sigrid dismounted without answering. She led her horse to a patch of grass while Leif followed with his horse in tow.

"I was going to say I want nothing more than to run away with you. I want what you already have. The opportunity to know everything about you. To just know you like you do me."

"That isn't what it sounded like."

"I know. I sounded like an arse. I feel like one too. You've made me think about things I never would have. I haven't spoken of feelings more serious than lust and battle since I was a child. I've barely thought about them. Now I can't stop thinking. I'm jealous. And I find I'm lonely too. Those don't make for conversation with my friends. Nor are they emotions I'm used to acknowledging."

Sigrid looked at Leif, who towered over her. He could break her into pieces, but the tortured look on his face showed what he must have looked like as a young boy. The guilt, remorse, and fear etched between his brows as he watched her. She stepped forward and wrapped her arms around his waist. She waited until he returned the embrace.

"Ours isn't how most relationships start. We're each jealous of phantoms. Jealous of pasts we can't change. I want you to get to know me, and I intend to share with you the same things I already know about you, but don't think there is nothing left for me to learn about you. I don't know the real you. I've seen glimpses, but I haven't seen all your life. I wish to know what you are like with your people, your family. I want to see what you will be like with me."

"Fair enough. I want the same."

They stood holding one another until the moon rose, and the night grew dark. When Sigrid shivered, they walked back to camp. No one said anything to them as they returned their horses to the pack and hobbled them. They sat next to each other to eat what someone had left for them.

After the women returned from seeking privacy, Sigrid laid down beside the fire. She had already said goodnight to Leif, so it surprised her when he laid down next to her. He tossed an extra fur over her and wrapped his arm around her as he spooned her back.

"Leif."

"Shh. Just let me."

It wasn't long before both were asleep. Sigrid fell into a deep and dreamless sleep she needed after the exertions of the day. Leif slept much lighter, always vigilant for disturbances in the night, but he was more comfortable than he could ever remember. Morning came far too soon for both. They laid awake but with their eyes shut for as long as they could, enjoying the feel of their bodies pressed against one another.

TEN

Leif looked around the campsite one last time. The other captains spoke with their crews as they readied the horses and covered any traces that they spent the night there. Leif walked over to Bjorn but kept Sigrid in his sights. They had spoken little that morning, but there was a peace between them after a night spent sleeping in one another's arms. Leif never actually slept with other women. He either left or sent them away before a full night passed where there was sleep involved. He dozed in between exploits some nights, but he never slept with a woman to actually sleep. Leif found he enjoyed falling asleep then waking to Sigrid snuggled into his body. He knew the chilly night and his body heat drove her sleepy mind to seek him out, but he basked in the joy of waking to her draped across his chest with one of her legs entwined with his. Her hair tickled his nose, and he enjoyed stroking the silken strands away then down her slim back. He forced the grin from his face before Bjorn could ridicule his happiness.

"We ride in ten minutes. We have fair weather, so we take advantage. Hakin is a madman to begin with by thinking he can conquer our land, and he's even madder for doing it so close to the season changing."

"He believes it will take him no time to squash us, so he doesn't feel a need to hurry." Bjorn observed.

"The man's pride knows no limits."

"That's clear since he underestimates Grímr and trusts Einar."

"How is Strian taking the news of his uncle's perfidy?" Leif glanced to where their friend stood talking to his crew.

"Better than I would have expected. I think he no longer feels guilty for distrusting and disliking his uncle. He's the only family Strian still has, so he felt he had to remain close. I think Einar exploited that."

"I'm sure he did. I also now assume he did so to gather information about our voyages. It must have been much easier for him to slip away from home when Strian wasn't there to notice."

"That's what I figured. How else could he have carried on with Inga if Strian was there to question his disappearances? I wonder why his wife nor children ever said anything. I bet they didn't feel safe speaking up." Bjorn frowned as he considered Einar's timid wife.

"I wonder where they used to meet. There's no way that Einar could travel all the way to Hakin's home and back without people noticing his absence. I know Inga didn't come to us. What was Grímr thinking allowing his wife to carry on as she did? He should have set her aside the first time a child was born looking like Einar."

"I think he couldn't beget a child on her. I haven't heard of him having any illegitimate children either. He needs the heirs, so he claims Einar's children as his own."

"How little Einar cares about anyone but himself if he would let another man claim six of his children." Leif's lip curled as he pictured his father's warrior captain.

"He cares little for the ones he has with his wife. Why should he care about those he has with Inga? After all, he's in love with your mother."

Leif's jaw ticked and his nose flared. Any man other than

his father touching his mother, thinking of her with desire, was enough to make Leif's blood run hot. "If Strian doesn't kill him, then I will."

Bjorn nodded and looked over at Sigrid. "You two seem to get along better than last night. What we heard didn't paint you in the best light, my friend."

"I know. You caught my rant just before I was about to say despite all of that, I want nothing more than to be with her."

"How can you be so sure?"

"I don't understand it. I just know. There is something about her that brings a calm to my soul that has never been there before. She fills a hole I didn't know was there."

"It sounds like *you* want to fill a hole you didn't know was there," Bjorn taunted.

Leif grabbed Bjorn by the collar of his shirt and lifted him onto his tiptoes. "Don't ever speak of her like that again. She isn't some whore for me to fuck and move on. She will be my wife and one day our *frú*. Don't forget that. Ever. Cousin or not."

Bjorn's laughter filled the air as he gripped Leif's wrist and twisted. "Simmer down. I was just testing you."

"Testing me? I doubt that."

"And you passed."

"How gracious of you."

"No, seriously. Leif, you have never taken more than a passing fancy in a woman. And it's always been an eagerness to bed her and little more. You would never have defended another woman so fiercely when it comes to talking about bedding her. Sigrid will make you a fine wife."

"And you make me sound little more than a whore."

Bjorn laughed at Leif's look of chagrin. "Who am I to judge?"

"I would say not one at all. You should count yourself lucky that your prick hasn't shriveled up and fallen off." Tyra walked up to the two men and glared at Bjorn. "Are you two done gossiping? We're all waiting." Tyra walked away to join Sigrid, Freya, and Strian.

"That woman has a forked tongue." Bjorn watched Tyra's hips sway as she moved further away. He shook his head. "I pity the man who tries to tame her."

"Perhaps it will be a wise man who doesn't try to tame her."

"Will you ride with me today?" Leif asked Sigrid as he stood beside her near the horses.

"Why wouldn't I? Do you not want me to?"

"Of course, I do. That's why I'm asking. But now I know you have your own horse, I wondered if you might prefer to ride alone."

Sigrid nodded before she looked around the party as men and women mounted. She noticed several of them watching them. Some curious, some wary, but a few were undoubtedly unwelcoming. Word spread of her spirit walk the previous night. Even though no one other than the captains knew what she saw, others figured out why she, Freya, and Leif disappeared for so long. Her prophecy from the rolled runes also became known to most of the warriors.

"You need not fear them. Even the suspicious ones. They know you're with me. None would dare act against you, and if they did, they know what consequences they face."

"I think I should ride alone even though I'd rather ride with you."

"Then why don't you? I can protect you better if you ride with me."

"No, I'd be in the way if you need to swing your sword. You're better off if I'm not in your way."

Leif pulled her forward, so their toes touched. He slid one arm around her waist as he took her hand in his.

"You are not in the way, and I am not better off without

you. I won't force you to, but if you ride alone, then you ride in the center."

"Fine."

The riders set off at a canter as they moved into their formations. Leif and Bjorn rode at the front of the line of warriors. Strian and his first mate rode at the rear. Freya, along with Freya's first mate, rode to Sigrid's right while Tyra and a man Sigrid didn't know rode to her left. They dispersed the other men between Leif and Sigrid, and Sigrid and Strian. Just as Leif had insisted, Sigrid rode in the middle of the entourage. The morning passed with Sigrid enjoying the sun on her face while she caught snippets of conversation. No one attempted to talk to her, but she didn't mind. She was used to the solitude of her hut. It was a struggle for her to be around so many people with no chance for time alone. The thought of carrying on a stream of conversation made her head hurt.

When they stopped to water their horses, Sigrid and the other women slipped away for a moment of privacy. Sigrid lingered as long as she dared at the side of the road, noticing one man watched her horse while it drank and nibbled at the grass. She enjoyed riding, spending hours on horseback searching for various herbs and plants she needed. Sigrid was skilled and strong, but she wasn't eager to get back on the horse. She would have preferred an hour of solitude instead.

"You have made your point to everyone else. You ride with me now."

Sigrid startled when Leif stepped out from a bush next to her. "High handed once again."

Leif pulled her back behind the bush and yanked her against him. "No, I've missed you."

His mouth descended to hers as her body reacted to their nearness. She wound her arms around his neck and moaned as his hands cupped her bottom to bring her closer. She opened to him without reservation and welcomed his tongue into her mouth. It felt like velvet as it swirled with hers, and she sucked lightly on it. Leif's grip tightened to nearly painful, but Sigrid found it only aroused her more. She rubbed her mons against his steel rod that pulsed against her. She felt it twitch as she rocked her hips.

"I will take you right here at this very moment if you keep doing that."

In response, she trailed her hand down his chest and cupped his manhood. She didn't know what to do, so she ran her palm up and down. "What if that is exactly what I want?"

"Leif!" Freya's sharp tone cut through their haze of lust.

"We must go, but you ride with me. I don't want to go another moment without touching you."

Sigrid nodded once and turned toward Freya's voice and the waiting riders. Leif watched the sway of her hips in the leather breeches one of the women must have lent her while they took their reprieve in the woods. They were snug and encased her bottom like a second skin. Her legs were slightly thicker than whoever owned the pants, so the leather left nothing to the imagination. Leif wanted nothing more than to drag her back into the woods, peel the breeches from her, and sink into her until he could no longer hold back and spilled himself there. He growled when he realized that what was on view for him was also on view for all the men. His jealousy slammed into him as he watched the men who avoided her now appreciated her presence. He marched over to her and kissed her neck before swinging her onto his horse. He was behind her before she settled into place.

"They already know I'm yours. You don't have to keep staking a claim. You're worse than a dog marking his territory."

"And I will keep doing so until they wipe their lecherous looks off their faces," Leif grumbled.

Sigrid's soft laughter was a fuse to the fire in his belly. He wrapped his arm around her as his horse leaped forward. The lurch made her body fall back into his.

"You did that on purpose. You don't have to. I'm where I want to be, Leif. You've claimed me, and the only person that should matter to is me. You've accepted me, and for that I breathe easy."

"It matters that they all know. I won't have there be any doubt. I saw the way the men look at you now that you wear Freya or Tyra's pants."

"They're your sister's. As for the men looking at me, let them. If looking is the worst they do, then I'm safe. I count myself lucky. I'm riding with you, you slept next to me, and you've announced I'm under your protection. I would rather think you do that because it's me you care for rather than you acting like a little boy who doesn't want to share his newest toy."

"I do care for you. Very much, and I find it has me acting out of character." Just as the day before, his hand cupped the underside of her breast, and the rocking of the horse pressed her hips back into his groin.

Sigrid leaned her head back against Leif's shoulder and allowed the horse's gait to lull her into a light sleep. Just before she dozed off, she murmured, "I like this version of you."

Sigrid startled awake. She looked around and realized the landscape they passed was what she saw only a few minutes ago. A dread slithered along her spine as her eyes swung from one spot to another. She sat rigid and leaned forward.

"What's the matter?"

Sigrid sat back up and looked over her shoulder. The look on her face must have told Leif more than she intended.

"You've had a vision."

"More a premonition. A feeling. We will be attacked. When we cross the next rise, there will be a war band three times the size of yours." Leif turned to issue orders, but Sigrid's nails bit into his arm. "Leif, wait. You must have Bjorn take Tyra away now. If you don't, one of the men will confuse her for me. We have similar color hair. The man will take Tyra and try to molest her if he gets her away from the group. They must wait to rejoin us until we're all away from here. Please Leif, tell him now."

"I will have Bjorn take you too. He can hide you both, and you'll be safer with two warriors."

Sigrid shook her head as she swallowed the lump in her throat. "No."

"What do you mean, no? Listen to me on this one, Sigrid. I won't argue."

"Neither will I. You must let Bjorn take Tyra. They will take me regardless. Save Tyra."

"No one is taking you."

Sigrid's sad gaze told Leif more than he wanted to know. He tightened his hold on her but swung around to speak to the others. "Prepare for attack. Bjorn and Tyra, ride into the woods. Bjorn, stay with Tyra until you are sure the battle is over."

"I'm staying here. I'm not running away, and absolutely not with him."

Leif opened his mouth, but Sigrid spoke first. "Tyra, please. It has to be this way." Sigrid and Tyra exchanged a look Leif didn't understand, but the warrior woman nodded her head before glaring at Bjorn. They broke off into the trees.

Freya rode up alongside her brother. She looked at the couple and then at the road ahead of them. "Do you want me to ride with Sigrid? I can take her in the opposite direction."

Sigrid shook her head. "I know what I saw, Freya. I know what will be."

Leif despised riding into what he knew was a trap. However, there was no other way to go. They were traveling along a strip of land bordered by fjords on both sides. While the strip was wide enough, so they couldn't see the water from where they were, Leif knew there were few places to go. At least, not if he wanted Bjorn and Tyra to get away. He had to choose between sitting and waiting for the attack to come to them or trying to control the situation by entering the attack aware it was coming.

"What do you think?" Leif looked to his sister.

"I think we're running out of time and luck. If there are as many as Sigrid believes, we'll be hard pressed to beat them. Our best bet is an attempt to ride through and around."

"If we do that, and we somehow make it through, then what of Bjorn and Tyra? They won't be able to catch us if our enemy lives. If we struggle to survive with our forty strong, how will two of them make it alone?"

"They'll be able to slip past much easier if there are only two of them," Strian joined the conversation. "If there's a chance for Tyra to slip away from Bjorn, and a chance for him to chase her, they'll find it."

Freya and Leif stared at him, but a small smile played at Sigrid's lips. Strian only shrugged.

"Sigrid, what did you see?" Strian looked to her.

"I saw the battle but couldn't make out faces. It was just bodies fighting until a man grabs me. He takes me away while Leif fights Einar. Einar sees they have me, and he runs. In the melee, he's able to slip away. I didn't experience what happens after that, so I didn't learn what happens to any of you or where they take me. I wasn't granted that, but I can only sense fate has shifted. It's not as I once saw. Einar never rejoined your father. Bjorn won't kill Einar, but Tyra and Strian will survive." The battle lust flowed through the warriors who surrounded her. She could feel it seeping into her like a pervasive winter wind. "I don't know which of your men will fall, but I do know the captains survive. I have seen each of you enough times to know this isn't where any of you will die."

"Little consolation," snarked Freya.

"I know. But use that knowledge for what you will." Sigrid looked at Leif. "You must let me ride alone."

"Absolutely not."

"This is what must happen. You cannot fight fate. You

shouldn't even try, even if I sense Einar is. I will be alive when this ends, and so will you."

"But in what state will I find you? Half beaten?" Leif grazed his fingers along the bruises that still marred her face from when Hakin's men stole her the first time. "Raped? What if I can't get to you in time?"

"You will." Sigrid swung her leg free and slid to the ground before Leif could stop her. She dashed to the back of the riders, found her horse, and swung onto its bare back. Sigrid didn't mind that there was still no saddle for her. Sigrid grew up riding bareback and preferred it. The horse had a bridle and reins which was all she needed. She rode abreast of Freya and Leif and reached over to Leif's saddle. Sigrid lifted her staff from where Leif tucked it under the flap of one of his saddle bags and checked that the rounded top that held her runes was secure. Sigrid ran her hands down to the bottom and pulled. A small cover came off the bottom and a wickedly sharp blade appeared. It turned the staff into a spear. Sigrid looked around and raised an eyebrow.

"My mother taught me to consider my safety when I ventured into the woods alone."

They advanced toward the location Sigrid pointed out. They were close to the rise when a wall of Norsemen streamed over it and barreled down the hill toward them. Sigrid wasn't far behind Freya when their warriors charged to meet the attackers.

Leif swung his horse around to bring it alongside Sigrid. His sword aimed at his first opponent and slid through the man's stomach. He pulled it free before swinging again, cleaving his next foe's head from his shoulders. Leif whistled, and Freya backed her horse so they could fight back-to-back with Sigrid locked in the middle. Leif knew they would have to dismount soon if they were to save the horses and not allow the enemy warriors to pull them off as the enemy poured forward on foot.

"We dismount! Sigrid, stay on your horse and ride. Don't

stop until you are clear of the fighters. You must try to get away."

Sigrid didn't answer. Instead, she swung her staff as a club, connecting the round top to the skull of a man who leaned forward to spear Freya's side. The impact was enough to make him fall from his horse. Sprawled on the ground, Sigrid stabbed him through the heart with the other end of her staff.

Leif stared in disbelief as the woman he thought of as in need of protection killed a man without flinching. He watched for a moment as she maneuvered her horse with her knees and swung her staff again into the gut of a man who charged her. She drew back and used the rounded end to drive into his sternum. As he doubled over, she swept her blade across his throat. Leif didn't have the luxury of watching much longer as more and more of Einar's men poured over the hill. It forced him to dismount, and he could only pray Sigrid would listen.

The battle raged on with Leif and the others holding their own despite being outnumbered. Leif fought as a berserker and lost all sense of time and space. He swung his sword and battle ax as sweat poured from his forehead and stung his eyes. He didn't have time to wipe it away in fear he would miss an attack that could maim him or end his life. Freya found his back, and they fought alongside one another. He watched as Strian fought his way toward them and joined them. The trio fought like this countless times in practice and in battle.

"There's Einar," Strian panted.

"I see," Leif grunted as he drove his ax into his opponent's exposed flesh where the man's shoulder met his neck.

"He's coming for you, Strian," Freya called out. She positioned herself to cover Strian's weaker side. He was left-handed, and Freya fought best with her right. This gave them a wider range to reach without clashing their own swords against one another. Leif edged to protect both of their backs.

Einar grinned as he saw his nephew and the children of his adversary fighting together. "You pups still look like you're tumbling about the whelping box. Let's see if you learned what I taught you," he taunted. "Nephew, you don't seem surprised to see me. Could it be the little tart Leif's humping told you? Where is the pretty, little seer?"

Leif didn't shift his gaze from Einar, even though he wanted to see if Sigrid made her escape. His heart knew she hadn't, even though his mind rebelled against the idea they would take her.

"Leif, tell me. Is she as tight as she looks? I shall enjoy having my turn with her. She will sleep in your bed every night, but it will be me she sleeps next to tonight."

"How can you be in two places at once? I thought it was our mother you coveted. Or have you already realized she will never accept you." Freya threw her own taunts at the man she had known her entire life. A man who had trained her both to fight and to sail. She couldn't contain her disgust as she looked at the traitor. "Do you think our mother will ever call out a name other than our father's? You think to make Sigrid yours, but what will you do when she turns your cods to lead? When she casts her runes, and your cock goes limp, never to rise again?"

"You can throw your words at me all you like, but we both know she's a seer not a witch. She can't do anything to my prick but take it wherever I shove it."

Leif roared as he surged forward. He broke away from the others to swing his sword in a rapid pattern of slices and jabs. Einar was prepared for the rhythm of the moves but not the intensity that came from a man protecting the woman he knew he would love for the rest of his days. Einar tried to capitalize on Leif's fury, banking on his anger distracting him. He swung his sword wide to draw Leif's attention while he tried to drive his knife into Leif's stomach. Leif was prepared and brought his ax down onto Einar's arm. Einar pulled back just in time to only receive a sharp cut through his leather bracer. Had he been any slower, his hand would have been laying on the ground.

"So, you did pay attention, pup," Einar goaded. Strian

moved around the back of his uncle as Leif continued to engage him from the front. "Would you stab me in the back, like a man with no honor, Nephew?"

"It's what you would deserve since you're nothing more than a backstabbing turd of offal."

"Such strong words for your own family. Your loyalty should have been to me not to Ivar and his brats. You would live to see tomorrow and could be the chief of my warriors once I kill Ivar and these two. Instead, you shall die too."

Strian didn't think twice before he drove his sword forward, except Einar shifted as he tried to attack Freya now. Strian's blade went through his shoulder instead of his heart. Einar grunted before dodging to the side to avoid all three as they attacked together. A sharp whistle sounded through the air, and Einar laughed.

"You're too late. The seer is mine, and she will cast fate to my control." Einar turned and sprinted for a horse that was being led to him by a woman on horseback.

Leif looked around and saw a flash of dark blonde hair swinging near the flanks of a horse. Sigrid was hanging over the back of it as it charged away. Leif searched for a mount, but he couldn't get to one soon enough. Leif ran to his man who attempted to control their animals. He pulled a mare loose and leaped into the saddle. Leif charged up the hill, but it was if the enemy vanished. There was no trace of any riders or even soldiers on foot. He scanned the horizon, but there was nothing.

"How could they simply disappear?" Freya asked as she rode up to meet him at the crest of the hill.

"Einar's ability to fade away is what made him ideal for training us. We must think as he would. Where would we go to hide and make our way to Hakin's army?"

"Einar will have boats to sail back down the fjord. He had to know we would give chase. He won't have attacked without a way out. Einar must have known something damaged our ships enough that we would come ashore."

Strian shook his head and closed his eyes for a long moment.

"You know none of this is your doing. Your uncle is his own man, and a rotten one at that. You are your father's son," Freya whispered, but her words carried weight. Strian nodded, but the haunted look lingered.

"Nobody would have thought him capable of this. None of us would have believed anyone other than a seer if they told us Einar would become a *niðingr*, a betrayer of our trust and disgraceful." Freya continued. "You proved yourself loyal when we were children. You don't need to prove it again now. We already know."

Freya nudged her horse forward knowing any more conversation about feelings would only make Strian baulk. There was a fine line between consoling and patronizing. Freya was careful not to cross it. She looked back at Leif, whose face was a thundercloud. Freya almost pitied Einar for when Strian and Leif met him again. He wouldn't be long for this world. He brought this shame upon himself, and she wished she had a claim to killing him too.

"We ride to the inlet instead of further inland. We'll waste hours having to ride back, but there is little choice if we intend to stand a chance to catch them. We meet our crew and go after Einar. He knows we will, and he knows he will lead us to Hakin and our father. This is one of those skirmishes Sigrid warned of." Freya's idea was the only reasonable one, and both Strian and Leif agreed.

"How many men did we lose?" Leif looked around but saw most of the men.

"We only lost three. Surri, Njáll, and Refur died as they should. We will take their bodies with us and prepare them for Valhalla tonight," Strian sat tall in his saddle as he looked back at the warriors who awaited orders to move out. He was once again ready to lead his crew. They rode out at a gallop as they followed the path south and toward the upcoming war.

ELEVEN

The party rode hard for the rest of the day. Leif couldn't settle his mind as it hopped from one horrific scenario to another. He couldn't shake the sense of foreboding that took hold of his gut. For the first time in his life, he wished he had the gift of sight. He was impatient to reach Sigrid and wished he could foretell what would happen to her. His shoulders ached from holding himself so rigid while leaning low over his horse's withers. The others did well to keep up with him when he pushed them all to the brink of exhaustion before slowing for the night. Winter approached, and the days were growing shorter. He would have ridden in the dark if he didn't know how foolish that could prove to be. If the horses weren't lathered and snorting, and if he were willing to go at a slower pace, then riding at night might have been an option. But as it stood, the horses and his men were spent. They made good time, and he was even sure he caught sight of sails the few times the path wound close to the shore. However, he couldn't be sure if those were Einar's or their own flotilla. They could even be someone else's, though he doubted that. Leif chewed on dried beef he always traveled with and drank deeply from the mead horn he hadn't touched since leaving home.

"Careful there. You shall end up in your cups and try to bed one of these hairy beasts."

Leif whipped around and grinned as Bjorn and Tyra emerged from the woods.

"Or it will be what I need to sleep through your snoring. I've confused you for a wild boar more than once," Leif laughed.

"You wouldn't be the first to make such a mistake." Tyra quipped.

Leif looked between the two captains, puzzled at Tyra's biting words. She always had a sharp tongue, but her words had more sting this time. Leif wondered what his cousin did to worsen an already tenuous relationship. Bjorn and Tyra had antagonized one another since they were children. Both had a dry wit that often was at the other's expense. Tyra knocked Bjorn down one too many times when they were training as teens, and Bjorn never seemed to forgive her. His patronizing manner rubbed Tyra's patience raw. While they trusted one another on the battlefield, admired one another's sailing prowess, and considered themselves friends, they were the ones who got along the least.

"Sleep next to me tonight, and you can keep me quiet," Bjorn taunted.

"If you're inviting me to suffocate you in your sleep, then I shall accept."

"I can think of plenty to do with that tongue besides talking."

"I shall remember that tonight when I'm not the one sleeping alone. Perhaps your horse will keep you warm."

"I have been called a stallion before."

"By the voices in your head. But wait, once again, you are alone. Be sure to warm your hand first."

Leif could no longer contain his laughter as his cousin snarled. Tyra's reference to Bjorn taking himself in hand while she found a bedmate struck home, and Bjorn looked like he was ready to strangle the woman as she sauntered away.

"Why do you let her goad you like that?"

"I have no idea. She is like a burr up my backside, but she's one of the finest warriors we have, and by far the best sailor. I can't help but respect her even when I don't like her."

Leif nodded before turning serious. "Did you see anyone while you traveled?"

"No. Not a soul. We couldn't hear anyone either. We passed close to the coast hoping to catch sight of something, anything, that could guide us. There was nothing." Bjorn settled next to Leif by the fire, and Leif passed him the horn, which Bjorn shook. "You've drunk more than half of this already. You haven't opened it since we left, and in one night, you've drunk most of it. That isn't like you."

"If I pass out, then I won't have to keep worrying about her."

"You know she's well. She has told you that the future holds a family for you. Together."

"That's still not a guarantee. Einar is very well ignoring what fate tries to bring him. He could rape her or beat her before she's returned."

"Would you turn her away if Einar did? Or would you wait to see if she carries his babe before deciding?"

Leif's hands balled into fists, but he kept them at his sides. "You are testing me too often. You know I will make her my wife no matter what happens. You don't need to question whether I would keep my word to her."

"I seek only to enlighten you to your own feelings. You aren't only quick to defend her, but you feel the offense on her behalf."

"This isn't just some passing fancy. I can't even explain how I feel. I know it makes little sense. I've known her only a few days, but I'm telling you, it's like she's filled a soul deep hole I'd been trying to ignore for years."

"I shall take your word for it."

"You will understand one day."

"I sincerely hope not. I have no intention of being so enraptured with one woman."

"You will. If for no other reason than you protest so much. And when you marry, don't fool yourself into thinking you will keep concubines. You shall find your match one day, and you won't want anyone else. And any woman willing to take you on, would cut off your balls before sharing you with anyone else."

"You're probably right," Bjorn chuckled as he took the last draw on the mead horn before handing it back. Leif turned it upside down and not a drop came out.

"Arse."

"So you've said before."

The next morning couldn't come soon enough for Leif. Just the day before, he dreaded the sunrise and having to pry himself away from Sigrid. This morning he couldn't be on his horse early enough. He set a hard pace once again, and by midday, they reached the inlet where they meant to dock. They looked around, but there was no sign of their crews. Leif paced along the pebble beach and shielded his eyes as he strained to see if there was even a hint of movement across the water.

"They should be here by nightfall," Freya stated as she walked past with an armful of wood.

"Why did we even bother going over land? We should have just stayed with the boats and sailed. Then she never would have been abducted." Leif huffed as Bjorn clapped his hand on Leif's shoulder.

"You know Sigrid couldn't have spirit walked anywhere else in Midgard without us coming ashore. We needed the safety and privacy the trees gave us. There was no way for her to do it on deck or in Freya's cabin. I wasn't even there, but I could tell from how you and Freya looked that whatever you saw wasn't something the others needed to witness. That is why we went ashore. And now we know of Einar's plan. We know of Hakin's and Grímr's too. We know we should be on the lookout for traps and attacks meant only to distract us and whittle us down to an army of none. We wouldn't know any of this without Sigrid being on land."

"I get it. You don't need to keep repeating yourself. It's tiresome."

"Just as tiresome as your moping and self-recriminations. That won't get her rescued or us to Ivar and Rangvald any faster."

Leif knew his cousin was right, but it didn't stop his heart from tightening every time he imagined what Sigrid was enduring. It didn't make him any more patient while looking for their longboats. He scrubbed his hand over his eyes, trying to wipe his headache away. Bjorn elbowed him, and he looked up.

"While you're hiding behind your hand, you're missing our boats' arrival."

Leif followed the finger Bjorn extended just beyond his nose. He swatted Bjorn's arm away but saw the outlines Bjorn spotted. Leif said a silent prayer of thanks to All Father, Odin, and Freyja. He hoped that Freyja would be on his side and protect her spirit walker. As a fellow seer, Leif prayed that Freyja would not abandon Sigrid when she most needed the goddess's protection. Bjorn and Leif moved back up the hill and along the cliff that served as a bank to the fjord the boats would maneuver into.

The crevice in the land was deep, allowing the shallow bottomed boats to move inland without running aground. Their longboats came into the inlet and could anchor close enough for the plank gangway to rest even with the rail. Crews went aboard their respective ships. Each captain inspected their boat before they were underway again. They sailed through the evening and into the night. The fjord was deep, but it was also narrow. For most of the journey, the boats sailed single file. Tyra's boat led the way. She was the most natural and accomplished sailor in their group. It was as if she had been born to the water. She seemed to sense the whims and moods of the seas, and she had never led them astray, even during the worst of storms. She always kept them on course, and the others learned to trust her implicitly for all things nautical.

TWELVE

Sigrid thought she would throw up again. She had little in her stomach, but the saddle bit into her belly, and the jostling of the horse made bile rush up her throat. Sigrid swallowed down the burning taste and tried to breathe through her nose. She was slung across the horse when Einar's man grabbed her then shoved her aboard a longboat to shiver and starve. She stayed that way until they returned to land and the horses. Putting up little fight once she identified her captor, she knew it was better for her to go willingly, or at least look like she went willingly, than to face being beaten again. The last time someone kidnapped her, Hakin's men beat her even though she put up no fight. They did it for the pure enjoyment of battering a woman. She suspected that Einar feared her supposed powers too much to risk harming her. She knew he stole her in the belief she would see for him. He thought her little more than a witch, despite what he declared aloud, and he intended to capitalize on that and have her cast spells for him to succeed in battle.

The time spent hanging sideways on the horse caused her consciousness to fade in and out. The moments of black allowed her to see more of the future. Sigrid no longer wanted to panic since she knew what course she needed to take. She forced herself to go against her very nature when she found patience excruciating. She worried Leif would do something impetuous in his attempt to rescue her. She didn't doubt he would come for her, and she looked forward to the rescue. However, she didn't want Leif making a foolish mistake that could alter their fate and see him dead.

The horse's hoof hit a rut, and the saddle bit into her skin just below her ribs. Sigrid couldn't contain the groan the pain elicited. Sigrid attempted to keep the men believing she was unconscious even during her times of wakefulness. Having thrown up three times already, the men believed she passed back out after each time. She had, but she was very much conscious now and regretting that she made her state known to the others. A hand landed hard across her backside and then squeezed. She ground her teeth to keep from yelping. The hand rained down several more spanks before pinching her.

"She's too scrawny for me. I would break her in half before I even sank to the hilt."

A chorus of laughs sounded from around her, and her cheeks burned at the humiliation of not only being manhandled but then insulted.

Leif doesn't seem to mind. His hands seem to end up there within moments of taking hold of me. I can't be lacking that much. And what does it matter if I am? I'm not trying to impress any of these heathens.

Sigrid slipped when the horse came to a sudden stop. The man she rode with dismounted and yanked her from the horse's back. She stumbled as her legs shook trying to bear her weight after hours of jostling.

"She's spindlier than a newborn foal." This time she recognized Einar's voice before the others chuckled. "She needs breaking in is all."

Sigrid's skin prickled as she watched Einar approach. He fingered a few strands of her hair before wrapping the length around his hand and tugging.

"Don't worry, little seer. I have a more important purpose

for you than rutting. Displease me though, and you shall make up for it with my cock down your throat. Do you understand?" Sigrid tried to nod, but Einar's hand held her head in place. He squeezed her cheeks together until her lips pursed. "I asked you a question. Do you understand?"

Sigrid stomped hard on his foot before bringing her knee to his groin. Einar doubled over but recovered enough to reach for her. Sigrid was faster. As his fingers brushed her throat, she pulled her staff loose from the saddle behind her.

"Touch me again, and it's not the future of the battle I change. It will be how you die. And when that happens."

Sigrid knew she had little control over changing the events of the future, at least not by her divinations. But these men didn't need to know that. A healthy fear of her and her powers would keep them at a distance. It was what kept Hakin's men from molesting her when they traveled away from her home.

"And I warn you not to wear out your welcome. I would have you cast your runes, but I can live without knowing. I don't need to know if I win, but how I can make it happen faster."

"And I shall make your cods shrink until they disappear. Or shall I make them fall off? Then no woman will call you a man, and no man will follow a eunuch. Do you wish to discover just what I have the power to do? Do you trust me to cast the runes only to discover the outcome of this war? Or is there the chance I cast a spell over you? Do you test me?"

"You are no more a witch than I am. You can't scare me into releasing you. Cast the runes and give me the reading I seek."

"If you already know what you crave hearing, what is the point in even casting the runes? You don't control fate. Perhaps you will die tomorrow and walk in Hel after the Valkyries fly past you and take Ivar and Rangvald to Valhalla."

Einar's hand flew out to grasp Sigrid's throat once again,

but she was just as quick and used her staff to block him. The rap of her staff against the inside of his wrist echoed among those who observed their standoff. Sigrid knew she was risking her life by thwarting Einar, but she had to establish the belief she might be a witch. It was the only way she could ensure they didn't touch her. When Hakin's men took her, their own seer traveled to meet them. They kept her untouched because the seer demanded she come to the sacrificial altar unmolested. She suspected had Leif and the others not arrived when they did, the old man had his own plans for Sigrid's body. Einar and his men had no one but her to convince them not to assault her.

"Take her away. Her tongue is sharper than my blade. My ears shall bleed if I must continue to listen to her hiss and snarl. Bind her. Gag her if you must."

Sigrid allowed two men to pull her away from the others, but as soon as they were a fair distance from the others, she enacted the true part of her plan.

"Before you bind me, I need to use a bush."

"No."

"Would you prefer I relieve myself on your boots as you tie me up?"

"You wouldn't. You couldn't even. You're a woman, so you can't aim, and you're in breeches."

"Do your boots want me to take my chances? Do you want to smell it while guarding me?" Sigrid smirked at the man on the left who refused to budge, but the man to her right wasn't as willing to risk smelling of piss.

"Fine. Be quick, and we are just on the other side."

Sigrid had scanned the area while she exchanged words with Einar. She knew where she needed to duck behind bushes.

"Where do you think you're going?"

"Right over here. You may need to guard me, but you need not watch. These bushes will do. Or better yet that large tree. I shall just be around its trunk."

Sigrid ducked around the bushes and made for the tree trunk. She heard the men following her. She searched the tree for its lowest hanging berries, breathing a sigh of relief when she found not only the yew tree with berries low enough for her to reach but mistletoe growing on its side. This unusual combination had to be fate. She plucked them as fast as she could and shoved them into the loose pockets of her vest. She made quick use of the privacy to relieve herself and found her guards staring as she reappeared.

"You took a long time," grumbled the guard who didn't want to allow her the privacy.

"It's tricky squatting with pants on."

The man grunted, and the two guards brought her back to the campsite. They allowed her to sit near the fire, which she welcomed for its warmth and its proximity to the stew being cooked. She looked around, but no one seemed to pay them any attention.

"What're your names? You look very similar."

"I am Olaf," said the more amenable of the two. "And this is my brother, Sven."

"You two can keep prattling like old women, but I shall find a rope," Sven spat as he walked away.

Sigrid turned back toward the fire but rubbed her hands over her vest as if to wipe them clean. She pulled the mistletoe leaves from one while keeping the berries in the other pocket. She would save the poisonous yew berries for later. She held her hands over the fire and rubbed them together as if to warm them. The motion tore the leaves into shreds before she dropped them into the cooking pot. The new ingredients would cause stomach cramps, blurred vision, and an upset stomach but should kill none. It would be enough to incapacitate her captors. She had to get close enough to Einar's bowl to add the yew berries. It was the seeds that would kill him, and she knew she would have to be even quicker poisoning him than she was with the large cookpot. She looked over her shoulder, but Olaf wasn't paying attention to her.

Sven returned with a coil of rope and didn't wait to wrap it around her ankles. "You shall keep your hands unbound since Einar intends for you to serve us. Make one wrong move, and I will gut you."

Sigrid nodded and looked at the nasty blade Sven pointed toward her. "I would ask one thing."

"You don't get to ask anything." When Sven pulled the rope around her legs, she thought she would tip over.

"I would just know whether I am to serve Einar first or last. I would save the best for him," she added just enough sarcasm to make her question sound bitter but frightened enough to make them think she intended to please Einar in exchange for her life.

"First," piped in Olaf.

Both men left her with nothing to do but stand there looking around. Sigrid could walk nowhere, and if she sat, she would have a hard time getting up again. She reached into her pockets as if to keep her hands warm in the chilly early evening. She smashed the berries into a pulp that would dissolve in the hot stew. It wasn't long before someone thrust a bowl into her hand along with a long spoon.

"For Einar," Olaf explained.

Sigrid nodded as she pulled her hands free and twisted to turn her back toward Olaf. She gripped the lip of the bowl, so she could drop the berries in just as she ladled the first spoonful. Sigrid poured more over it and stirred it before handing it back to Olaf.

A line soon formed with the men and women delighting in insulting and taunting her. A few even spat on her. She kept her bearing with pride. Her shoulders remained back, and her chin tilted up. She would accept their degrading behavior, safe in the knowledge they would receive their comeuppance soon enough.

Once everyone else was fed, she was given a bowl of her own. She made a show of serving herself, but in actuality, she took the tiniest amount she believed she could get away with.

She hobbled over to a tree and sat with her back against it and pretended to eat. With so little in her bowl to begin with, it would look like she finished if anyone walked by. She brought it to her lips but allowed none to pass. As everyone else finished, she put her bowl aside. She watched through half-slitted eyes as Einar sat down to eat. Even though she served him first, he had been too busy drinking to pay attention to the food. He had just finished eating when she could see the effects of the leaves taking hold and many stumbled while walking and a few rushed into the bushes.

Einar noticed the strange behavior and came to stand before her. He kicked the sole of her boot. "What have you done? Poisoned the food?"

"How could I do that? Do you believe I carry poison with me wherever I go?"

"Then why are my warriors ill for no reason?"

"I warned you, but you didn't believe me. Perhaps you should have heeded my warnings that I would use my dark arts."

"You are no more a witch than I am."

"But you would trust me to see the future?"

"You are a seer and nothing more."

"That isn't what you believe, and we both know it. Protest all you want. I brought no poison with me, and yet as you claim, I have made your army sick. Look around." She swept her arm out and gestured to the men and women who were becoming ill. "I served myself from the same pot as all of you, but I haven't taken ill."

Einar paused at that and looked at Sigrid. He could feel sweat breaking out on his forehead and his vision had him seeing two, then one, then three of the woman.

"You have done it to me too. What is happening?" Einar swayed before stumbling against the tree trunk Sigrid leaned against. His chest tightened, and he gripped the front of his tunic. Sigrid sat, knowing it would only be a matter of moments before the man's legs gave out.

Einar slumped to the ground and convulsed. He looked like many other warriors now lying about the campsite, except Sigrid knew the effects wouldn't wear off for him. She leaned over him as he doubled over in pain, both from his stomach and his heart.

"You shall not suffer long but suffer you shall. Your body will ache, your stomach will seize, and your heart shall feel like I am pinching what's left. Your mind will see what is not there, and the air will not fill your lungs. You shall die the fitting death of a traitor." She pulled his sword free from its sheath on his back and tossed it away. She pulled one knife from his boots and sawed the rope that bound her feet together. "You shall die a *níðingr*, an oath breaker and a traitor. You shall find yourself trapped in *Náströnd* with no burial since you have seen fit to abandon all honor. Your soul shall find its home there, not even making it to Hel. You shall remain in the realm of darkness and horror just as you deserve."

Sigrid stayed just long enough to watch the last breath escape Einar's now blue lips. His eyes stared lifelessly at her. She pulled his sword further away from him, leaving no possibility for his spirit to claim it. There would be no hint of Valhalla for him. He wouldn't even rest where those who died of age and disease went to rest. He deserved none of those. She straightened and looked around. Some of Einar's warriors were still conscious, but they were writhing with stomach pain or rushing back to the bushes. She had added just enough mistletoe leaves to keep their stomachs churning until morning, but unless they had a weak constitution to begin with, they would survive.

She knew it would be difficult to travel in the dark, but she had to put distance between herself and the camp. If she could make it into the hills and find a cave, then she could wait until morning before she attempted to find her way. She went to the horses and found one she could mount without help. She saddled it and was about to ride out when a shadow blocked her way.

"What did you do?"

It was Olaf. A moment of panic coursed through her. Of course, it had been too easy. She took for granted no one else accused her of poisoning the camp. Now she was alone with a man who weighed three times as much as she, and she had no one who would stop him from killing her. She stood rooted in place.

"I believe you poisoned us. You obviously poisoned Einar," Olaf accused. Sigrid's eyes flashed wide. "I heard you. I heard all you said to him. I saw you deny him Valhalla."

Sigrid tried to ease the horse around to use its large body as a barrier, but Olaf was more agile than he looked and sidestepped to stay even with her.

"Does Swen live?" Sigrid feared the answer.

"Yes. My brother lives but will be shitting in the woods for hours."

"How are you not ill?"

"You were careless, and a large piece of a leaf made it into my bowl. I recognized it from when Sven and I were young. We made ourselves ill eating mistletoe berries."

"And you warned no one?"

"No, I did not."

"Not even your brother."

"Not even him. I don't like the man he has become since he joined Einar, so I came only to keep him out of trouble. I don't agree with Einar's plan, but I must go along with Hakin for he is my jarl. I have no say. I don't have to follow Einar though. There is no love lost on my part now he is gone."

"And what will you do now that Einar can't use me as a seer?"

"I will tell you that if you head due east, you will come to a rocky wall that leads up a hillside. If you stay to the left and go halfway up, you will find a stocked cave with firewood and furs."

Sigrid's mouth dropped open before she nodded once.

"Know that I will be compelled to hunt you down once the others are well, but I will lead them far from you if I can."

"Why are you doing this? Why would you help me? It has to be more than disliking Einar."

"My wife, Torfa, came to Hakin's land from yours. She was a thrall given to Inga just before Inga married Grímr. I bought her freedom after we fell in love. We have a daughter, Dalla, who is close to your age. I would kill any man who thought to steal either of my women. Your uncle and cousin have been fair men when they trade with us. Hakin oversteps, risking business vital to our homestead. He believes he will own all the land and will have the resources to no longer need trade. I don't have such faith as he. Your man, Leif Ivarrson, is not an enemy I wish to make." Olaf broke into a wide grin. "And his sister terrifies me. I saw her fighting and have no wish to meet her on a battlefield again."

"Thank you, Olaf. If I can, I will see you spared."

Olaf shook his head. "I would reach Valhalla when the All Father decides it is my time. If that is soon, then I shall go with honor."

Sigrid nodded. She wouldn't argue about the man's right to die in battle, but if she had the chance to keep the kind warrior alive a little longer, she would. She mounted and rode out without looking back. Sigrid knew Olaf would no longer be standing there, and there was nothing she wanted to remember from the camp.

THIRTEEN

Leif drew his sword as they approached the campsite. They could see bodies settled around the campfire and near the bushes. It was unnaturally quiet. Leif looked to his friends and raised his eyebrow. Tyra shook her head, the doubt obvious. Freya signaled she would move around to the left as Strian moved to the right. Bjorn, Tyra, and Leif moved forward further as they surveyed the scene that lay before them. The crews from their longboats followed as they encircled the camp. There was only one man who sat awake by the fire.

"Leif Ivarrson!" the man called out. "She is gone. No harm has come to her, but I cannot say the same for my people."

Olaf didn't move from his position by the fire. His sword rested across his lap as he continued to stare into the flames. His voice roused several of the warriors who spent the night suffering. With the early morning light, most had recovered enough to sleep off the effects of the last night.

"Who are you?" Leif called back.

"The only one who knows where she went."

Leif teeth clenched. He wasn't inclined to go around in

circles with the man, but he couldn't risk not finding out where Sigrid was being held.

"Tell me where she is being kept, and perhaps you will live to see a fair fight."

"She isn't here. She's a very resourceful young woman."

Leif might have been proud if his bloodlust wasn't coursing through him hotter and faster than lava down a mountainside.

"I'm in no mood to speak in riddles. Tell me now, or you shall find one of my sister's arrows sticking from your chest."

That made Olaf look up as a bush rustled across the fire from him. The tip of an arrow poked through. The movement and Leif's warning were enough to make Einar's warriors come to their feet with swords drawn.

"That man is mine. I am sure he knows where she is. And I think he helped her, but I'm not convinced," Leif whispered to Bjorn and Tyra. The others nodded, and Leif released a bird call that had his army surging forward. He charged to the man who now stood beside the fire.

"Where is she?"

"She left last night. She's in the hills."

"Why would she be there? How did she escape? Why do you know this?"

"You speak a lot for a man in battle," Olaf smirked as their blades whistled along each other.

"I want my woman back, and you know where she is. I'm only letting you live, so I can find her. If you serve no purpose, I will kill you now." Leif pulled away and swept his sword back to make a slicing move that caught the older man in the ribs. Blood poured forth from the wound.

"She poisoned most of the camp. She put mistletoe leaves into the stew Einar forced her to serve. He thought he could humiliate her, but he gave her the perfect chance to exact her revenge. The others have been ill all night. It's why they put up little resistance now."

Leif's eyes shifted for only a second as he took in the battle that was already winding down.

"You don't seem to have suffered."

"I did not. I recognized the leaf in my stew and chose not to eat it. Your woman, the seer, reminds me of my daughter. I would kill the man who thought to take her from me."

"And that is what I shall do once I am done with you."

"You're too late. Sigrid already took care of Einar."

Leif leaped back from the man's reach and stopped fighting. Olaf welcomed the break and pressed his hand against his side.

"Einar is dead?"

"At Sigrid's hand. She poisoned him with something stronger than she gave the rest of us. She took his sword and left the carrion birds to eat his body. No one has stirred enough to realize he is dead, so no one has given chase."

"And you saw no reason to rouse everyone. To chase the woman who killed your leader."

"Einar was never my leader. I followed only to keep my brother alive, but he has changed since Einar's greed filled his head. As I said, Sigrid reminds me of my Dalla. I don't make war on women, and I don't mistreat them either." Olaf lowered his sword and lowered his voice. Leif leaned forward to hear better but caught himself before bringing his neck closer to Olaf's sword arm. "She has a horse, Einar's as it would turn out. I told her to ride due east and find the rocks. There is a cave there with provisions. She should be there now."

"I still don't understand why you would help her."

"Let's just say I would have the Valkyries not confuse me with my brother. I would be sure the All Father knows of my good deed before it is my time to leave this world."

"You understand that time has come?"

"I would expect no less."

"Leif!" Freya ran toward him, but he never took his eyes

off Olaf. "We found Einar. Looks like someone poisoned him. He's been dead for hours."

Leif jutted his chin toward Olaf. "Take this man. See to his wounds and bind him. He shall live, but he is now my thrall. Kill the others."

Olaf swung hard at Leif as he roared his anger. He wouldn't live out his life as anyone's slave. He was a warrior who would die on the field of battle. Leif thrust his sword through the man's stomach as another point drove toward him. He looked over Olaf's body as it slumped against Leif's sword. Bjorn stood on the other side. They skewered Olaf between their blades.

"You knew he would accept nothing else." Freya stated.

"I know. But he helped Sigrid get away. I offered for her, not for him."

Tyra and Strian joined the other three. Tyra grimaced before saying, "They put up little fight. This places stinks of a shit hole."

"Sigrid poisoned them with mistletoe leaves. She gave something much stronger to Einar. But they've been shitting themselves since last night," Leif shared.

"That would explain why the fight was so easy. She did us a favor," Strian observed.

"I imagine she knew that too."

"Now that you killed this man, there is no one left. What would you have us do with their bodies?"

"Build a pyre and send them on to Valhalla. Even if they were weak, they still fought." Leif looked around and spotted Einar. He walked over to the lifeless body and spotted the shorn rope that lay near his head. He sensed they used it to bind Sigrid. Guilt washed over him for the hundredth time as he imagined what she endured. "Leave this piece of offal for the birds. Let them pluck his eyes out, and perhaps the wolves will eat him. No burial for him."

Leif made his way to his horse after cleaning his blade across Einar's chest. He mounted and looked at the other captains. "Ride to my father's side. I shall find Sigrid and meet you near Stjordal." Leif didn't wait for the others before he spurred his horse toward the east.

Sigrid traveled throughout the night before she found the rocky hillside Olaf told her to find. She pulled the horse along behind her as they wound their way over the loose rocks and shale until she found the entrance to the cave. Just as Olaf predicted, there was firewood and furs stored in the back of the cave. Sigrid could find no signs of animals that made a home there, so she unsaddled the horse and brought him inside. She set about lighting a fire and looking for something to eat. She wasn't lucky enough to have both food and warmth. Too exhausted to care about her hunger, she would deal with that later in the day. Sigrid stoked up the fire and sank under the furs. It was only a moment later that she was asleep.

Leif picked up Sigrid's tracks once the sun was high enough to see. He wound through the woods and across a valley before he spotted the rocky edifice Olaf instructed Sigrid to find. As he reached the base, flurries fell about his ears and shoulders. Leif looked up and saw a steady stream falling from the fluffy clouds that followed him all day. It was still exceedingly early in the season for snow, but this far north, it wasn't unheard of.

I must find her before the temperature falls any further. She isn't dressed for this weather and only All Father knows what condition she is in. I must get to her before this storm takes hold. I doubt she has anything to eat either. Sigrid, I'm on my way. Just wait for me. I'm almost there.

Leif prayed these last thoughts would travel to her. He didn't know what to expect when he found her, but he knew his worry wouldn't subside until they reunited. Leif rode to the bottom of the rocks and was about to lead his horse up when movement in the bush caught his attention. He pulled his bow from his saddle and nocked an arrow in time to see two rabbits dash out from the underbrush. He fired one then another arrow as he caught both animals. He gutted them where he stood because he didn't want their entrails and blood to draw larger predators to him once he found Sigrid.

Leif led his horse up the rock face until he saw the shadowy glow of flames lapping against the inside wall of a cave. Leif drew his sword and edged forward until he could look inside. The scene that met his eyes brought tears to them. Sigrid was nestled under a pile of furs with a fire burning beside her. Her blonde hair glowed like gold in the light of the flames. He could see the furs rise and fall enough to reassure him she lived despite the falling temperatures outside.

Part of him wanted to scold her for the large fire. After all, if he spotted it, anyone could have. But the stronger part of him wanted climb under the covers with her. Leif brought his horse in next to hers and unsaddled the animal. He slipped over to the wood pile and found three sturdy branches he made into a spit, then set the rabbits on to roast. He laid out their skins nearby. Sigrid stirred when he laid down next to her and slipped under the covers.

"Sigrid, my love, I'm here."

She sighed, and even in her sleep, his name was on her lips. She didn't stir again until Leif forced himself from her side to keep the rabbits from burning.

"Leif," her voice was husky from sleep. "You came."

"Always, Sigrid. I'll always come for you."

"I seem to make a habit of needing you to rescue me."

"Not really." He jutted his chin toward her. "You seem to do well enough without me."

"Not true. These things were already here, and I was too tired to make sure I had food. You must have met Olaf if you are here." Leif hesitated before nodding. "He's dead, isn't he?" It was more a statement than a question. Sigrid nodded her head even as sadness flashed across her face. "He wouldn't have accepted anything else."

Leif stood up and crossed over to her. He sat and pulled her into his lap. "He was kind to you?"

"In a way. He knew what I did, and he didn't stop me. Just the opposite, he told me how to get here. Finding this cave saved my life. And he must have told you where to find me. So yes, I suppose he was kind."

"He said you reminded him of his daughter."

Wistful, Sigrid smiled. "His wife was one of Inga's thralls. She came with Inga from my home. He bought her freedom, and they made a life together."

"We gave him and the others a proper burial while we left Einar to the scavengers."

Sigrid's jaw tightened as she looked into Leif's eyes. "He deserved nothing else. He changed fate by demanding more than his due. The gods don't appreciate that."

Leif looked over Sigrid and saw no injuries, but he understood that didn't mean they didn't exist. He stroked his hand over her hair, then cupped her cheek. He brought his lips to hers with a soft brush of skin to skin. Sigrid cupped his jaw in both of her hands as she opened to him. The kiss was exquisitely slow as they nipped at one another before sinking into a long mating of their tongues as they tangled with one another. Leif lowered them to the ground as he covered her body with his. He lifted his head to look into her eyes. When he saw no fear, and she didn't rebel at his weight, he caressed his hand down her ribs and back up over her breasts.

"I can't seem to get enough of these in my hands. My palms itch to feel your breasts' weight resting against them."

Sigrid reached between them to unfasten her vest, but Leif's hand covered them. His were large enough that one hand swallowed both of hers.

"You don't have to do anything. I don't expect anything. If this isn't what you want, we'll stop. I'll never force you. Not ever, Sigrid."

Sigrid's smile lit up her face, and Leif thought its brilliance might blind him. "I know you won't. But I might if you stop me again. Leif, no one hurt me. No one even tried to touch me." She raised her head to press a kiss against his jaw. "I want this more than anything I've ever desired before. I want to know you as your wife would and share my body with you."

"Sigrid, know that if we do this, you'll be my wife from now until Ragnarök. I don't care we aren't following the customs. We can do that when all of this is over. We can have a proper feast and all the rituals, but right now I pledge myself to you before Thor, Freyja, and Freyr." Leif rolled off Sigrid and helped her sit up. He lifted a gold necklace over his head and kissed the hammer that dangled from it. He placed the hammer into Sigrid's lap. "I know this isn't even close to large enough, but it's all we have."

Sigrid looked at Leif before tilting her head back and saying, "Mighty Thor, I call upon you in this moment that we might seal this marriage with your blessing. Goddess Vár watch over us as you would at our wedding feast. See that our union bears fruit in the moons to come."

Leif watched as Sigrid invoked the names of two gods known to influence the fertility of a newly married couple. He felt his cock twitch when he thought of making a child that day with Sigrid. He had strived never to impregnate a woman ever since he first discovered the pleasures a man and woman could share. Sitting in the cave with Sigrid, he wanted nothing more than to spill his seed and create a life with the woman he knew he loved. His mind knew it was unreasonable to believe he was in love after such a short time, but his heart and soul yelled for his mind to be silent.

"Freyja and Freyr, we have no sow or boar to offer you. Thor, we have no goat, but we shall make this right when we can offer you our sacrifices." Leif continued their prayers. "We bind ourselves to one another with the promise to fulfill our duty to be wed with reverence to you, our gods."

Sigrid placed Leif's necklace around her neck and let the

hammer hang between her breasts. She stood, and when Leif reached for her, she patted his shoulder. She walked over to Einar's saddle and pulled something from one saddlebag. Sigrid returned and showed Leif the full mead horn she found earlier in her journey to the cave.

"It isn't enough to last us a moon, but Einar seems to have favored honeyed mead. It will have to do for tonight." Sigrid uncapped the horn and passed it to Leif, but he shook his head and guided the opening to her lips. She drank from the horn before pulling back. She moved to wipe her lips, but Leif was faster. He licked the sweet liquor from her swollen skin, still puffy from their earlier kiss. He took the horn and drank the rest before setting it aside.

"I promise you, we will do things the right way. Not just the feast, but it all."

Sigrid laughed as she stroked her fingertip over his nose. "Do you think I shall need to bathe away my virginity after tonight? I lost my *kransen* somewhere near my hut before they took me. So, I lost my virgin crown a while ago," she giggled as the mead warmed her insides. "I shall wear my hair down for you though. It has already come undone enough."

Sigrid pulled the leather thong from her hair, and Leif ran his fingers through it untangling it before spreading it about her shoulders.

"And I think you won't need to dig up a sword to prove you are no boy but a man. I have already felt your manhood." She giggled again.

"I shouldn't have let you have the first drink from the horn. The mead seems to be going to your head already."

Sigrid tried for a serious face but laughed instead. "Don't confuse my happiness and giddiness to become your wife for drunkenness. I promise you, I will remember all of this in the morning."

"Are you worried I will change my mind by then?"

When her answer was not fast enough, Leif pulled her into his lap again before cradling her skull in his large hand.

His other hand gripped her hip as his mouth descended once more. This was a punishing kiss that was a spark that lit the blaze between them. Neither held back as their desire for one another came back to life. Leif slid his hand into her tunic and at last felt the satiny skin of her breast against his bare hand. No longer was there material as a barrier to his explorations. Sigrid's fingers went to work loosening the lacings of the vest and then the neckline of her tunic. She pulled away just long enough to whip the two away from her body. Leif took in the fresh pink nipples that called to him as the fire reflected off her skin. His thumb whirled over her nipple until it became a tight dart he rolled between his finger and thumb. Sigrid arched her back into his hand as she pried his tunic loose from his belt. Her insistent yanking forced Leif to let go long enough to pull his own shirt over his head. As soon as his bare chest came into view, Sigrid scored her nails down his chest and back as she nipped at his shoulder. Leif's responding growl made the knot in her belly tighten. He pulled her tight against him, so their skin rubbed against one another.

Sigrid shifted to straddle Leif as she pressed her breasts together for him. Leif watched as she pulled her lower lip between her teeth. He loved her brazenness, but he understood she was nervous about how he would react to her body. He understood his actions would convey more than any placating words he could offer. Leif pulled one breast to his mouth and latched on. He took as much into his mouth as he could, and the pressure he exerted as he suckled had Sigrid tipping her head back and mewling. His hand pinched the nipple of her other breast hard enough for her to yelp before she ground her mound against his rigid cock.

"You like that, do you? You like it a little rough." Leif's voice had a wolfish timber that sent a shiver across Sigrid's skin.

"Yes," she breathed as she arched once again in invitation. Leif's responding growl was feral and deep. She shifted to unlace his breeches and pulled the flap wide enough to release him. She looked down and gasped. Leif was a large man all over, but she never imagined a man's rod could be both so long and so thick. Leif slowed and stroked her back before kissing her forehead. She looked up at him when his manner changed from lusting to loving.

"Are you afraid?" he murmured. She shook her head as she tentatively reached out her hand to wrap her fingers around his length.

"Not afraid. Surprised and unsure, but not afraid. I'll never fear you." Sigrid's eyes met his for a moment before she returned to examining his iron cast sword that throbbed in her hand. She stroked him and smiled enigmatically as she watched a pearl seep from its tip.

"Do you understand what will happen between us?" Leif remembered her mother died while she was still young. She came across as knowledgeable, but he wasn't sure how much was bravado.

"Of course, I do. Remember." Sigrid scowled as her own memories of seeing him with other women flashed before her.

"That's not what I meant. I know you understand the mechanics. I meant, do you understand the feelings that come with it?"

"How can I when I have never done this before?" She opened her mouth for a snarky comment but bit it back. She wouldn't ruin the moment with her own jealousy. Leif stroked the pad of his thumb over her cheek and then along her jawline.

"I know what you saw. I wish I could wipe those memories from both of our minds. There will be no one else, Sigrid. The past is just that. I give you my word."

Sigrid leaned in for a kiss as she resumed her stroking. This kiss was slower than before. The urgency remained, but it wasn't as frantic as it was only moments before. Leif unlaced her breeches and helped pull them down her hips as he shifted them once again to the ground. Once she could kick them free, he removed his own pants.

"I am going to make love to you for the rest of the day and all of tonight, wife." Leif smiled as he realized he said two things he never had before Sigrid. Two things he had studiously avoided until now. He never considered what he did with other women as making love. It scratched an itch and relieved a need. It had nothing to do with love before Sigrid. And he willingly called her wife. He had avoided falling into any woman's trap before he met Sigrid. Now he understood why he was so opposed to the notion because he was equally adamant that Sigrid would be—was—his wife.

"I shall hold you to that, husband."

Leif's heart squeezed at the sound of his new title. He wanted nothing in his life as much as he did at that moment. Leif wanted to be a good husband to the woman beneath him. He wanted to love her as she clearly loved him. Leif recognized the sacrifices she made and how she risked her life more than once to be with him and to support his family.

"Fate has truly smiled upon me to bring you into my life. I don't know that I deserve it, but I will spend the rest of my life proving that the gods were right to bring us together. Sigrid, I will be worthy of your love."

"You already are. I've always known that. It is I who must earn your love. I will be a good wife to you."

"You already are. Sigrid, what I have seen in the past week has shown me you are the bravest, most fearless, woman I know. Before you disagree," he pressed a finger to her lips, "I can't think of any warrior who would willing allow men to kidnap them twice because it aids other people's cause. You sacrifice your own wellbeing, even your soul, to walk about with the spirits, so my tribe might win a war. You brought Strian peace fate's deprived him of for years. You made my sister, who prefers few friends and confidants, warm to you in a matter of days. I believe you know the futures of all my friends and my sister, but you keep your own counsel and only guide them to their fate as they want. You could manipulate them or control them by holding their fate in your hand, but you would never abuse your gift or your relationship with others by doing something so self-serving. Your beauty goes so far beyond your shimmering gray eyes and flaxen hair or your luscious body. You exude beauty in the way you smile, laugh, and bring kindness to those who have only known a battle-weary life. I have never met another woman like you. That you already know me better than I know myself doesn't frighten me. No, it gives me a sense of peace. You know me as I am. You have seen me for better and worse, and you haven't tried to change your fate. We both know you have the power to do so. I don't think you are with me out of duty alone."

"I am here because I choose to be."

Those were the only words Leif needed to hear. "I love you," he breathed before taking her mouth in an achingly tender kiss. They poured their devotion and intentions into that kiss. Leif caressed every inch of her he could reach. He resumed his worship of her breasts as he suckled and kneaded the firm flesh. Sigrid arched as her body responded to his ministrations. Her hands roamed over his back and chest. She felt the muscles ripple under her fingers as he shifted and rocked against her. His cock rubbed against her mound creating an aching need unlike anything she had ever felt when she eased her own longing. It was so strong that it rested on the cusp of pain but resided in pleasure. Her soft moans were music to Leif, and as his fingers found her sheath, they grew louder. This symphony swirled around Leif as he pressed one finger into her entrance, testing her to see if she would accept his questing digit. When her knees fell wider, allowing him to settle between her legs, he pressed another finger into her as the head of his sword coated itself with the dew now dripping from her sheath.

Sigrid didn't know if she should continue to arch her back to offer her breasts to Leif's starving mouth or arch her hips off the ground to angle his exploring fingers deeper into her core. Her head thrashed as she longed to take more of him into her.

"Easy, little one. I would bring you to release before I enter you. It will ease the pain if you bask in the euphoria of a climax while your body adjusts to the fullness of having me deep within you."

His words only spurred her on rather than soothed her need.

"I ache for you, Leif. It consumes me, and all I want is for you to fill me. My body is searching for yours, and your fingers aren't enough. Leif, please. I feel like this fire within me will scorch me alive if you don't take me now."

Leif increased the pace of his fingers as he hooked them to stroke the inside of her womb. His thumb pressed against the engorged flesh that was the center of her pleasure. Leif watched as she broke apart, her mouth dropping wide in a silent scream of release. He withdrew his fingers and replaced them with the tip of his cock. Leif watched her eyes drift shut as her body relaxed. He seized his opportunity and drove through her barrier to encase himself in her molten sheath. Leif struggled to hold himself still as her body went rigid again. He knew this time it wasn't pleasure that made her arch off the ground. He would have given his soul in that moment if he could have traded her pain and taken it in him to give her the glorious feelings she gave him. His cock ached painfully, and his bollocks demanded he thrust, but he waited until she calmed again.

"I'm sorry, *elskan mín*." Sigrid registered the endearment, my love, and it eased the tension that radiated from her. Once her body unwound from the sharp, piercing pain of a moment ago, she appreciated the sensations of having Leif seated inside her. She shifted, and Leif's responding groan had her rocking her hips.

"Do you like that?" Her question was timid.

"More than I could ever tell you. You must be part Valkyrie along with seer for Freyja is calling me to *Fólkvangr*. She has chosen me to live in her realm of love."

Sigrid's laugh tightened her muscles around Leif, and he

thought he would spill himself in that moment. He clenched his jaw to keep himself from thrusting once and being done.

"You haven't died, in battle or in me, so you can forget about finding the goddess and making your home with her nor can Rán's daughters have you either."

"You fear the nine temptresses will claim me in the afterlife? Why would I want nine of them when I have the only one I need right here?"

Leif rocked his hips, the pace gradual to acquaint Sigrid with the feel of their joined bodies. He knew he was well endowed even for women with plenty of experience. Sigrid's body's response was immediate. She wrapped her legs over his and rose to meet each of his thrusts.

"*Faen!* Sigrid, what are you doing to me? I can't hold on much longer. By Thor's hammer, I am about to spill. You're so damn tight. You feel so damn good."

Leif was panting as he tried to slow his pace, but when Sigrid unhooked her legs to drive her heels into the ground and slam her hips into his, he lost all control. His mind couldn't take in anything other than the sensations her body offered him.

"More. Don't stop, Leif. By the gods, yes." Sigrid released a long, deep moan as her muscles began to spasm. She gripped his buttocks and dug her fingers into the taut muscles as Leif supported himself on his forearms. "Don't stop."

Leif slammed into Sigrid as she drove him over the edge. His movements were frenetic as he poured his seed into her. Even after he knew the last of his essence had drained into her, the aftershocks kept him rocking his hips. He felt Sigrid tense again as a second climax came over her. Her body trembled as she floated back to earth.

Sigrid stared up at Leif with such awe and surprise that in any other situation it might have made him laugh. Instead, he knew his face mirrored her expression. He couldn't hold himself up any longer, but rather than crush her, he attempted to roll them. Sigrid once again wove her legs over his and pulled him down to her.

"I will crush you."

"I would feel the weight of you press into me as our bodies come together."

Leif let some of his weight settle over her as his forehead brushed hers. Lowering his body gave his arms the reprieve they needed.

"You are holding back," Sigrid accused.

Leif laughed, and his cock twitched to life inside her. Sigrid moaned and shifted. "If you believe I had any more to give, then you believe me to be Thor because it has been nothing like that before."

As his cock rose back to life, he set a languid pace as he kept his thrusts short but deep. Sigrid's hands skimmed his back.

"You do seem to have at least a little more left." She cocked an eyebrow, proud of her double entendre.

"You know what I meant, you little minx." He nipped at her neck, and she tilted her head away to give him more access.

This round of lovemaking didn't have the frenzy of their first time. They took their time, looking into one another's eyes as they climaxed together. This time, when Leif tried to roll them, Sigrid didn't fight him. She lay stretched over him. Her hair cascaded over her back and his chest, creating a web that seemed to bind them together. They lay for a long time as their hearts and breathing slowed. They basked in the afterglow of their joining.

"Sigrid," Leif breathed. She lifted her head and strained to kiss him. It was a gentle exchange before she rested her chin on top of a hand she placed over his heart. "I meant what I said before. That was more than I could ever put into words."

Sigrid smiled, timid she wouldn't live up to what he was accustomed to. "You enjoyed it?"

Leif's disbelief showed on his face, but she mistook it. Leif felt her retreat. "Oh no, you don't. Don't shut me out. You once again misunderstand. Or rather, you don't hear all I have to say. I can't believe you need to ask whether I enjoyed making love to you. That was the singular most exquisite experience I have ever had. I swear I saw the gods float alongside me when I came. I have never felt my spirit connect with anyone else. In these moments we shared, we became one in more than our bodies coming together." It was Leif's turn for a moment of insecurity. "Did it seem the same for you?"

"Leif, I never imagined coupling could be like that. I knew it was pleasurable, but is it not the same each time? It's the same acts."

Leif choked at her naïve comment. "I promise you it is not always the same, but it should always be pleasurable. It can be different because of the positions—"

"Believe me, I already know that," Sigrid cut in, but then flushed as she admitted once more that she had seen Leif at his most intimate moments.

"So, you also know I have never been like that before. Never been that out of control with want and need. I've never felt anything like that. Sigrid, that's the first time I've ever made love. I've only ever made love with you." He once again stroked her back as she shimmied higher to kiss him without straining. "I will show you, you are the only one. I understand your jealousy because you don't have experience yet. But with time, you'll realize what we share is beyond anything you saw in my past."

"I'm ashamed of my jealousy. I have no hold over your past, and I feel guilty for having seen parts of your life you didn't intend for anyone other than your partner to see."

"Did you ask the gods to show you those moments? Did you watch them with the pure purpose of pleasuring yourself, or did the gods show you those moments because they led to other more impactful events?" Sigrid inhaled before sighing. "You know I am right. The gods are sometimes capricious and cruel. I believe they tested you to be sure you could accept your fate. While I'll never stray from you, life as a *frú*, a jarl's wife, is difficult. You're made of sterner stuff than most. You've proven you are meant to be at my side through all things. You didn't reject me when you saw me with women who weren't you."

"You've become quite sage all of a sudden. How did that happen?"

Leif tickled her ribs and pinched her backside. "Cheeky minx. How do you know I haven't always been this wise?" Sigrid dissolved into laughter and almost rolled off his chest. "Fair enough. That wasn't the wisest question to ask."

That only made her laugh harder. "I'll believe you, *minn*, though thousands wouldn't." She teased.

"You believe me wise enough to counsel the gods? Then you shall have to believe me in all things."

It was her turn to tickle Leif's ribs, and it surprised her to discover he was even more ticklish than she was.

"Hardly," she snorted as she tickled him again.

"Enough! No one has tickled me since the last time I pushed Freya into the mud for doing it when we were children."

"I imagine you didn't fare well for that."

Leif laughed at the memory. "No, I didn't. She blackened my eye, and our mother blamed me for the whole thing."

They laughed together until they both shivered. Their bodies had cooled, and the fire burned down. Leif slipped out from beneath her and threw two more logs to build the blaze. He slid back next to Sigrid and pulled the furs around her. Sigrid looked over at him and curled her nose.

"I didn't notice the horrible smell of burned meat until now. Those two rabbits have disappeared into the ashes."

"I know. I regret not moving them. It was snowing when I entered, and I am sure it covers the ground by now. I won't find more furry beasts."

Sigrid ran her hands through the curls on his chest as she snuggled closer. "I have mine right here."

"Beast, am I?" He peppered her shoulders and chest with kisses.

"No. I meant furry." She ran her hand from his chest along the trail of hair that led to the thatch above his hardening rod.

"You're awakening the beast."

"Then I shall have to find a way to soothe him."

It was the early hours of the morning before they fell into a deep sleep, satiated and in love.

FOURTEEN

Sigrid woke to feeling as though someone pitched her onto a funeral pyre. There was a suffocating weight and heat that enveloped her. That heat was also breathing into her ear. When she and Leif slept under the stars and shared a fur, the air temperature was chilly enough that she didn't realize how much heat he could generate. Laying naked next to him was like being burrowed away for a winter hibernation. Once she realized the source, she tried to roll, so she could snuggle closer, but Leif wrapped his body around her in such a way she couldn't press any closer. She sighed and drifted back to sleep.

It wasn't until a sense of urgency overtook Sigrid that she awoke. Leif shifted enough for her to slither out of his embrace. She looked around and found his tunic by the other clothes strewn near the fire from the previous night. She slipped it on, along with the boots Tyra lent her, and made her way to the cave's entrance. A world blanketed in a thin white layer greeted her. The snow that fell the night before accumulated but wasn't thick. It was just enough to make travel inconvenient. Sigrid slipped out and found a scraggly bush near the entrance, and after she used it, she grabbed a chunk of snow to wash her face and neck. She checked on the horses as she returned to the cave. She assumed Leif was still asleep, but it was only moments after turning to look back out at the dusty world that she felt arms slip around her waist and a warm chest pressed against her. Sigrid felt the evidence of his interest pressed between the cheeks of her bottom.

"You didn't think you would slip away, and I wouldn't notice, did you?"

"I certainly didn't hear you approach."

"I'm a light sleeper, Sigrid. Even when nestled away with you, or rather, especially when I'm nestled away with you."

"Afraid I will harm you in your sleep?" Sigrid looked back over her shoulder, only half teasing. She felt a moment of true trepidation that he didn't trust her.

"Of course not. But I would harm anyone who came near you."

"Don't you feel perpetually exhausted from never relaxing all the way when you sleep?"

Leif kissed her temple, marveling at how she understood what he would never volunteer. "At times. When we returned home, just before Rangvald arrived, I looked forward to sleeping like the dead in the comfort, and safety, of my chamber. Being away for so long, in other people's company, sleeping on deck or on the ground isn't the novelty it was when I first began my voyages. But last night was the best night of sleep I've ever had, followed only by the last time I slept next to you. I was still alert to an extent, but I slept better than I ever have before."

"But you would be in your bed if you hadn't had to chase me."

"That's not true. I would still be away, but instead of with you, I would be with my father now."

Sigrid nodded as she looked out and noticed flurries were falling again. Leif's hands splayed over her belly as he clasped her against his chest.

"I have no desire to return to that bed until you are in it next to me."

"You would share?"

"Did you think I'd expect you to sleep on the ground?"

Sigrid shook her head but bit her tongue until Leif nudged her shoulder with his own.

"I assumed you would visit my chamber when you, well, when—"

"After what we did all night, you can't bring yourself to say the words?" Leif chuckled. "I will visit your chamber," Sigrid tensed, "because it shall be the same as mine. We are not living apart, Sigrid. You're my wife, and I intend to spend every night I am home with you."

Leif ran his hands over her belly before continuing.

"And until you are carrying, I would like you to consider traveling with me. Selfishly, I don't want to have to miss you. I would have you by my side everywhere I go. But for your own safety, I wouldn't want to leave you at home unless one of the others is there too. And since Strian, Bjorn, Freya, and Tyra almost always travel when I do, that would leave you without their protection."

Sigrid turned in his arms, and her soulful gray eyes looked up to his darker ones. His eyes matched the heavy clouds laden with snow that hung over the treetops.

"You don't feel safe with me in your village? Even living in your parents' home? Even with your parents?"

Leif tucked a strand of hair behind her ear and cupped her skull. "I'll never trust anyone to protect you as I would. I admit that, but until I'm sure they accept you into our tribe, I won't take any chances. We haven't had a seer in at least a generation. The last one died when I was a child, and she had no living children. I don't know how some people will react, and until I'm sure that my father accepts our marriage, I won't leave you behind to face his temper." Sigrid looked down to where his bare toes brushed her booted ones. "My mother will stand beside us both, and she has a way with my father that no one else does, but he can still be a bear to deal with."

She nodded but didn't look up until Leif lifted her chin.

Even then, she wouldn't look him in the eyes again. "I don't want to come between you and your father. I don't know what that part of the future holds. I have no idea if your father will ever accept us or what'll happen with your relationship."

"That wouldn't be your fault. Your mother told him the prophecy before we were even born. If he believes he can control fate, then that's a matter he must resolve with All Father. Fate brought us together, but I believe we found love because our souls intended to join."

Leif kissed her as he led her back toward the fire. He tossed another log onto the fire before lifting his tunic over her head. Sigrid took the time to explore the tattoo that scrolled the length of his arm from his knuckles to his shoulder. The intricate scrollwork wrapped around a sea monster battling a bear. It was the most impressive artwork she had ever seen adorning a man's arm. Her fingertip traced over the knots and twists that wound their way over his wide forearm and bulging upper arm. She marveled at how smooth the skin felt even as his muscles rippled just like his back had the night before.

Leif stood still as he watched her ministrations. His breath grew ragged with every pass of her fingers. She roamed over his shoulder and to his chest, but he groaned when she stepped around him to examine the tattoo as it traveled over his shoulder blade. Sigrid ran both hands over his back and then down his trim waist. She caressed the small of his back as her hands slid into the grooves at the side of his hips. She continued around his other side until she stood before him again. Her hands returning to the indentations that fit her palms.

"Do you like what you see?" Leif asked, his voice gravelly as he tried to draw in air to combat the lightheadedness he felt. It was like being heady with drink except he had never been soberer. Sigrid looked up and nodded before tracing her hands over his chest and down the grooves of his stomach. She cupped his bollocks in one hand as she wrapped her fingers around his length.

"You know I do," her voice equally husky.

Leif's hands gripped her backside as he drew her closer, but she kept enough space between them, so she could continue to stroke him. She strained her neck, and he met her halfway with a scorching kiss she broke long before he would have liked. Sigrid sank to her knees before she licked him from stem to tip. Leif's head fell back as he groaned. His muscles tightened against the urge to rock his hips toward her. He felt her tongue, tentative at first, glide along his length before swirling over his tip. He ground his teeth to keep from calling out as he felt her satiny mouth slide down over him. His head whipped forward in shock as she took most of him into her mouth. Even the most experienced women he had been with couldn't accommodate so much of him. He brushed the hair from her face and gathered it in his hand as he watched her work his cock. Once again, he steeled himself against rocking into her mouth when his body screamed for him to thrust. Her eagerness to please more than compensated for her inexperience. It was only seconds before the need for release pulsed through him.

"Sigrid, stop," he gasped. When she continued her endeavors, he pushed her shoulder as he stepped back. Surprise and pleasure quickly replaced the look of hurt and rejection that flashed across her face when Leif lifted her in one swift move from kneeling before him to her legs wrapped around his waist as he thrust into her.

"I couldn't wait any longer. This wasn't the time when I wanted to come in your mouth. I want to be inside you when I find my release. I would bring you to yours along with me."

He sank to his own knees and used the new position to thrust into her as he held her in a crushing embrace. In turn, Sigrid unwrapped her legs and braced herself to match each of his thrusts. Her head rested to the side as he rained scalding kisses over her neck and shoulder. His teeth found her earlobe, and as he nipped, his warm breath sent a shiver of arousal spiraling to her core, tipping her over the edge. She clenched her inner muscles around his pulsing cock and rubbed her mons for the friction she needed. Leif's fingers bit into the skin of her backside as he cried out his release.

"Sigrid!"

"*Feun*! Leif, don't stop. Not yet." She pleaded as her release carried her through another wave of pleasure. It was several long moments before their bodies stopped twitching against one another, and their breathing steadied enough to speak.

"I didn't know you swore like that, little one."

"You said it last night when you climaxed. It seemed appropriate in the moment," Sigrid grinned with no remorse for shouting the expletive. She had never used the word "fuck" before, but it seemed to be the only one that fit in the moment. She rather liked the message it conveyed when no other word would suit.

"I must think on how I feel about that," he gave her a playfully reproachful stare.

Sigrid rocked her hips, grinning again when Leif groaned and grasped them. "I can think of something else to feel."

"I have unleashed a ravenous appetite, haven't I?"

"I believe you have. One that only feasting on you can satisfy."

"Well, you shall not dine alone."

Once more, Sigrid found herself being lifted, but this time it was Leif's turn to slide down her body. She lay back but watched as Leif's tongue darted out to taste her. They spent the rest of the afternoon and night feasting and exploring one another.

FIFTEEN

It was early the next afternoon when the snow stopped, and Leif helped Sigrid onto her horse. Mounted, they rode away from their cavernous hideaway. Neither was in a hurry to return to reality, but they both knew responsibility and duty wouldn't disappear because they discovered they were in love. Leif led them down the backside of the rock face, and while it was precarious in parts, it saved a great deal of time than to travel back the way they each came, then going around. The air grew warmer as they descended, and there was less snow at the base of what Sigrid looked back to discover was a small mountain. Once again on level ground, they set a hard pace, galloping south to the vicinity of the upcoming battle. They made camp that night under the stars but forced themselves to tame their desires enough to sleep before another long day in the saddle. Leif looked over at Sigrid countless times, regretting how rough their first-time making love was. He knew she had to be sore, but she never even grimaced. She pushed ahead in silent challenge more than once to race when they were on flat, even ground. It took two full days of riding before Leif reined in. They set off that fourth day of travel before the sun rose over the horizon. It was only mid-morning when Leif cocked his ear and listened. There was no mistaking the sounds he could make out coming from the valley below. He knew once they broke through the tree line, they would see the battle raging in the valley. He inched them along, ever vigilant for enemy scouts in the trees waiting to pick them off.

Leif swore under his breath. He watched as the three armies came together in a melee of swinging swords and axes. His father's army fought to the left while Rangvald's was to the right. They stuck Hakin and his men in the middle as the two flanks pressed inwards. Leif looked over to Sigrid who watched just as intently, and he was torn between keeping her away and safe, and joining his father's army and his friends. Sigrid decided for him when she yanked back on her horse's reins and came around his other side before racing toward his father's army.

"Sigrid! Sigrid! Wait!"

Sigrid was leaning low over her horse's neck as the pair flew along the ridge until she found a slope that would take them to the valley. It was rocky, but it was the best path she could see. She knew Leif followed her, and she knew he would be irate when he caught up to her and could scold her. But she also knew he wouldn't leave her if he believed she was unprotected. He would choose her over the battle, and she refused to force that choice. Rocks slid from under her horse's hooves as she gave the animal his head and allowed him to find his own footing. When she reached the base of the embankment, she skirted around the fight before looking back at Leif. His expression was thunderous, and she wondered if she would live to see the end of the battle. Sigrid tilted her head toward the fight, but he shook his. She looked forward again until the last few men fighting came into view. She rode past them and looked back at Leif again. He reigned in, still a distance from her, but nodded. He dismounted and brought the horse to her. After he handed over the reins, he turned and charged into the fight.

Leif's chest tightened and his mind rebelled at leaving

Sigrid out in the open, but he knew he must join. He swung his sword and ax as he plowed through any man who came toward him. He fought several women as well before he spotted his sister fighting at their father's back. Leif leaped over fallen bodies and shoved others away as he neared his family.

"About bloody time you showed up, Brother."

"I'm happy to see you too."

Freya edged over to allow Leif to fit between her and Ivar. The three fended off the onslaught of Hakin's men. Leif caught sight of Strian, who fought alongside Erik Rangvaldson. They were being pushed back toward Leif as a new wave of Hakin's men seemed to materialize behind them. Leif didn't have time to wonder how Erik made his way to this side of the battle when his father's army was at the other end. He shoved his father aside in time to block a double-sided battle ax from cleaving the older warrior as Ivar fought two men using his own battle ax and sword. His sudden change in position left Freya open. A loud roar sounded as Leif caught a blur speed past him. From the corner of his eye, he made out the wild hacking of a crazed berserker before he could see Erik crash through four men who surrounded Freya. Freya attempted to hold her own, but Erik swung before anyone could come near. If he weren't trying to keep his own head on his shoulders, Leif might have laughed at the sight. He pitied poor Erik for when the battled ended, thanks weren't what he would receive from Freya. Erik turned his back against Freya's, and they fought together once Erik allowed Freya to swing her sword again.

"We move to Strian, Father."

"On three. One, two, three." They charged through more men as they made their way to him.

"Thank All Father," Strian panted. He had a large gash across his left thigh and blood trickled from his mouth. He continued to fight with the power of three men, but now that he had two allies to watch his back, the frenzy left him.

The battle carried on well past the sun passing overhead. Leif's body ached, and the sweat stung his forehead and eyes as it dripped from his hair. His position had moved farther into the center of the fight, and there was no way for him to see if Sigrid was where he left her. He feared she would be taken again or injured as the fighting shifted with each surge of men clashing together. Leif plowed on, taking down any enemy who stepped within his reach.

The sun was nearing the western horizon when Ivar's army met Rangvald's with only a few of Hakin's men left in the middle. It was only a matter of minutes before they defeated the last of Hakin's army. The plan to trap their enemy in the valley between them brought victory to Ivar and Rangvald.

Leif wiped the blood, sweat, and mud from his face as he pushed his hair back. He examined the deep cut he had taken to his side and knew it would require stitches. His mind raced back to Sigrid as he wondered if she knew how to sew him closed. He tried to make out the last place he saw her, but the distance was too great, and the sun was no longer strong enough to illuminate the end of the valley. He turned to slog his way back to where he left Sigrid when a bellow stopped him.

"Help me! Leif, Strian! I need you."

Leif turned to see Bjorn carrying Tyra as he tried to make his way through the mounds of dead bodies. Blood matted his hair red, and his right arm held Tyra at an odd angle. He hobbled as he found ground that had no body parts or debris. Leif ran to meet him, and he took Tyra from his cousin. The woman was unconscious, and there was a gaping wound across her chest where a battle ax must have landed.

"No!" Freya screamed as she ran forward. She whipped around and thrashed when Erik caught her around the waist. "Let me go!"

"So, you can knock your brother over? Let him get her

somewhere a healer can examine her. You can't carry her, so let him."

Freya lashed out again, but Erik wrapped his arms around her. He guided her to walk alongside Leif. She settled and slumped against Erik when she could see where Leif carried her closest friend.

"What happened?" Leif called over his shoulder to Bjorn, who Ivar and Strian supported.

"The tide swept us along when Hakin's men meant to draw back, but then Rangvald's men caught them on the other side." Bjorn was panting as he tried to tell his story.

"That is how I came to fight alongside your army," Erik interjected. Freya snarled at him for interrupting and hissed when Erik swung her into his arms to carry her.

"Put me down, you goat. I can walk just fine."

"But I like you here better, and my legs are long enough to keep up with Leif without running. You'll trip here and break your neck."

"It separated us from the rest of you, but we fought together," Bjorn continued as though no one else had spoken. "I have never seen Tyra fight like that before. She was magnificent, and she kept me alive more than once. A giant of a man came out of nowhere, and before I could warn her, the ox swung his ax. I pushed her aside, and it meant she kept her head, but she still took the ax to the chest."

Bjorn pushed away from Ivar and tried to catch up to Leif. Strian allowed him to walk alone but prepared to catch him despite his own injury.

"I thought she was dead," Bjorn whispered as he looked at Tyra's ashen face. "I was sure he'd killed her until the giant leaned forward to steal her torque. She shoved her blade through the bottom of his chin into his throat. He fell alongside her before she passed out. I pulled her to safety and defended her where she lay. Once it became obvious Hakin would lose, I carried her back here." Bjorn reached out to touch Tyra's hair but snatched his arm back. "I've been such an arse to her."

No one denied his statement, and no one offered false reassurance. They trudged along in silence until Erik looked back as a horn sounded.

"My father. He sounds the horn of victory. He lives for no one else would use that horn." Freya looked up to see the silent relief in the handsome man's eyes. He looked down at her and smiled only to receive a scowl in return. "One day, princess, you shall smile when I carry you."

Sigrid tried not to pace as it was only making the horses anxious, but she didn't want to wait any longer to see if Leif fared well. She picked her way through the littered ground but didn't make it very far before she saw a group of warriors walking toward her. She couldn't make out who it was, and as she looked around, she realized there were none of Ivar's men nearby to protect her. Sigrid pulled a knife free from one woman's hand and an ax from another man's. She had the weapons, and she was comfortable using them, but she was no match for such a large group. She looked around for a place to hide, but there were few options. She moved back toward the horses, but she knew she couldn't ride out of the valley easily. Sigrid chose the embankment she and Leif rode down earlier. She scrambled up the side when she heard her name called.

Leif recognized Sigrid before she recognized him. He knew the sight of five men carrying two other warriors had to be disconcerting. He watched Sigrid change her mind from going to the horses to trying to climb out of the valley on her own.

"Erik, put my sister down. I need you to take Tyra." Leif spoke for their ears only. Both Erik and Freya looked at him, and he jerked his chin toward Sigrid. "Take her, please."

"Yes. Put me down and help for once," Freya bit out. Erik

grinned as he put her back on her feet and transferred Tyra into his arms.

As soon as he was free, Leif bolted toward Sigrid. It shocked him that he still had the strength to run, let alone sprint toward her. Leif called to Sigrid until he was sure she heard him. He watched her pause on the hillside until she could see him, then she was running toward him. Leif caught her as she launched herself into his arms. Their mouths came together with a hunger born of fear and panic. Sigrid clutched the front of his clothing as Leif's hands skimmed over her checking for any injuries. When they tore their lips apart, Sigrid laughed.

"I should check you for injuries."

"And you will soon enough. I shall gladly have you look at all of me, but first I would know you are untouched."

"I'm fine, Leif."

"That doesn't answer me. Did anyone try to harm you?"

"Only two men came near me, but once they saw my staff, they backed away. I believe they recognized it and thought me a witch. Only one other man tried to attack me, and he is dead now, so the only worse for wear is him."

Leif pulled her close again as their kiss resumed with a different intensity. Gone was the need to prove they were both alive and well, and now there was a need to exchange love and hope. Leif's tongue stroked across Sigrid's as she drew him into the recesses of her mouth. They crushed their bodies together attempting to fuse them while layers of clothing kept them apart.

"Stop devouring my cousin, you rutting bastard."

"Don't call my brother a bastard, you son of a pig farmer."

"Tell your brother to let go of my innocent cousin, and then I might not call him names."

"Are you five? Who calls names? And your cousin isn't so innocent."

"What does that mean? What has your rutting bastard

brother done to her? And while we're at it, you called me a son of a pig farmer. So much for not calling names."

Sigrid rested her forehead against Leif's chest as she tried not to laugh.

"Enough," roared Ivar. "I would know what my son thinks he's doing mauling a woman I specifically told him to avoid."

Leif kissed Sigrid's forehead before resting his against hers. "And so, it shall start," he murmured.

"Perhaps I should give you some space. Is that Tyra being carried? I will see to her injuries. And don't think I haven't noticed yours."

"Tyra needs help. Her injuries are grave, but she's alive. Bjorn is beside himself since he was the one fighting by her."

"She will survive, and it won't be long before she is well again. But help Bjorn. He will suffer much guilt over this, even though Tyra will never blame him." Sigrid looked pointedly at him as she moved away and waved for Erik and Freya to follow her. Leif walked down to Ivar, Bjorn, and Strian.

"Bjorn, Tyra will live."

"How can your little witch be so sure?"

Leif balled his fists to keep from swinging at his cousin, but he bit out his warning. "Tyra's injuries may upset you, and we're all exhausted, but don't ever, ever call her a witch again. You have no right to risk her life like that when all she has done is help this tribe, knowing your words in the wrong ears could get her killed. She practices the black arts as much as you or I. She is a seer, and you know that."

"And where was she to warn Tyra? To warn me? Off fucking you, I suppose."

Leif stepped back surprised at the bite in Bjorn's words. "I will overlook your words said in the aftermath of battle lust because if I don't, I will kill you. Cousin or not, you don't get to insult my wife."

"Wife?" Ivar interjected. "I believe I told you to stay away from her. What spell has she cast over you, son?"

"Not you too. You know it has nothing to do with her casting a spell."

"No, it's the spell her mother cast."

"What are you talking about?" Strian stepped between Leif and where Ivar stood shoulder to shoulder with Bjorn.

"Sigrid's mother saw our fate before we were born. She told my father that Sigrid and I would be together, but Father believed he could change our fate."

"I am choosing the fate of our entire tribe over the fate of one woman who isn't even part of our people."

"She is one of our people now. I pledged myself to her. I gave my oath."

"An oath made that you weren't to give. You made a promise you shall now have to break, but since you didn't have a proper wedding, it won't anger the gods."

"Only me," Leif growled as he turned to follow Sigrid and the others.

"Don't walk away from me. She is going back with Erik. It is obvious you should have married ages ago, and you shall make an advantageous match as soon as spring comes. Mark my words."

The look of ice and loathing Leif sent his father made the older man realize he may have pushed too far.

"Don't make me choose," was all Leif said before walking away.

SIXTEEN

Leif found Sigrid leaning over Tyra near a slow-moving river. Erik was standing at a distance with his back to the women. Freya was helping Sigrid bathe Tyra, and Leif noticed a kit set out to sew Tyra's chest. He went to stand next to Erik as both men gave the women privacy.

"My cousin isn't an innocent anymore."

"I'm glad to see you survived the battle too. I'm well. Thank you for wondering."

"I wouldn't test me right now. She is more like a sister than a cousin."

Leif swung around and shoved Erik's shoulder. "If that's the case, you should have had men set to guard her when you couldn't."

"You don't know Sigrid well then, after all."

"I know she would have disagreed with you, but I also know there isn't anything I wouldn't do to keep her safe."

Erik looked over Leif's shoulder and then drew him farther away.

"I did have men guarding her," Erik whispered. "I didn't want her to know, but someone slaughtered them. They might not have harmed her when they kidnapped her, but I can't say the same for the four guardsmen. Experienced warriors but gutted like a spring calf. Necks slit and guts torn open. She would never forgive herself if she knew those men suffered because of her. She knew I often had men positioned to watch her land because she lived some distance from the village, but she never knew they guarded her. The men who took her were far more violent than I ever want her to know."

Leif took in what Erik shared with him and nodded. He could understand the man's reasoning. Sigrid's guilt would be acute, and she would blame herself for the lost lives. She understood the way of warriors and wouldn't have denied them their right to die with honor, but he also knew she would have argued they deserved to make their way to paradise in a real battle, not babysitting her.

"You love her."

"I do."

"How can you be so sure so soon?"

"Has she told you anything of what she's seen of me?"

"No. I didn't even know she had."

"Her visions of me started when she was nine winters. They've come to her often, surrounding an important event or a battle. But she's also seen us together with our children. She's seen us wed and happy." Leif paused to watch Erik as the other man looked over his shoulder. When Erik looked back at him and nodded, Leif continued. "I can't explain how I've fallen in love with her in such a short time. I can only say I've been offered a chance to witness and learn much about Sigrid in the past two weeks. It is more than me accepting a prophecy. I am inextricably linked to her, and I won't give her up."

"Your father doesn't agree. He'll send her back."

"And I'll choose my wife."

"You may have pledged yourself, if that's what you've done, but you know, like I do, even an oath given such as that won't be enough to make you wed in the eyes of our people or our gods. They cleansed neither of you, and you made no sacrifice. Your pledge doesn't bind you to one another."

"Then what good is my word if I can offer it, and it has no value."

Erik shook his head. This time when he looked back, Leif realized he was watching Freya. "When you figure that out, be sure to let me know."

"Have you made any pledges to my sister?"

"No. Though I would this moment if I thought either of our fathers would agree."

The two men looked at one another and a sad smile passed between them. It wasn't long after that Sigrid called to them. They went to check on Tyra and saw her eyes were open, even if they were only slits. Leif grasped her wrist in a warrior handshake. He nodded his head and swallowed down the lump that sprang to the back of his throat.

"Leif, I should see to your wounds now. Yours and the others." Sigrid's soft voice penetrated his hazy mind.

It took Sigrid the better part of the night to tend to the wounds sustained by Leif and his family along with Rangvald, who showed up halfway through Sigrid stitching up Strian's thigh. Her bruised uncle had a slash across his forearm that needed tending, but he had fared no worse than the others.

"How many men did you lose?" Ivar asked as Rangvald walked into the tent erected before the battle began.

"Not as many as I imagined. Maybe a hundred. I don't know why yet, but something split my forces just after the initial charge. It was those not with Erik and me who faced the greatest threat. You?"

"The same. Hakin wasn't so lucky."

"True, but has anyone found him? Or Grímr?"

"Not that I know of," Erik spoke up. "We shall look through the dead in the morning before we prepare ours for the funeral. But I don't think we will find them."

"I lost sight of Grímr halfway through the battle," Strian

bit out as Sigrid drew the needle through his skin again. "He was there one moment and then like a phantom the next. He wasn't still fighting anywhere near me."

"Same for Hakin. I saw him toward the beginning but then not again, and Tyra and I made it almost the entire length of the valley," Bjorn said from beside her. Sigrid had found herbs she could make into a tincture that eased the injured woman into a deep sleep. Bjorn never looked away from the still form.

Sigrid looked up from Strian's leg, and whispered to Bjorn, "She sleeps now, but she will blister your ears soon enough, and you will wish her asleep again."

"I would never wish this on her. I welcome her scolding. I have been far too hard on her for far too long, and now my pride has given me no opportunity to say goodbye."

"Bjorn, don't tempt fate. She isn't going to die." Sigrid was so emphatic that everyone looked at her, but she ducked her head to finish sewing up Strian. "I know this already."

"If you know so much already, seer, then tell us where Hakin and Grímr disappeared to." No one could miss Ivar's disdain, and Rangvald couldn't ignore it.

"Ivar," he warned, "My niece has done nothing but serve all of us. Sigrid doesn't deserve your or anyone else's ire. She does the best she can and more. She can only tell us what the gods will her to know. And she can only share with us what fate will allow. Don't blame her that fate isn't under your control."

"That may be true, but I can blame her for seducing my son."

"Father!"

"You've lain with her when I expressly told you to stay away. She sank her talons into you only because her mother told her some story that none of us can know is true."

"I know it's true."

"Because you're thinking with the wrong head."

"I'm still here," Sigrid bit out as she tied off the last of

Strian's stitches. As she looked at each of the other men, her dismissive glare stung Leif when her expression didn't soften for him. She turned back to Strian. "It's done."

To the others, they thought Sigrid referred to his stitching, but Strian stared for a long time before he whispered, "My father."

Sigrid nodded before dunking her hands into a bowl of water and scrubbing off the blood. She dried them on a linen nearby and walked out of the tent. She said nothing else and didn't look back.

"Sigrid, wait." Leif pursued as she made her way to the river. "Don't walk away. Please." She shook her head and held up her hand. "Fine, but I'm still following you. I won't let you walk near the river alone in the dark. And before you argue, I would say the same to Freya and any of the others. There might still be Hakin's men out there, or you could fall in. I don't allow my men to wander alone, and I won't let you too."

"Fine."

Leif shook his head. He had just declared how much she mattered to him, or at least he thought he had made it clear, and all she had was one word to respond. Sigrid walked down to the bank and found a rock to sit on. One that was only large enough for her. Leif stood back to give her space, but he wanted to pick her up and cradle her in his lap, telling her that everything would be all right. He believed it would be, but that wasn't what she wanted in that moment. She knew what the future held, but that didn't make the present any easier.

The minutes ticked away before Sigrid held out her hand to Leif, even though she didn't move over for him. His approach was tentative, and he took her hand before he pulled her to her feet. When she didn't protest, he stepped into her embrace and tucked her head against his chest. They stood that way for some time before Sigrid leaned back to look up at him. The moonlight twinkled in her eyes, and Leif's breath caught as he remembered once again how beautiful she was. The bruises from her first capture were close to healed, so her face was almost unmarred. They came together in a tender kiss that held promise and remorse all bundled together. It was the first time their kiss didn't fire into a conflagration of need and arousal. It felt innocent as they held each other, only their mouths and hearts moving. When at last they stepped apart, Sigrid and Leif knew they reached an understanding. Leif framed her face before kissing her forehead then the tip of her nose.

"No matter what happens, I will always come for you. I will never let you go. No matter what anyone else says or does, you are my wife."

"And you are my husband. I'll always wait for you, even if I would prefer to find you instead."

"Cheeky minx." He kissed her nose again before they walked back to camp hand in hand.

SEVENTEEN

Leif walked Sigrid back to the tent erected for Freya. Leif noticed the other women who would have stayed with Freya were in another tent. Leif looked at his sister, worried the women rejected Sigrid and refused to share a tent with her, but Freya's knowing gaze made him more suspicious of his sister's plans. He knew the look but didn't know what she was up to. Leif and Sigrid exchanged a brief kiss before Sigrid ducked into the tent. Freya stepped over to Leif and looked around before leaning forward conspiratorially.

"Wait an hour, and I will bring her to the river. I would bring her to you, but Bjorn and Strian will be there. And I don't trust you two to be quiet."

"No."

"What do you mean 'no'? Why not?"

"As much as I want to see my wife, I want her to face Father's wrath far less. I don't want to bring any more attention to the situation than necessary until we can discuss it properly."

"Discuss it properly. Are you not right in the head? Father will never discuss this properly. The best thing you can do is get a babe in her belly, and even then, Father may say she can't be more than your mistress."

"I won't accept that." Leif arched an eyebrow at her, and Freya laughed.

"You want me to convince him. You trust my powers of persuasion that much?"

"When have you not gotten your way in the end?"

Freya opened her mouth then shut it with a snap of her teeth. She knew her brother was right, and she was more than willing to try, but she feared this would be the one time she wouldn't get her way. Their father seemed adamantly opposed to a union between Sigrid and Leif. She wasn't sure how Rangvald felt about the match either. He defended Sigrid against Ivar's insults, but he hadn't exactly pushed the couple together either.

"I'll make my best case for you, Leif. I believe you two are fated, but more than that, I believe you make each other happy. There is an air about you I've never seen before. You seem more settled and calmer. You seem more satisfied with life. When we returned from the last voyage, I sensed you felt restless and caught between wanting to continue sailing and wanting to stay home more. Sigrid might be the answer to you remaining at the homestead more, and you could take her with you when we do travel."

"I'd thought much the same. I was growing tired of spending night after night somewhere different and unpredictable. I am proud of what we accomplish and what we bring home, but I also feel guilty for not being home sooner. Perhaps we would have discovered Hakin's plans sooner if we were the ones out patrolling."

"You can't know that. We've done what our father needed us to do, and we have done it well. I know you love being on the water as much as I do, but even I long for quiet from time to time. The only one who would choose to live among the fish every day for the rest of time is Tyra. I think Strian is feeling the same. I think he is lonely with little family, and now that Einar is gone along with his aunt, there isn't much left for him at home, yet I think that's where he wants to be. Bjorn is probably the one who might still be eager to explore. I don't know if he'll ever settle down. Anyway, I think you should meet with her, if not to tryst, then to make plans for when Father refuses. I can't promise to change his mind within a day, though I will try."

Leif nodded. He resigned himself to the truth Freya spoke, but he most wholeheartedly wouldn't resign himself to giving up his wife. If he had to let her travel back to her people, he would follow. He knew deep within he would give up being a jarl to be with Sigrid. He didn't think, and hoped, it wouldn't come to that, but that was the strength of his feelings.

"Before I do this, you're sure it isn't just infatuation. Not just lust?"

"I'm sure. I've lusted over other women before and bedding them ended it. If it didn't, then I bedded them more than once, but never did I long to wake up next to them. Never did I desire more conversation than how to pleasure one another. Never did I feel a need to protect, care for, and provide for another woman. This is as different from the past as it could be."

Freya nodded once. "Then meet us by the river in an hour. And for the love of the gods, be quiet with her."

Sigrid listened intently to the conversation between brother and sister. She knew she shouldn't be eavesdropping, but the conversation pertained to her. She felt a twinge of guilt, but it wasn't strong enough to send her to her bedroll. Sigrid listened to Freya's cautions, and she knew the other woman was right. Ivar would send her away. Sigrid didn't need to divine that. She also knew she would obey in the moment, but she wouldn't deny herself or Leif their future. She would find a way back to him. Hearing Leif's feelings relieved her. He'd expressed them to her more than once, but she still held a fear he spoke out of lust and infatuation. To hear him declare his feelings about her to someone else made her breathe easier. She didn't want a man who came to her out of obligation. She wished she hadn't told Leif of the prophecy so soon, instead waiting to see if he developed true feelings for her on his own. It had seemed right in the moment to confess to him what she already knew, but hindsight is always clearer than being impetuous. When Sigrid heard Freya's final instruction to meet by the river, she scurried to her bedroll and slid under the covers only seconds before Freya lifted the flap. Sigrid forced herself to calm her breathing, even though her heart jumped in her chest.

"You needn't pretend. I know you aren't asleep, and I know you were listening." Sigrid folded down the blanket and looked over at Freya, nervous about being caught. "Leif couldn't see your shadow, but I could. I should chastise you for listening to his conversation, even as his wife, but I believe you needed to hear Leif's feelings. He may not have said he loves you, and I think he's already told you that, but he described it."

Sigrid didn't know what to say or how to react, so she watched Freya as she prepared to retire.

"I wonder if you assume he feels that way because the gods have dictated you be together, or if you see that he feels that way of his own free will." Freya stopped and stared at Sigrid, and Sigrid knew the other woman would wait her out.

"That fear has crossed my mind more than once," Sigrid admitted.

Freya sat down crossed legged on her furs, and Sigrid sat up. "My brother isn't a selfish man by any stretch, but he can be self-involved. Too much time spent with Bjorn, I suspect," Freya snickered. "It's no secret he's been with other women. What man his age hasn't? But he's never spoken to me before about his feelings for a woman. He told the truth earlier. He's had none of any real depth or consequence. He coupled for the sake of fun and release. Now he is with you because he cares. The gods and fate could make him accept his destiny to be with you, and he would do so by his own will, but they can't make him love you. He does that by choice. Or perhaps more so because it's obvious there is no choice but to love you. I know I consider you a friend, and I barely consider anyone but Tyra to be one. I don't think fate paid much attention to me when it matched the two of you. I think of you as a friend because I like you and admire you in many ways."

Freya laughed at the shock on Sigrid's face.

"Don't look so surprised. You are a woman who has survived living on your own for years," Freya held up a hand to keep Sigrid from interrupting. "Don't tell me it's because fate was waiting for you to meet my brother. There are those who would fight against it, and that can alter each of ours. You've lived well on your own, surviving and defeating those who would kidnap you, not once, but twice. You've accepted your gift and now use it to help people you don't know. Your uncle and cousin obviously care for you, but they also respect your knowledge and skill. They believe *in* you just as much as they believe you, if that makes sense."

Sigrid nodded but kept silent.

"I see these things, and it makes me admire you. And I like how you put my brother in his place from time to time. He needs it. So, this's why I consider you a friend. I hope you think the same of me."

"I do."

Freya grinned before laughing. "I hope you still feel that way the first time you see my temper unleashed."

"Um. I have. Several times."

"Oh, right. Well, that would make sense. And you still consider me a friend. I would say that's a boon for me."

"Is that why you're willing to help us?"

"I would do anything for my brother. He is the person I trust most in life, and I love him, so I help because of that. But I also help because you are my friend, and I would see you happy."

"I admire your loyalty and fierceness. I am lucky to call you friend and to be counted among yours."

"I wouldn't underestimate your own fierceness. I saw you swing that club. How did you learn to do that? And who fashioned the blade at the bottom?"

"Erik. When we were children, and I was just discovering my gift, the other children were sometimes unkind. Some older boys would try to frighten me by encircling me and not letting me pass. Most of the time, they taunted me, but once when I was fourteen winters, one boy tried more. I fought him well enough, but he was much larger than I was and a skilled warrior already. Erik found him and beat him within a hair's breadth of his life. His family believed the boy would die and even demanded Uncle Rangvald pay a *weregild* for the loss of the boy's life. Fortunately for all, he survived, but he was bitter about Erik humiliating him. He blamed me and tried to attack me again. This time he didn't intend to rape me. He wanted to kill me. Once again, Erik saved me. I was so angry I couldn't defend myself that I demanded Erik teach me. He knew I wouldn't move into the village, not when the others our age still harassed me. But he worried just as much about me living alone, away from the homestead. Erik spent months training me how to take advantage of being smaller and often faster and more agile. Erik also taught me to use my staff, and since then, I never go anywhere without it. He fashioned the blade for me, intending it to be a weapon more against animals than men, but it has served both purposes more than once." Sigrid shrugged.

"Who taught you to ride like that? I've seen few women who can ride and fight with the ease you did, and you ride bareback well too. Was that Erik too?"

"No," Sigrid paused with a wistful smile. "That was my mother. She had a way with animals and an affinity for horses. She took me with her wherever she went, and often it was a good distance from home to gather herbs and plants to tend the ill. My mother was our healer before she died, and I took over. She made sure I knew how to ride well, so I could travel or escape."

"Escape? She knew they might attack you? And she agreed to let you live alone before she died? Or did you decide that on your own?"

"Both. She wanted us to always prepare since we didn't have the easy protection of the village if there was a raid. However, living alone kept most eyes off us, and that was its own type of protection. She grew ill, but we both recognized it wasn't something herbs and prayer could heal. She encouraged me to move into Uncle Rangvald's longhouse, but she knew I would remain alone. I like the solitude, and I must admit it is taking quite a bit of getting used to being around so many people, so much of the time. It's overwhelming after the quiet I've enjoyed. Uncle Rangvald, my Aunt Lorna, and Erik urged me to move in with them, but I couldn't leave the house my father built for my mother. My only memories of him are the stories my mother told."

"Lorna? That's not a Norse name. It's Scottish."

"Yes, Uncle Rangvald met my aunt during a raid. He saved her from being made a thrall by his older brother. Uncle Harrold died not long after that battle. Anyway, Uncle Rangvald gave Aunt Lorna the choice between running away, and he would not sound the alarm, or coming back with him. He wouldn't make her a thrall but a free woman. The raid killed Aunt Lorna's family. She had no family or home to stay for, and since Uncle Rangvald would make her a free woman, she agreed. Uncle Rangvald had already taken a liking to her, so he brought her back intending to woo her." Sigrid raised her hands palms up. "They've been wedded almost thirty years. Apparently, she agreed."

The two women laughed, and an easy silence fell between them. They were both deep in their own thoughts, but before long, Freya put her finger to her lips.

"It's time. We must be silent."

They rose and moved to the flap of the tent. Freya looked

around and stepped out but didn't move aside to let Sigrid out. Freya counted to forty before she moved. They crept out of the camp and to the riverbed. They were almost there when a shadowy figure stepped around a boulder. Freya whipped her sword from her back and stepped in front of Sigrid.

"Easy there. I'd like to leave with all the parts I came with."

Sigrid pushed around Freya to look at Erik.

"What are you doing here?" Freya asked as she put her sword away, and her hands came to her hips.

"I assumed Sigrid would try to meet Leif, and I came to ensure her safety while she waited."

"You came to spy on her and my brother."

"No. Is that why you came? Are you going to spy?"

"Of course not. That's ridiculous."

"I take it that means you came to ensure the same thing."

Freya hmphed and crossed her arms. Erik stepped forward and smiled at Freya but then turned to look at Sigrid. "Prickly one, isn't she?"

"*She* is still standing here, you uncouth boar."

"Calling names, and I'm the uncouth one?" Erik's grin made Sigrid almost cough as she tried to stifle her laughter, but when she heard Freya rattle off a string of curses, she could no longer suppress it.

"You two are a fine pair. I'm glad to see you get along."

"We don't," the pair barked in unison.

"Mm-hmm," was Sigrid's only response before a pair of sinewy arms wrapped around her waist.

"She's safe now, so you can both retire."

"Not a chance. I'm not leaving my cousin."

"How is she supposed to get back to our tent?"

"Fine, but I suggest you turn away or find something else to occupy your time because I plan to spend mine enjoying my wife's company."

Leif didn't wait before leading Sigrid further along the

river to a bend that made it impossible for anyone else to see them from the camp. Leif wrapped his arms around Sigrid, and they came together with a crushing need. Their kiss was calmer than after the battle ended, but it conveyed far more need. Now that they could fulfill the longing to come together, there was little patience between the two of them. They stripped each other of their clothes as their hands roamed to any place they could reach. Leif lifted Sigrid and sank into her as her legs wrapped around his waist.

"We haven't much time, Leif."

"I know. I doubt it will take me long. I want you so badly I'm struggling to hold back."

"Don't hold back. I need you just as much."

Leif lowered them to the ground, and Sigrid hung on. As soon as her back touched the grass, they set a punishing pace. Sigrid's hips rose to meet Leif's with the same intensity as he slammed into her.

"I don't want to hurt you," Leif panted.

"If you slow down, *I* will hurt *you*. Gods this feels so good."

Leif needed no other invitation. His warm breath was against her ear and neck as he bent over her. Sigrid's hands searched for his hips until she found the deep grooves that allowed her to hang on.

"Do you have any idea what you do to me? How I long to spend every damn minute of every day and night buried inside you. I wish to make love to you over and over, and that still won't be enough. Right now, I want to pump my cock into you until your body trembles, and I know I'm the one to bring you release. I crave hearing you breathe my name as you shatter around me."

"Yes. I'm so close already. Don't hold back. You won't break me. I need to feel how much you want me. Want this. Gods, I pray it's as much as I do. I can't stop aching for you."

Leif thrusted faster and harder until his body would allow for nothing more. He felt his release coming from the base of his bollocks. He reached between them to find her breast. He rolled her nipple as she exhaled a moan, the urgency growing by the thrust, until her neck arched, and her eyes shut. He pinched hard, and she flew over the edge. The sight of her climax pushed Leif along. They buried their faces in the crook of each other's neck to silence their screams of pleasure. As their bodies stopped rocking together of their own volition, neither was in a hurry to draw apart.

"I would keep you here all night, but you shall freeze. As it is, you don't have warm enough clothing for how the weather has changed."

"You generate enough heat to warm an entire longhouse. It's not possible for me to be cold with you on top of me, and I should like it very much if that is where you stay a while longer." Her soft laughter clenched her muscles around Leif.

They looked at each other, both feeling the new wave of arousal building momentum. Leif slid his arms under Sigrid's shoulders and wrapped his hands up and over them as he held her against his overheated body. Sigrid's legs wound over his as Leif rocked against her. Gone were the hard and long, then short and intense thrusts. This rocking gave Sigrid the same friction she needed, but the drawn-out pace made the fire in her core burn hotter. Their bodies pressed together, their faces nose to nose, melded their souls in another dimension from their more frenetic lovemaking. Even their wildest moments were never just about two bodies coming together. They kissed as they explored the nooks and crannies within the velvety warmth of their mouths. Sigrid's hands caressed over Leif's back and shoulders.

"I love you, Sigrid. No matter what happens in the next few days. I am your husband just as you are my wife. You are mine."

"Just as you are mine."

"Only ever yours. Forever, Sigrid. I won't let you go in this life or the next."

"I love you, Leif. I will always find you."

Their kiss conveyed a deep and abiding love that neither

of them expected but appreciated. Their kiss brought on their slow release that drew out as they refused to let go. When they settled back into reality, thanks to the loud hooting of an owl, Leif rose and passed Sigrid her clothes. The air chilled Sigrid as she keenly felt Leif's absence. She shivered, and Leif helped her to dress before wrapping his fur cloak around her. She looked up at him unsure.

"You're keeping it."

"Your father will know you saw me tonight if I come out of the tent wearing this tomorrow."

"Because you are my wife, and I shall provide for you."

"Don't you think it would be better not to antagonize him? I don't think he'll look with favor on this. What if it does more harm than good?"

"You not catching a chill that leads to a fever is what's good. If he takes issue with it, he will address it to me."

Sigrid could only shake her head. "If it weren't so cold, I would refuse, but I would be stupid to turn it away. What about you?"

"Bjorn has extra."

Sigrid raised one eyebrow. She had seen no sign that Leif's cousin had any extra furs to lend him. The cloak was longer and wider than the ones used for sleeping. That was why they used more than one fur for a bedroll.

"I will manage just fine."

Sigrid opened her mouth to argue but snapped it shut when Erik and Freya appeared.

"You've had enough time with my cousin. I'll be taking her back to camp now." Erik stepped forward and wrapped Sigrid's arm through his. "We will see you on the morrow."

Erik led her away, but he faced south toward his own tribe's camp.

"Just where do you think you're taking Sigrid?" Leif charged forward.

"Back to our camp and our family."

"She is at her camp and with her family."

"Be reasonable. Until your father agrees to acknowledge your marriage, she is an unwanted person in your camp. The others will follow your jarl's example. I won't have her among people who don't want her."

"*Her* is standing right here. *Her* can make *her* own decisions." It annoyed Sigrid that the two men who were most influential in her life were arguing over her like she was a child. However, now that she made her pronouncement, she didn't know who to choose. She knew Erik was right. But she also didn't want to reject Leif or be far from him.

"Sigrid, I know what you're thinking. If he has any sense, he'll know you aren't rejecting him. You're being prudent and giving him an opportunity to speak to his father." Erik's gaze locked with Sigrid's before her eyes darted to Leif then Freya.

"If I'm going to trust anyone with Sigrid's safety in that camp, it is you, but that doesn't mean I agree with her leaving." Leif stern expression as he spoke to Erik softened when he looked at Sigrid.

Freya walked forward and dumped a heap of furs on the ground. No one had noticed that she slipped away and back. "You're both being ridiculous. *I* will see to her safety. We shall sleep here. We're halfway between the two camps. Hakin's men ran scared, so they won't regroup and come back tonight. They will search for their so-called leader. Both of you, go to your tents. We shall see you in the morning. I don't know about Sigrid, but I'm exhausted. I want to sleep."

Freya bent to pick up a fur, but Erik pulled it away first. He stepped back before snapping it open as he called over his shoulder, "See to your own woman."

Freya bristled as she elbowed him out of the way. "I can make my own bed. I am my own woman."

"As you say."

Erik continued to lay out the furs as Freya stood and fumed. When Erik finished, she bit out a terse, "Thank you."

Leif gave Sigrid a peck on the forehead before pulling the

covers over her as she settled on the ground. "Good night, my love," he whispered.

"Until the morning, my darling."

As Leif and Erik walked to their respective camps, Leif's heart soared at Sigrid's term of endearment. No woman had ever said it to him without the intent to seduce him. He found it now had great meaning.

EIGHTEEN

Leif tried to keep from losing his temper. His nostrils flared as he ground his teeth, and his lips pulled in to make a hard, flat line.

"You're being unreasonable," he said to his father through clenched teeth.

"I am being reasonable."

"How can you say that when you already know this is fated? How can ignoring the gods' will be reasonable?"

"I have no way of knowing this is fate. It was the tale of a woman who I never saw again. How do I know she didn't make that up just to win her daughter a future jarl?"

"You believe Rangvald's sister, Sigrid's mother, had that little honor? She traveled to our home to retrieve her sister, who you rejected. Do you think she enjoyed the humiliation of that? She came because of her loyalty to her family."

"If that's the case, then why hasn't Rangvald tried to settle a betrothal between you two?"

"Because he respects Sigrid and her independence. He has forced nothing upon her."

"And she has grown too free in believing she can live as she wants. What woman lives alone in a hut away from her village's protection? Just what does she do there to keep herself occupied?" There was no missing Ivar's meaning.

"Father, you push too far. She was a virgin until we pledged ourselves. Don't besmirch her honor. She doesn't deserve that, even if you don't agree to this. But I'm telling you, Father, don't make me choose."

Ivar ran a hand over his chin and stroked his beard as he studied his son. He had always marveled at how little they looked alike, and yet they were the same person in mannerisms and personality.

"Bring her here. I would have her cast the runes to see how things will play out. Once this business with Hakin is over, we can settle on your marriage."

"To Sigrid." Leif knew his father was vague on purpose, so he could claim later that he never agreed to their marriage.

Ivar gave him a hard look before nodding once. "Get the woman."

Freya pushed the tent open. Standing just behind her was a shockingly pale and shivering Sigrid. "We're here already."

Leif brushed past Freya and pulled Sigrid into his arms. She trembled all over, but she wasn't feverish. Her eyes were distant but not glassy. "What's happened?"

Leif was asking Sigrid, but when she didn't respond, didn't even wrap her arms around him, he looked at Freya.

"Sigrid had a horrible nightmare just before dawn. She hasn't said a word since she called out in her sleep. She's just shivered and been withdrawn. Sigrid's done everything I ask, but it's as though she's in a trance again."

Leif scooped her up and set off for his tent.

"Where are you going now?" Ivar demanded.

"Our tent." Leif kept walking. He disappeared into the tent next to Ivar's just as Rangvald and Erik walked up.

"What's happened? Why is your son carrying my niece?"

"Freya says she had a nightmare and hasn't spoken since she woke up. She's just shivered." Ivar shrugged. Rangvald and Erik looked at each other before turning to him.

"She's only been that way twice, and both times it signaled death. When she was eleven winters, she had one of these episodes just before an illness swept through the homestead, and we lost close to a quarter of our people. The other time was three years ago before a fierce battle in Scotland. Sigrid was with us while Erik was gone. We didn't know how accurate her prediction was until Erik returned with less than half of his crew."

"I'm going to check on her." Erik backed out of the tent. Freya looked over, tempted to follow, but she knew Leif would only send Erik back, and she needed space from the unsettling Norseman. Rangvald and Ivar stood staring at each other until Rangvald broke into a wide grin.

"Your niece believes death is upon us, and you grin like a simpleton."

"I grin because you still refuse to believe my sister. I shall not force the issue. She made me promise not to, but you'll have to accept that you may be the master of your men, but you're not the master of fate."

"Why would you encourage this? We are already allies. You would serve your own purposes to find another tribe for her to marry into."

"My niece hasn't had an easy life. She never knew her father because he died before she could remember. Her mother died when she was thirteen winters. She lived alone because her gift scared the children her age. Her only friend has been Erik for most of her life. He's protected her as much as he's been a companion. She is the most loyal woman I've ever met. She will always put others ahead of herself and will risk her life to do so. I would think those would be the exact qualities you'd look for in your tribes *frú*. It is assuredly what I will look for in Erik's future wife."

Freya listened to the conversation and agreed with Rangvald. She would help her brother when he became jarl, but she would never replace a wife and that woman's duties. Freya also knew she wouldn't live in her village forever. They would marry her off, and as she thought about that, a nagging sense of relief swept through her when she realized Rangvald revealed Erik was neither married nor betrothed. She shoved that feeling aside as it served no purpose.

Ivar listened as Rangvald spoke, but nothing in his expression hinted to him changing his mind. The opposite seemed true. He appeared more irritated by the more he heard how wonderful a wife Sigrid would make. The two jarls came to an impasse until Rangvald shrugged and looked toward the flap as Erik returned.

"Leif wouldn't let me in."

"I could have told you that," sniffed Freya.

"Perhaps you could have saved me the trip."

"I doubt that. You wouldn't have listened."

Erik stepped over to Freya and spoke for her ears only. "I would listen to just about anything if you were the one saying it."

"Listen to this. Go away." Erik guffawed as Freya glared at him. "People will get the wrong idea about us," she huffed.

"What if it's the right idea?"

"That you annoy me? Then I suppose the truth is obvious."

"If you say so."

"Enough. You two sound like children squabbling," Ivar grumbled. "When will the girl be well enough to return? We need her to cast the runes before we encounter Hakin or Grímr again."

"Father, she isn't a girl. She's a woman just like I am. And if you'd like her help, perhaps you should try being more pleasant." If anyone else said such a thing to Ivar, they would have come away minus a tongue, but Freya gave him her large adoring gaze to soften the bite. Ivar couldn't deny she was right. "And Father, she's my friend, so for my sake at least, please be nice."

Ivar's eyes bulged as he looked at his daughter as if he'd never seen such a creature. "You've made friends with her?"

"Why does everyone seem so surprised by that? I'm plenty capable of making friends. I just choose not to. I don't know many people I would want to spend my leisure time with, let alone call a friend. Sigrid happens to be one of the few."

"How lucky for my cousin," Erik muttered.

Freya was ready to turn on him when she caught the ever so brief look of disappointment before the expression slid from Erik's face, and his mocking tone was back. Freya didn't know what to say, so she kept quiet instead.

"Can one of you not see if she will hurry?" Ivar broke the silence with his frustrated utterance.

"No need, Father. We are back," Leif announced as he carried Sigrid back into the tent.

Leif had sat in a chair in the tent he shared with Bjorn and Strian and held Sigrid in his arms. She had stopped trembling, but she was still ashen. It had taken him what seemed like ages to get Sigrid to stop shaking. When they entered his tent, he swore under his breath because there was no way for him to have a hot bath prepared for her. Taking her to a freezing river certainly wouldn't stop her shivering. The best he could do was wrap them both in furs as she burrowed into his chest. It was only a matter of moments before she calmed as she took in Leif's unique scent, but her body didn't cooperate as it continued to shiver. Sigrid ran her hand absent-mindedly over his chest as he stroked her hair. She kept her eyes closed as she breathed to slow her racing heart. Leif's kisses on her forehead and cheek were so tender they made her breath hitch. If she hadn't been so consumed by the visions she had seen in her dream, she might have better appreciated the loving care Leif put in each of those kisses. She used Leif's presence to ground her back in the present, even though fear coursed through her with every shiver.

When she stopped trembling, Leif tilted her chin until she opened her eyes, and then he waited a moment longer before raising his eyebrows. He didn't want to ask her in case she wasn't ready, but he wanted her to know he was interested and was prepared to listen.

"It was so horrible," she whispered. "It was unlike any other dream I have ever had. I've been able to sense other people's emotions and even feel them, but this time, the emotions swallowed me whole. There was no longer a separate me from those I saw. Not only could I feel what they felt, I could also feel the events as they happened. The pain their bodies experienced, I experienced along with them."

She shook her head and rested her forehead in the crook of his neck.

"Whatever happens with the next battle, it still won't be over. The battle will be bloody and fierce even with Hakin's diminished forces. That wasn't the part of the dream that affected me. It was after that. Ivar insisted that I return home with Uncle Rangvald and Erik, but he was at least willing to come to a feast in Uncle Rangvald's hall. We were all there when the hall smoldered. People tried to get out, but the doors were all barricaded. Before anyone could do anything to break down the doors, the roof caught. The fire spread faster than it should have. Something was on the thatching that made it burn faster, and so the ceiling caved in. It trapped everyone. Chaos erupted as people panicked. Most were already too drunk to understand what was happening until it was too late. They thought the yelling and pushing were all part of the revelry. You could get to me, but just as we embraced..." Sigrid shook her head. A sob escaped her throat as she pulled back from Leif. "A beam fell, and you pushed me out of the way. It was aflame and landed on top of you. I watched as you burned to death. I tried smothering it with cloths and even found water, but it wasn't enough. The hall filled with smoke, and I died lying next to your remains as the smoke suffocated me. Suffocated our child." Sigrid dissolved into sobs that wracked her entire body.

Leif held her as she clung to him, trying to take in all she told him. The part that echoed over and over was that their child died. He understood Sigrid said it killed them both, but the notion they were having a child and the baby would be harmed was more than he could digest. He felt a sob rise in his own chest as he looked down at the small figure tucked next to him. When Sigrid could look up again, her watery smile was hollow.

"I don't know when this will happen because I couldn't tell if the next battle happens today or in a week or even three months from now. I don't know if I'm already with child, but I was when this happened."

Leif blinked hard to keep his own tears at bay. He hadn't cried since he was a child, and he didn't intend to fall apart in front of his wife, who needed his strength and support.

"This whole nightmare was so different than anything else I have ever dreamed. It was so real I thought it was happening in that moment. It was almost like a spirit walk. The most significant difference was rather than this being a foregone conclusion, an unalterable prediction, I knew through the entire thing that if I awoke, I could keep it from happening. It was as though I knew I was dreaming, even though my mind was sure the fire was happening. I don't know if I've described that in any way that makes sense other than in my own head."

"I understood. I can't imagine how terrifying all of that must have been. I'm sorry I wasn't there for you."

"You're here now. That's all I need."

"That doesn't stop me from being angry for giving in when I should have insisted."

"Leif, you couldn't have stopped that dream. You wouldn't have even been able to wake me up. I had to see what I did. Your support only helps me now that it's over. The dream wouldn't have let me go until I did." They settled for a few minutes before Sigrid took a deep breath and pushed the furs down. "We can't stay here any longer. Hiding won't make my duty go away. I would have done with it all now rather than later. I need my staff from Freya's tent, and then we can speak to the others."

It wasn't long after that Leif asked Bjorn and Strian, who had vacated the tent as soon as the couple arrived, to join them in Ivar's tent. Strian offered to fetch her staff.

"I know what I saw," Sigrid finished retelling her tale now that she, Leif, Strian and Bjorn had joined the others. "We have the chance to prevent this, but if we do, some other event will have to replace it. I don't know yet what fate's other option is."

"Would casting your runes tell you?" asked Strian.

"I believe so. I don't know in advance whether they will answer the exact questions I have. Sometimes they do, but at the same time, they create more questions."

"Sigrid, what do you need?" Erik murmured. He still stood near Freya, and she secretly enjoyed the heat that radiated from his large body. Listening to Sigrid's prophecy chilled her to the bone. She wondered what she would have been doing during the feast and how she would have died. She looked over at Erik as he chanced a glance at her. Her thoughts seemed mirrored in his eyes. He brushed the back of his hand against hers. It was only for a second, but it was a comfort Freya didn't realize she needed.

"I need someone to build up the fire."

Bjorn stepped forward and threw two more logs into the fire, and they all watched as the flames grew taller before dropping back to a normal size. The snapping and popping were a brutal reminder of what Sigrid shared about their fates. Sigrid stood from Leif's lap, and when he moved to follow, she tapped his shoulder. She walked around the fire clockwise twice then counterclockwise once and used her staff to draw a circle around the fire pit. Sigrid marked off the points that divided the circle into four before coming back to where she started and kneeling before the flames. She etched marks into the dirt that only she understood.

She twisted the rounded top off her staff and dumped the runes into her hands. She clasped the bones and small stones in her hands as she reached them over the fire and then overhead. Sigrid recited an ancient prayer before beginning her chant. As her voice rose and fell, she cast the runes before her and waited for them to settle into position. Her chant came to a close, and she leaned over to study what lay before her. She picked up one bone and turned it before replacing it. A rock landed on top of another, so she slid them apart. Sigrid studied each individual piece as images formed in her mind then grouped the mixture of rocks and bones into different configurations before settling them back into their original positions. She rocked back onto her toes before gracefully rising. Sigrid gazed into the flames once more before turning to face the others. It was with a sense of dread she explained her reading.

"This battle was only the first of many. The war with Hakin isn't over for he shall recruit mercenaries from a faraway land to come and join the fight. I can't explain how he can afford this, even after his homestead burned, but he will. I see a man with two heads, and I believe this to be Grímr because I believe that as much of a danger as he is to us, he will play his brother false. The only way for this to end is when two adversaries become lovers. It is a shared love that forges a bond that connects our clans. This isn't about Leif and me. It is two warriors who I see. The death doesn't end until these two fight side by side in unity. A cloud shall pass over us if this doesn't happen. I sense this is where my dream plays out. We shall see great loss before we see our victory."

"Who do you see?" Freya inquired. She refused to look at anyone but Sigrid.

"I can't say. The runes are not that specific."

"But what about the past, your other visions?"

"I can't link the events I've seen to a specific time. My visions tell me what will come to pass, but I don't always know how long until it happens. Sometimes the visions are flashes from the past, too. I can't tell you any more than I have. I'm sorry."

Sigrid bit her lip. She knew she was being evasive, but she couldn't risk sharing all she knew. Fate had to work itself out without her intervening. She had to leave the others to their own destinies and warning them might change their actions.

Leif stepped forward and wrapped his arms around her. It relieved him to see the color back in her cheeks, and she seemed more settled. There was a moment where she remained rigid before a deep breath escaped, and she settled into the warmth of his embrace. He knew she was keeping something from them, but he had faith that whatever it was, it was something not meant for the others to know yet. He hoped she would share with him, but more because he wanted to share her burden than be privy to her secrets.

"Do you at least know when the next round of fighting will come?" Rangvald asked.

"Soon. It was before the snow in the hills melts from the other night."

"Then we shall return to my homestead to regroup and celebrate this victory."

Sigrid shook her head vehemently.

"Rangvald, remember Sigrid had a nightmare last night. She dreamed we did just that, and your longhouse was set ablaze with everyone locked inside. There were no survivors." Leif ground his teeth, annoyed they could forget Sigrid's dream in favor of planning a battle. Both mattered.

"Where would you have us then, niece?"

"That I don't know. I'm not a strategist. I know there can't be a feast at your home until Hakin and Grímr are both dead. If we don't wait, it will signal our deaths." Sigrid fought her desire to protect her belly with her hands. She couldn't give away anything else. Leif knew, and that was all that mattered to her.

"Come. I'll take you back to Freya's tent to rest." Leif

stroked his hand over her back and turned them toward his sister's tent.

"Wait." Ivar called to them. "Rangvald, if your niece has nothing more, she can tell us, then perhaps it would be best if she returned to her home. She's not a warrior and would be safer with your wife than on a battlefield."

"Father! You believe my wife is safer away from me?"

"She's not your wife, and I am in no mood to hear otherwise."

"She is my wife. But even if she wasn't, how do you propose she travel back to her home?"

"I will take her," Erik stepped forward.

"Over my dead body. She stays with me."

"I can arrange that. Your father is right. A battlefield is no place for her."

"And your land is. Where they kidnapped her."

"They kidnapped her from you too, if you don't recall."

Leif and Erik came toe to toe as they glowered at one another. Sigrid tried to pull Erik away just as Freya shoved Leif's shoulder. Sigrid couldn't make Erik budge, but at least Freya forced her brother back a step. Leif swung his attention to Rangvald.

"Rangvald, this is unbelievable. You'd send her on a journey, even with your son, that might take her straight by the enemy? You would send her back to her hut to be alone when she's already been a victim to Hakin's plan twice."

"I understand your concern, Leif, but I still have well over a hundred men guarding the homestead, and her Aunt Lorna is there to receive her."

"I don't accept that."

"Leif, it's not your decision to make." Ivar growled. "You are sorely testing my patience."

Leif opened his mouth, but Sigrid stayed him with a hand on his arm. He looked to her, but her expression showed she didn't want him to continue the argument. Rather than relent and agree with his father, Leif shook his head and took Sigrid's hand.

"I'm taking her to rest. It's been a rough night and morning. Sigrid deserves a reprieve. She's aided us all today."

When they arrived at Freya's tent, Leif tucked Sigrid into the bedroll. He didn't know what to say to her since he didn't know what to do. He wanted to rebel against his father, but he couldn't do that in the middle of a battlefield where their warriors needed to see their leaders as united.

"Don't worry so much, my love," Sigrid said as a yawn escaped her. "It will work out one way or another."

"I would have that way be where I can see you and touch you to know no one harms you."

"I feel the same, but you may have to accept that we need patience." Sigrid tried to stifle the next yawn, but she could only clap her hand over her mouth.

"Rest now. We will decide later." Leif kissed Sigrid's forehead as her eyes drifted closed. He slipped from the tent before looking for his sister.

Sigrid heard Freya enter the tent, and even though her body clamored for sleep, she forced her eyes open.

"You're awake."

"Yes, though I wish I weren't. I was waiting for you to return. Freya, you have to take me home."

"What? No. Leif would kill me. He might very well kill Erik if Erik tries to leave with you."

"You know Leif would do no such thing. You're the only one he would without a doubt trust with my safety. I would go alone if I thought he wouldn't follow me. Or if I thought Erik wouldn't follow me. I don't need those two traveling together, or worse racing each other, to find me. I can't stay here driving a wedge between Leif and your father. I know you would rather fight than play nursemaid, but I need to leave."

"Sigrid, this isn't a wise idea. Leif will be a terror if he doesn't know where you are. Do you think sending him into battle distracted will do him any good?"

"He will know I'm with you. Besides, if we sail, we can take Tyra with us. She can get the care she needs from my aunt. She is an even better healer than I am."

This made Freya pause. She had only stopped thinking about her friend long enough to pay attention to the arguing among her family and Rangvald's. "Leif won't let me sail away with you even if it means getting Tyra help."

Sigrid thought for a moment before she knew what they needed to do. "Make sure that Leif, Erik, and Bjorn go scouting. Tell Leif and Erik they both need to cool their tempers, and send Bjorn to keep an eye on them. Strian will help us get Tyra aboard your ship. You've felt the wind all morning. It will sail us in the right direction, and we are close enough you shouldn't need a full crew to row. We leave before nightfall."

"And you think no one will notice our disappearance?"

"Of course, they will, but it is what both Ivar and Uncle Rangvald want. No one will rush to tell Leif or Erik. By the time they return, we'll already be on the boat and under way. Freya, please. I can't cause a falling out between Leif and Ivar. This isn't the solution I would choose if there was a choice, but there isn't. It has to be this way."

"Have you seen this in a vision? Are you sure?" Sigrid shook her head. Freya blew a long breath out through her nose before agreeing. "I hope you're right."

NINETEEN

It didn't take Freya as long as she thought it would to convince the three men to be part of the scouting party. It didn't thrill Leif and Erik to be riding out together, but they both needed time away from their fathers. Bjorn needed a chance to escape his guilt whenever he looked at Tyra. Strian took a little more convincing to help them get Tyra aboard Freya's longboat. It was an uneven and jarring ride to get to the fjord and the anchored boats. They had to travel at a slow pace for Tyra's sake, but Sigrid worried someone would alert Leif or Erik they were missing. She prayed they were far enough in the opposite direction to not be able to catch up with them, even if someone notified the men of their disappearance.

"Thank you, Strian. If they ask, don't feel compelled to hide what we have done. There's no point in lying about it because it will be obvious enough. I hope they don't blame you." Sigrid squeezed Strian's forearm as the trio stood on the longboat's deck.

"They won't be thrilled, but Bjorn and Leif know Freya, and I get the impression Erik is catching on. There would be no stopping Freya, so I can say with honesty it was better I helped and saw you safely away than not."

"I heard that."

"And I meant you to. May the gods be with you." Strian extended his arm for Freya to clasp about the wrist. They shook before Strian pulled her in for a quick hug. Strian hugged Sigrid before going back ashore.

It was only a matter of a few minutes before Freya was navigating her longboat through the fjord and away from the two armies. Sigrid closed her eyes as she tried to get a sense of whether she made a wise decision or her greatest mistake.

"There's no use praying now. We're underway. We shall just have to meet whatever comes our way with our swords and our wits."

Sigrid nodded as she looked out over the blue expanse that stretched before them. Time would tell soon enough.

The men were tired and muddy by the time they returned to camp late that night. Leif wanted nothing more than to shuck his clothes and jump in the river to scrub away the dirt and grime before going to see Sigrid. It drizzled while he was on patrol and mud splattered over his legs with each clop of his horse's hooves. They found tracks they were sure belonged to Hakin or Grímr since they were solitary prints. But the rain washed them away. They went the rest of the time with no other signs. They agreed they should return when the sun sank, and the moon didn't come out from behind the clouds.

Leif returned to camp with Bjorn, but Erik said his goodbyes before heading to his own tribe's camp. Leif knew something was wrong the moment he saw the looks on the men's faces. He ran to his tent, but no one was there. He moved to Freya's, and finding Strian sitting alone surprised him.

"What's going on? Where's Sigrid? And Freya?"

"They're gone."

"What do you mean gone?" Leif interrupted. "Who took them? How?"

"No one took them. They left. They took Tyra back to Sigrid's aunt. She's a renowned healer."

Leif squinted at him as a rock settled in his gut. "Just how do you know this?" He bit out.

"Because I helped them move Tyra there."

"Move Tyra where," Bjorn walked into the tent.

"Strian helped Freya smuggle Sigrid away."

"I did no such thing."

"Where's Tyra?" Bjorn demanded.

"Freya agreed to help Sigrid when Sigrid asked to go home. She didn't want to continue to cause trouble between you and the jarl. She knew you wouldn't agree to her traveling alone, and she didn't want you to argue anymore with your father. Sigrid also made the sound argument that Tyra needs more care than Sigrid can give her here. I helped them to Freya's longboat."

"When?" Bjorn's voice came out as a dangerous whisper.

"Several hours ago. I didn't know until after you left the reason Freya didn't suggest I go with you was because she would ask for my help. But I wasn't going to turn her down. She and Sigrid would have left regardless and taken Tyra too. I would rather know they made it to the longboat in one piece than wonder if they were alive or not."

"You think the fact they sailed away guarantees they'll stay alive?" Leif was incredulous.

"Of course not. But I know that it improves their odds since Freya will be better able to protect them on her boat than if she ran into danger on horseback."

Bjorn pulled Strian forward by the front of his fur cloak until his face was almost touching Strian's. "If anything happens to her, to them, I will hold you responsible. This will be on your head."

Leif and Strian stared at Bjorn. It was out of character for Bjorn to get involved in another man's argument, even if he was the most hot headed of the group. Bjorn shoved Strian away before stomping out of the tent.

"He's right. I will blame you, too. But why's he so upset about my wife and my sister leaving? I know he's family, but he's always let Freya do whatever she wants."

"I don't think it's about either of them. I think he feels guilty that he didn't prevent Tyra's injuries and believes it now binds her fate to his, and he feels responsible for her."

"Maybe you're right. Either way, I'm not staying here."

"I doubted you would. There is food packed for you and Bjorn aboard your boat."

"You're staying here?"

Strian laughed. "I can't leave. Who will stand as one of your father's captains if we all disappear? As it is, I will need to be sure Tyra's and Bjorn's crews can sail when the time comes."

Leif clapped his hand on Strian's shoulder. "You're a good man and a better friend. Thank you."

"I shall remind you of this. Don't doubt it."

Leif left the tent in search of Bjorn. His cousin was already remounting his horse while holding the reins to Leif's.

"Strian made sure there is food aboard my boat. We ride to the fjord then sail."

Bjorn said nothing as they galloped out of camp. Leif looked back over his shoulder as he considered what his father would think when he discovered Leif chose Sigrid over him.

The journey home was uneventful for Sigrid. Compared to everything that happened since she left, she almost felt uneasy because nothing went wrong. She helped on deck when she could, and when she could not, she tended Tyra. The woman's eyes fluttered open from time to time, but Sigrid's tinctures kept the pain at bay enough for her to sleep. Rangvald's guards who recognized her on the dock greeted them. They ceased the alarm and helped the crew come ashore. They brought a stretcher for Tyra, and they made their way to

Rangvald's longhouse where Sigrid's Aunt Lorna greeted them. Freya was unprepared for how much the woman looked like her son. She believed he looked like Rangvald until she saw Lorna. The woman was tall and statuesque but still smaller than Freya. She piled her auburn hair high on her head making the fine bone structure under her alabaster skin more prominent. Lorna was one of the most beautiful women Freya had ever seen. Freya felt like a bull stomping about compared to the elegant Lorna, and even Sigrid made her feel as though she paled in comparison.

"She makes every woman feel that way when they meet her, but they learn she is the kindest and most selfless woman you'll ever meet. It would seem her beauty is lost on her." Sigrid leaned over and whispered as Lorna approached. Sigrid stepped forward to exchange kisses on the cheek with her aunt. "Aunt Lorna, I'd like you to meet Freya Ivarsdóttir. Freya, this is my Aunt Lorna. We've brought our wounded friend, Tyra, home for help."

"It is a pleasure to meet you, Freya. Welcome to our home. Please, come to the longhouse. I'll see to it you are both fed while I check on your friend."

Freya paused for a moment, torn between wanting a proper meal and staying with her friend.

"Aunt, if it's all right with you, I think we would rather eat while staying with Tyra."

Freya shot Sigrid a grateful smile, and Sigrid nodded.

"Of course. Let's get Tyra settled. Then I'll arrange for someone to bring in two bathing tubs and some food. It won't be one of the finer chambers, but there is a women's chamber that will be large enough to accommodate all three of you. Sigrid, I'm assuming you're staying rather than returning to your hut." Lorna made the statement in the lilting brogue she still held, but the order was clear.

"Yes, Aunt Lorna. I will stay here. If I don't, not only will Uncle Rangvald and Erik have my head, Leif will too."

"Leif?"

"My brother," Freya interjected.

"Yes, dear. I know who Leif is. So, it would seem things are going well if you're worried about Leif's reaction, Sigrid."

"Things are well between us, or at least they were before we left. But things are not well with Jarl Ivar."

"He's still fighting the inevitable? The old goat does like to have his own way." Her light laugh took some sting from her words, and Freya nodded in agreement.

The women followed the stretcher bearing Tyra into the *frú's* longhouse. A thrall showed them into a spacious chamber that was a bit sparse but would host them with comfort. Lorna's hushed tones floated to them as she gave orders to a thrall before making her way over to Tyra. She removed her cloak and examined Tyra. Her face remained expressionless even as she lifted the bandaging off the younger woman's chest to see the freshly stitched wound.

"You've done well, Sigrid. The stitching is clean and even, and you've packed the wound with yarrow to fight infection. She needs monitoring, and her wound needs ongoing care, but I think she will pull through as long as a fever doesn't develop. Has she been flushed or overheated?"

"Not yet. I made sure she received willow bark tea every few hours, and she's been sleeping. Even during the voyage."

"Good. I will clean around the wound and add a fresh poultice while you both bathe."

On cue, the chamber door opened as a line of thralls entered with two large bathing tubs along with soaps and linens. Sigrid and Freya looked at one another before grinning. After the days without a proper bathhouse, neither was shy about stripping off their filthy clothes and sinking into the hot water. Both declined help from the thralls as they scrubbed their hair and their bodies. It was only toward the end when they needed help to rinse the soap from their hair and then the final dunk of cold water did they ask for help.

"Freya, I know these aren't what you are used to, but these are what I have that will fit you."

Lorna held up a dress and apron with embroidery around the neckline, cuffs, and hems. The dress was close to floor length and fitted Freya's lean frame as though a skilled seamstress designed it for her. Its apron did nothing to disguise her shapely body, and if anything, accentuated all the right parts. The combination was feminine but still practical.

Freya wasn't sure what to think since she wore dresses at home when she had no other choice, but it was a rarity. She preferred the linen or leather breeches that the men wore. She rolled up the sleeves of her tunic to above her elbows and wore a vest to hide her breasts. This outfit accentuated her more than ample bust. Sigrid looked at her with a cocked eyebrow before offering a knowing smile. Freya responded with a scowl.

"We have women warriors here, of course, but most are away with Rangvald and Erik, so I can't ask to borrow their clothing. I hope this suits you."

"It is lovely. Thank you, *Frú* Lorna."

"Just Lorna, if you please." Lorna's gaze slid to and away from Sigrid with such speed Freya wasn't sure the woman ever looked away.

"That is most gracious. Lorna."

"Sigrid, I had some of your clothes brought here after you left. I would like you to stay here until your uncle returns. Going back to your hut is not an option." Once again, the burr in her accent removed the bite from her stern words.

"That's what I was hoping to do, Aunt."

The three women sat down to the table full of food a servant laid out while Sigrid and Freya bathed. They spent the rest of the afternoon and evening eating and talking. Sigrid sighed as she settled back to let Freya and Lorna do most of the talking. She missed Leif and wondered when he would arrive. She wanted to check on her hut, but she knew there was no need. The hut was no longer her home. There was little there she needed when she would leave for Leif's village. Even if there had been, there was no chance Lorna would allow her to go, and she would ask none of the guardsmen to take her after what happened to the others tasked to watch her. Her eyes drifted closed, and her mind floated above her as if she drank too much mead, but she had drunk none. She allowed her body to relax, recognizing the signs of what was to come. She breathed as she allowed the images to take shape behind her eyes.

The images began hazy. Sigrid sensed people rushing and panic hung in the air. As she relaxed her body more, her mind grew sharper. She saw the village outside the longhouse as women ran with their children to find shelter. The guardsmen hurried to close the gates, but the raid happened too fast. Sigrid watched as a man she recognized as Grímr led an army of men into the village. They carried lighted pitch torches they threw onto the thatching of the longhouses. They dismounted and fought the warriors who remained to protect the jarl's family and land. Rangvald's warriors seemed to be prevailing until embers from the blazing roofs rained down. Sigrid felt herself squinting. No, it was not the roofs that caused the fire to fall. It was the arrows that were on fire. Grímr's men killed many of the children on sight and only took the boys and girls who were old enough to serve as thralls and bed slaves. They bound and gagged Rangvald's surviving warriors before making their way through the women.

Sigrid heard the screams as the women fought their attackers. She heard the laughter and grunts as the men overpowered their victims. She saw the children watching the attackers abuse their mothers. Then she saw herself as she and Freya tried to protect a group of women and children who hid in a dugout. Freya stood below the hatch with her sword and ax drawn, ready to hack apart anyone who attempted to breach their refuge. Sigrid held her own ax and knife as she stood in front of the huddled group. She looked around but couldn't see her aunt. Even in her vision, she felt the bile rise as she understood Lorna hadn't gone into hiding. She wouldn't have hidden when her people continued to fight, and so it was with certainty Sigrid knew some screams belonged to her aunt. Sigrid's eyes popped open, and when she slid her gaze over to her aunt, she knew she was wrong about one thing. Her aunt would never give her attackers the satisfaction of screaming.

"We have to go. Now." Sigrid stood from the chair so fast it skidded backwards.

"Go? You just got here." Lorna smiled as she reached a hand out to take Sigrid's.

"No, you don't understand. They will attack us tonight. We must get all the women and children away from the homestead. Send them to the hidden glen. We must do it now or only a handful will survive. Lorna, you will not be one of them. They will take Ofeig and Kormack as thralls to train into Grímr's warriors. Your sons will not stay here alive. They will make Astrid and Isla bed slaves after someone assaults them in the village square. We must go."

Lorna gave Sigrid a long, hard look before she called orders to her thralls. Sigrid hurried to Tyra's bedside and prepared her for yet another journey. Freya disappeared before Sigrid could ask where she was going. Lorna gathered extra furs and blankets along with sending thralls to gather clothes from all the chambers in the longhouse. Lorna and Sigrid were about to walk outside when Freya returned.

"I have a cart and oxen ready outside. We load Tyra along with the youngest and oldest onto it. We send them ahead now. The others remain here to gather what they can carry. I have alerted your warriors." Freya looked at Sigrid and offered a tight smile. "None argued with me once they knew you'd had a vision."

Small consolation that my visions are appreciated now.

Sigrid forced the bitterness from her mind as she listened to her aunt and Freya issue orders. She followed the others out as they loaded the cart with the people who were too frail to flee on their own feet or too small to keep up. Sigrid walked up to a male thrall she recognized and whispered to him.

"Take them to the hidden glen. You must hurry, but don't take the shortest way. You must stay away from my hut. There will still be men watching it, and if they see you escaping, they will either attack or alert our enemies. It will be longer to go north before turning east, but you must."

The man nodded as he used a switch to urge the oxen to move. Women and children trailed behind the cart as a quarter of the warriors accompanied them. They all saw Sigrid give instructions to the oxen driver, so they would listen to him as they fled.

Sigrid looked around and saw Freya speaking with the captain of the guard. Lorna reappeared but looked unlike anything Sigrid had ever seen her aunt wear. The woman was in leather breeches and a leather vest. She had pulled her hair back into tight braids. She carried a double handed broadsword that anyone would recognize as Scottish but made for her size. She had an ax shoved into her belt with knives sticking out of her boots, her belt, and strapped to her wrists. As she approached, Sigrid saw a mace in the sword sheath on her back.

"After this is over, I shall tell you the whole story of how your uncle and I met." She winked at Sigrid as she handed her two of the knives sheathed in her belt.

"I will hold you to that, Aunt."

The remaining warriors, Freya, Lorna, and Sigrid settled in to wait. The sun was setting when a call went out about a longboat docking. Freya looked at the captain of the guards who called out orders to ready the fire and arrows. Sigrid inched forward to see beyond the gates. She saw two men come ashore but couldn't see their faces. One man took three steps forward, and Sigrid knew. She raced forward as Freya tried to catch her arm. She wrenched free as she sprinted toward the dock.

Leif saw Sigrid running toward him. He observed how silent the village was as they anchored, and it filled him with trepidation when no one came out to greet them. Bjorn commented on it, and both men along with their crew had drawn their swords before even stepping ashore. Now the one person who meant the most to him was flying toward him, and he couldn't think of anything but getting to her faster. They met halfway, and Sigrid threw herself into his arms. Leif caught her and squeezed so tightly he was sure he heard her back crack. Her arms wrapped like iron bands around his neck, and he wasn't sure he could fill his lungs with enough air to slow his galloping heart. She was safe and in his arms. His mind couldn't work past that.

"What the blazes is going on here, Freya?" It was Bjorn's question that had Leif and Sigrid coming back to reality.

"Sigrid envisioned an impending attack. We've evacuated everyone who cannot stay to fight."

Leif looked at Sigrid as he placed her back on her feet. She nodded before looking around him to Bjorn.

"You need to move your longboat further down the coast. Grímr will seize it or fire it if it remains here."

"It's your husband's longboat, and I would like to know how you can be so sure it's Grímr who comes."

"Cousin, did you not hear me? Or Sigrid? Ask your questions later. There is still much to do. Move Leif's boat and hurry." Freya turned her back on Bjorn, who let loose a stream of curses as he headed back to the boat. It was already shoving away from the dock by the time Leif walked up to the village with the women. Leif pulled Sigrid aside once they were inside the wall.

"Don't think for even a moment that this settles things. You may find yourself over my knee when this finishes. You have scared years off my life."

"And I will gladly bend over if you promise not to get yourself killed."

Leif's cock found that inopportune moment to harden fully when his wife's innocent words sunk in. His cock awoke the moment he saw her, and it came to attention when he felt her body pressed against him. Now the notion of bending her over had it twitching.

"I will take you over my knee, but when I bend you over, it will be with me thrusting inside you," he whispered.

Desire flared in Sigrid's eyes, and Leif felt her nipples harden as he pulled her against him again. "Don't say things like that if you can't follow through right away," she breathed.

"How do you think my cock feels when you talk about bending over?" His warm breath tickled her neck as he whispered in her ear. "If I was sure we had five minutes to ourselves, I would prove it to you."

"Only five minutes?"

"I hate to admit it, but it probably wouldn't take even that long."

Sigrid's back arched as she pressed against him. His hand slid down to grasp her backside as he squeezed enough to make her yelp. She pulled his head down to her as she brought their mouths together. The kiss was short and intense. Their lips and teeth mashing together until they slowed enough to allow their tongues to glide against one another, and Sigrid welcomed him into her mouth. Leif's response, somewhere between a growl and hum, made her core clench as she felt moisture on her inner thigh.

"Why don't the two of you find a storeroom and take care of things." Freya's voice broke them apart. "It's not as though either of you will concentrate while your blood is running hot. We have spotted no boats nor horsemen. You should be able to find that five minutes you promised her, Brother."

Leif wanted to throw an angry retort at his sister, but he wanted his wife more. He took her hand and pulled her away.

"Where?" He bit out. Sigrid guided them toward a storeroom filled with sacks of grain.

"Are we really doing this? Now?" Sigrid wondered aloud.

"Do you feel too guilty?"

"I do, but I admit not enough to stop."

"I know what you have seen, but I also know what could

happen. I want to make love to my wife in case this is the last opportunity we have."

Leif's hands skimmed her legs as he pulled the tunic up around her waist. His fingers sought her entrance, and he hummed as he felt the dew coat his fingers as they brushed her inner thigh. He thrust two fingers into her and wrapped his arm around her waist to brace her as her hips shot forward to meet his thrusts. Sigrid's moans filled the small room as she did nothing to contain her pleasure.

"That's it, little one. No need to keep quiet this time."

Sigrid ran her fingers under Leif's tunic as she scored her nails along his chest. Her other hand cupped his shaft through his pants. She alternated between rubbing and squeezing until Leif growled and gripped her hand.

"The only place I shall come is deep inside you. Keep doing that, I shall spill right now, and our time will be over in less than five minutes."

Sigrid undid the lacing that kept his pants in place and pushed them down over his lean hips. "Then you had better hurry because I'm already close."

Leif thrust all his fingers inside her as he pulled her tunic and apron up over her head. Naked before him, he feasted his eyes on her body. His fingertips grazed the peeks her nipples became. He brought his head down and licked the tip of her nipple before whirling his tongue around the puckered flesh. Sigrid leaned back against the table behind her, and Leif helped her ease onto it. She pushed herself back as he climbed over her. He opened his mouth and took as much of her breast into the warm cavern as he could. Sigrid panted as she let her knees drop wide as he settled between her legs.

"Now, Leif."

Now that they were alone, Leif had no intention of being rushed. He pressed his thumb over the sensitive skin of her pearl and rubbed until her hips arched off the table. He withdrew his hand and thrust hard until he was seated to the hilt.

"By all the gods, the feel of you entering me is nearly enough to finish me."

Leif grunted as he set a punishing pace with his hips. Sigrid wasn't to be outdone. Her hands found her favorite place on his body, besides his cock, and slid into the grooves of his hips. She dug her fingers into his chiseled buttocks as she pushed him down toward her as she simultaneously thrust up to receive him.

"I don't want to hurt you. I'm being too rough," Leif tried to ease his pace.

"If you slow down now, I may never forgive you. Don't you dare stop. And don't keep making me say that."

"But—" Leif tried to catch his breath enough to speak, "—your body isn't used to this."

"Do you feel how wet I am? How ready my body is for you? I know what I want, Leif. And how I want it."

"If this could be our last time, I should be slow and gentle."

"No." The one word was drawn out on a moan as Sigrid's head tilted back. "We don't have time for slow. And that's not what I want right now. It can be slow next time. Right now, I want you to fuck me."

"We shall talk about that foul mouth of yours while we discuss you running away. But for now, I will indulge you, wife."

There was no more talking after that. The only sounds were Sigrid's moans as their bodies slapped together, and Leif grunted with each thrust. Their passion was a symphony to their own ears. While Leif dominated their pace, Sigrid had no problems keeping up. It was only a matter of minutes before they were both tipping over the edge into release.

"*Sigrid!*"

"*Leif!*"

They wrapped themselves in each other's embrace as sweat streamed between their bodies and coated them in a light sheen. Leif stroked the hair from Sigrid's sticky forehead as her hands continued to hold his backside, only her caress was tender.

"No matter what happens, you are mine."

Sigrid looked into Leif's iron gray eyes and a warmth spread through her before a small twinge coursed through her womb. Her eyes flickered wide as realization dawned on her. She reached for one of his hands and slid them between them. She placed his hand over her belly and covered it with her own.

"We're both yours."

Leif could only stare as he accepted what Sigrid implied. He brushed his lips across hers.

"I love you," he whispered.

"And I love you," she returned.

"Always and forever," they said together, laughing as their minds spoke what their hearts knew.

TWENTY

Leif didn't want to leave the love nest the storeroom became for them, but he knew being gone was irresponsible to begin with, and staying any longer pushed the boundaries of selfishness. Now he knew he and Sigrid conceived a child, he wanted her as far from the ensuing battle as he could get her. He would have Freya take her away. He would find ways for her to join the others wherever she sent them. Leif helped her dress, and they slipped out of the small shed. He held her hand as they returned to the group of warriors who mingled in the center of the village. Plans were being discussed as they counted and sharpened weapons. Blades were checked, arrows counted, and the weight of swords tested in the warriors' hands.

"About time," Bjorn grumbled but the ridiculous smile on his face told Leif his cousin wouldn't forget to tease him about his tryst later.

"Remember, she's my wife," Leif muttered for his cousin's ears only. Bjorn nodded, and his smile softened as he nodded to Sigrid. "Freya, I need you to take Sigrid to the others. She can't stay here."

"Leif, no." Sigrid gasped. "I have to stay. I'm not leaving you. Or the others."

"Circumstances have changed. You are not remaining here in danger."

"What circumstances?" Freya looked between the couple, but she couldn't tell what her brother meant.

"Sigrid, be angry with me all you want, but you are not staying here. Not now. You know I can't take you, but I trust Freya to keep you safe."

"I'm not leaving."

"Sigrid," Leif's tone was harder than she had ever heard it. She knew it was the one he used with his warriors. She bit her lip but shook her head. "Sigrid," Leif practically barked.

"Leif, no. Please don't send me, us," she mouthed the last word, "away. I need to stay here. What if I have another vision, and I'm not here to warn you?" Sigrid felt panic trying to claw its way into her heart. She looked around for anyone who might side with her. The looks of surprise told her they had all understood what she had tried to say silently.

"Brother, we will return when we can. If anything happens, I will send someone." Freya stepped toward Sigrid as the seer shook her head.

"No," she tried to scream, but no sound came out.

Leif kissed her once more, and she tried to cling to him as Freya pulled her away. His hands caught hers and gave them a quick squeeze before pushing them away. His heart felt like it was stone as the pain of rejection flared in Sigrid's eyes. Leif shook his head. He couldn't do it.

"Wait."

Freya looked over her shoulder as Sigrid pulled away. Leif once again caught her as she threw herself into his embrace.

"Boats!" A loud cry went up from near the gate.

Leif looked down at Sigrid. It had taken the choice from him. He realized Sigrid's stalling would keep them alive. If she and Freya had tried to leave only moments sooner, they wouldn't have made it out of the gate, anyway. And if they had, they would have been exposed to the warriors about to come ashore. His gaze swung around at the various buildings scattered around the border of the village square. He couldn't think of a safe place to hide his wife and unborn child.

"Don't worry. There's a hidden trapdoor in the storeroom we were just in. There's a cellar I can hide in."

Leif looked at her as she smiled bravely up at him. "I know you don't want to hide but thank you. I couldn't fight while worrying about you."

"I know. We'll be fine."

"Leif, go with the others. I will make sure she is well hidden," Lorna spoke up.

Leif watched for a moment before the two women walked away. He ran to join the others as they prepared for the enemy to come ashore. It was only moments later before he saw Lorna join them.

"She's safe," Lorna reassured him as she lifted her sword.

It took little time for the wave of enemy warriors to move from the docks to the bottom of the hill below the village. Leif and the warriors defending the homestead lit their arrows, and on Bjorn's command, they fired. They listened to the screams of those struck by the arrows as the slain fell to the ground. Grímr's warriors meant for the chants and banging of sword hilts against shields to intimidate them since Grímr knew his numbers were diminished, but Freya's laugh was infectious. Roaring laughter met the battle chants as Bjorn ordered the archers to let loose another round of arrows. Leif and the others used the height of the hill to their advantage as they launched not only arrows but long spears at the approaching enemy.

As the numbers thinned, the men on the walls prepared to drop burning pitch along with a limestone and sand mixture. The screams filled the air as the counterattack gained momentum. Leif, Bjorn, Freya, and Lorna led the charge as Rangvald's guards spilled out of the gates. Leif swung his sword at anyone who approached. He slashed across arms and legs as he thrust his sword into the bodies of the men who charged him. Bjorn fought at his side as they made their way toward the next wave of attackers. Freya and Lorna fought together, and Leif noticed that Lorna fought with a ferocity he recognized in Freya and Tyra. The woman was a notably well-trained warrior, which cleared Leif's conscience to focus on those who tried to cut him down.

"More boats," Bjorn panted.

"*Feun!*" Leif swore.

He and the other warriors struggled to hold off defeat. If more men and women arrived to support Grímr, who he only caught one brief glance of before other combatants separated them, then Grímr would defeat them.

"Rangvald!" He heard a woman's voice yell. "He comes!"

Leif swung again to block a sword that would have cleaved him in half and squinted at the approaching longboats. He recognized the sail. As warriors spilled over the side of the boats, a horn sounded from behind the walled fort. A new wave of warriors stormed toward the beach in a wedge formation. The new fighters plowed through many of the attackers as the numbers evened.

"Leif," came a great roar he would recognize anywhere. Leif didn't dare turn his head, but his face split in a grin.

"Father! It's about time you caught up."

His father's grunt came from beside him as the older man joined Bjorn and Leif. He fought alongside them until he spotted Freya.

"Your sister." Ivar charged through four men to take his spot fighting alongside his daughter and Lorna. The smell of burning wood joined the acrid stench of burning flesh. Rangvald torched one of Grímr's boats as he and his warriors came ashore.

Freya turned when she heard a deep baritone call out, "Mother." She watched Erik hack his way to his mother's side. Freya shifted as her fight ended with another man dead at her feet. She caught motion behind Erik and lunged forward. She let her battle ax fly over his shoulder as a man raised his mace to club Erik in the back. Erik glared at her until he heard a thunk. He turned back and saw the dead man lying sightless with an ax through his throat, his head half severed. Erik nodded before he turned to find another warrior to fight.

Another horn sounded from near the shore. Grímr's men retreated. It was only as Leif and the others charged after them that Leif's forces saw the other boats waiting. Bowmen stood on the decks ready to fire as Grímr stood, giving orders to the men wading to the boats. They pulled the last of the warriors onto the decks, and the oarsmen rowed in unison.

"Cease! It's not worth it. They are gone, and I would not lose any more people when the fight is over." Rangvald called out.

Rangvald's and Ivar's warriors lowered their weapons as they watched Grímr laugh as he offered them an obscene gesture by way of saying goodbye. Freya and Leif found Strian who fought despite his leg injury. He sustained a few more cuts but nothing serious. Bjorn limped over with Ivar and Rangvald, who held his wife against his side, her feet dangling against his shins.

"Put me down, Rang." Lorna laughed as she wiped hair from her husband's eyes.

"I shall put you down in our bed and not before," he kissed her soundly.

"Who am I to argue with you, my jarl."

"You two are worse than newlyweds," Ivar grumbled.

"You haven't a clue," Erik chuckled as he came to stand beside Freya. "Thank you."

Freya swallowed as she looked up at him and nodded. Her exhaustion kept her from doing much more. She watched as Bjorn, Strian, and Leif stood with her father. She could hear their conversation but was far too tired to join in. Freya felt Erik shift subtly next to her. He brushed his arm against her side before moving it back. It gave her the space to lean against him without it being too obvious.

"You saved me," Erik murmured. "I am grateful for that."

"Then we are even."

When Erik didn't respond, Freya glanced up. She couldn't read the look on his face, but his arm welcomed her against him.

"You shouldn't have run off like that," Ivar began. "Wait."

Leif shook his head and was ready to walk away when he heard the change in his father's tone.

"But I must admit when I am wrong. I'm not pleased that you and Bjorn left without telling me, but I'm glad you both went to protect Freya and Sigrid. It was what needed to get both me and Rangvald here in time. I can't deny any longer that Sigrid's visions are not happenstance. If she hadn't left, you wouldn't have followed. We saw the women and children evacuating with their guards. They told us Sigrid warned them they had to escape. Leif, I owe you and Sigrid an apology."

"Thank you, Father, but I only want to get my wife."

Leif didn't wait any longer. Instead, he raced back through the gates and across the village square. He threw open the door to the storeroom and stopped as all the blood drained to his toes. He took in the open trapdoor, the dead body lying beside it, and his wife standing with a bloody knife in her hand. Sigrid looked up at him, and when she recognized him, she dropped the knife. She calmly stepped over the body and leaned into Leif. After a few long moments, Leif found his voice.

"Did he hurt you?"

"No more than pulling my hair to get me out of the cellar."

"You overpowered him?"

"He didn't expect I would have a knife. When he bent over and grabbed my hair to pull me out, it put him in the right position for me to sink my blade into his throat. He stumbled backwards, but I fell when he released my hair. I banged my head, but I could still scramble out and finish him."

"I never should have left you alone."

"Shh. That's not true. It was the right choice. You could fight, and since only one man made it in here, I assume you were victorious."

"We won. For now, at least. Grímr got away again. But Rangvald and my father are here." Sigrid froze. She wasn't sure if Ivar's arrival boded poorly for them. "My father wants to apologize to you. He admits he was wrong about you and your gift. He's seen enough proof now to know he shouldn't have argued against your visions."

Sigrid smiled wanly but acquiesced as Leif guided her to the door. "Then let us see your father."

TWENTY-ONE

Leif could tell Sigrid was less than eager to see his father, but she broke out in a wide smile when she saw her family. Erik was speaking to Freya, or rather arguing from what Leif could see, but he stepped away when he saw Sigrid. He rushed to her and wrapped her in a hug Leif was sure would break her in half. Her laughter was the only thing that reassured him she could still breathe.

"I was so worried when I heard that you and Freya ran off. What were you thinking? On second thought, I don't want to hear your reasoning. I've already heard Freya's, and I'm no more pleased than I was when I discovered you gone. I don't know which of you is the worse influence."

"She is a wonderful influence, and I'm happy to call her sister." Sigrid smiled as she gave Erik another squeeze.

Erik pursed his lips and looked doubtful as he put her back on her feet. Next, Rangvald seized her in a bear hug. Leif was becoming tired of watching his wife, who he hadn't spent nearly enough time with in the past two days, being passed around like a rag doll.

"I'm well, Uncle. I promise. I'm just relieved we made it here in time to warn Aunt Lorna and the others."

"Praise the gods for that. You kept our tribe from being

wiped out. Lorna told me you got the women and children evacuated in time. I've already sent men to retrieve them."

"How long will that take, do you think?" Bjorn interjected. He looked like he could barely contain his anxiety. Sigrid hid her smile by leaning in for another embrace from her uncle.

"Two hours at the most. Are you waiting for someone?" Freya taunted.

"You know I would be sure Tyra is well. It's my fault she's injured. It's my responsibility to be sure she survives."

"Yes, duty." Freya once again taunted.

"Cousin," Bjorn warned. Freya settled for smirking. Ivar cleared his throat as he stepped forward.

"I owe you an apology and a debt of gratitude. You've been a hero to my tribe and your own more times than any young woman should have to be. My ambition and pride have helped my tribe prosper, but it also almost cost my son his fate. I see now what everyone else did days ago. You are the best match for my son, and you will be an asset to our tribe. One day you will be our people's *frú*. It's a blessing to have you. And I don't mean because you are a seer. That is a benefit for our people, but it's your spirit that makes you a treasure. I should have listened to your mother all those years ago. I'm sorry I have been unkind and unreasonable."

Everyone stood about with their mouths agog as they listened to Ivar apologize. The mountain of a man stood contrite before a woman who looked more like a wood sprite next to him than a now experienced warrior. Sigrid reached out to take both of his hands. Ivar's eyes widened as an energy shifted through their hands and along his arms to his heart.

"Your mother." His hushed words echoed in the silence of those who watched.

"Yes, she is here."

"She forgives me too?"

"I am sure she does, Jarl Ivar. She would have you know she is glad we will be family at last. It wasn't the right time all those years ago. It wasn't the right couple."

Ivar nodded as Sigrid released his hands. She was prepared to step away when he cautiously embraced her. It surprised Sigrid at how safe and natural his embrace felt after feeling like adversaries. Ivar must have felt it too because he tucked her more firmly against him.

"I know you never knew your father, but it would honor me if one day you might consider me your father." Sigrid thought he sounded almost bashful.

"I think I already do."

"Welcome." And with that, Sigrid finally felt a part of Leif's family.

"Father, I would marry Sigrid tonight. Marry her again that is. In front of you and the others."

"No—"

"*Father—"*

"Hear me out before you get your hackles up. Your mother would spear my bollocks if she missed her only son's wedding. I'm more than happy to consider you married, but the wedding must wait until your mother can be present. I can't deprive her of that. She would want to welcome Sigrid into the family."

"I don't mind waiting," Sigrid interjected as she smiled up at Leif.

"Thank you. I don't want Mother to miss it either. If my father recognizes you as my wife, then I don't mind delaying the feast."

"I would offer to host the feast, but I am sure you are eager to be home and check on your own people." Rangvald made it easy for Ivar to leave without causing offense. No one voiced a reminder of Sigrid's nightmare.

"I invite you to travel with us. If you feel safe leaving again, I would have Sigrid's family with her when our clans join by blood."

"We can be ready within the hour." Lorna shot forward.

Rangvald's laughter caught on. "The Scots like a feast

almost as much as a Norseman. She never turns down an opportunity for merriment."

"Then how did your son end up so sour?" Freya muttered. Her face flushed scarlet when she realized everyone heard her. Rangvald's laughter boomed as his wife's giggles doubled her over.

"The tartest apples make the sweetest treats." Erik replied. He leaned over and murmured in Freya's ear, "and I'm sure that makes you the tastiest treat I shall ever sample."

As unbelievable as it was, Freya's face flushed an even deeper shade of red as she shoved past Erik.

"It'll be hard to taste anything when you're missing your tongue," she hissed before storming off. The warrior's laughter joined that of his parents.

Once the women, children, and guardsmen returned, they brought a goat forward for sacrifice to the god Thor. They collected animal's blood and placed it upon the village altar as the people said a prayer of thanksgiving for the two victories their armies already claimed. Sigrid led the ceremony as the tribe's seer. Leif watched as she went through the rituals and felt a surge of pride as he looked at the woman who he'd known such a short time but who'd become vital to his very existence. He tilted his head back and looked at the stars overhead. When he saw a blaze shoot across the black backdrop, he smiled. He was sure it was the gods' way of showing their pleasure with the outcome of their plans.

Customarily, feasting would have continued throughout the night, but Sigrid's nightmare was still present in the forefront of everyone's mind. Instead, people retired early to prepare for sailing the next morning. It was already the wee hours when they each sought their beds.

Morning came abruptly for Leif. His eyes slid open expecting to see his wife sleeping next to him, but her spot was empty. He threw back the furs in a panic he dreamed their happy reunion.

"Calm down. I'm right here," Sigrid said from behind his shoulder. Leif turned to find his wife had a small bundle packed with the few belongings she would take with her. Leif noticed someone perched a *kransen* on top of the pile. Sigrid followed his gaze.

"Freya brought everything this morning. She slipped away to my hut to gather my belongings. She found the *kransen* on the ground near the trail. It doesn't seem fitting for me to wear a symbol of virginity, even if we haven't performed all the wedding rights. I'm taking it for our daughter."

Leif stood and came to stand before her. His large palm spread across her belly. "Daughter?"

Sigrid smiled up to him. "At some point. I saw her in my vision of us, but I haven't tried to learn which comes first. A son or a daughter. I would rather learn that with you. Unless you would rather I tell you." Sigrid seemed hesitant to do that, so Leif shook his head.

"I would prefer to learn just as every other couple does. The day our babe is born and placed against your breast. I want to share the joy and surprise with you when the time comes."

"And you wouldn't mind if the gods give us a girl first?"

"As long as the gods keep you and our children safe, I don't mind what we have or what order they might come in." Leif kissed her tenderly as their love flowed freely between them.

"I'm sorry if I startled you by not being next to you when you woke. You slept like the dead, so when I heard someone at the door, I got there before there was even a knock. It was only a few minutes ago."

It shocked Leif that he slept through anyone moving around. He was a light sleeper for the exact purpose of knowing who was nearby and to be alert in case of attack.

"Come. You can protect me in our sleep tonight. Now we

need to leave." Leif chortled as he followed his perceptive wife into the early morning rays. "And it doesn't take being a seer to know that's what you were thinking. It was written across your face."

Leif sighed as he wrapped his arm around her and kissed the top of her head. They had fallen asleep in each other's arms as soon as they laid down. Leif didn't mind in the least. The intimacy of spending the entire night with Sigrid held its own magic and power over him. They caught up with the others as they brought Tyra aboard Freya's longboat. Sigrid looked about for Bjorn and found the man scowling on the deck of his own boat.

"He must let go of his guilt. Tyra won't blame him. I'm sure of it." Leif mused. "The only thing Tyra won't like is if he binds his fate to hers because he feels a life's debt for her injury. She might kill him to be rid of him. They have never gotten along that well."

"I remember hearing that." Sigrid said nothing more as she looked once again at Bjorn before returning Strian's wave. Captained by her first mate, Tyra's boat shoved off with the rest of the flotilla that included Ivar's, Erik's, and Rangvald's boats along with the five captains. The voyage was quiet, and Sigrid suspected no enemy was foolish enough to take on such a contingent on the water. The wind was at their backs, so they made the journey with ease. Sigrid shaded her eyes from the early evening sun as they drew close to Leif's home.

"That's my mother." Leif pointed to a solitary figure who stood at the top of a cliff.

"Wife!" Ivar's call could be heard as his voice bounced off the fjord's cliff walls.

"Husband!" Came a softer, albeit sure, response.

Leif waved to his mother just as Freya did too. Leif smiled down at Sigrid as he watched her bite her lip as she watched Lena move along the ridge to meet them at the docks.

"You have nothing to fear. She'll be on your side. My mother often reminds my father that his pride will be his downfall. She'll love you soon enough. Mother's much more reasonable than Father."

Sigrid inhaled as she felt some tension release from between her shoulder blades and around her neck. She watched the boats pull in along the docks. Those that didn't fit anchored close to shore. Leif jumped into the low surf and lifted Sigrid into his arms as he carried her to the beach.

"Let me enjoy it. My mother and my people won't think you weak. They will see I am a husband in love with his wife."

Sigrid's lips twisted to the side before she offered him a half smile. He tickled her, and her responding laugh made Leif know that, at least for the moment, life was as it should be.

TWENTY-TWO

Lena watched as the war party made their way toward her. She spotted her husband and two children. She watched with curiosity as Leif approached carrying a young woman. Her breath caught as she recognized the young woman's face.

"Signy. You must be Signy's daughter." Lena beamed as she stepped forward to welcome Sigrid. Leif felt his bride relax in his arms when she heard the warmth in his mother's tones. "I would recognize you anywhere. You look just like her."

Leif set Sigrid on her feet and encircled her with one arm as he embraced his mother with his other. Leif would never admit out loud what a relief it always was to receive this first hug from his mother whenever he returned home. He knew he would never outgrow the sense of peace and safety it brought him. He knew she understood, and it was a secret they shared between the two of them, though he suspected Freya felt the same way.

"Mother, I would like you to meet Sigrid. My wife." Leif's smile slipped when he saw the flash of hurt in his mother's eyes.

"My lady, we married by making our pledges to one another, but we should very much like it if we could hold a proper wedding here." Sigrid stepped in. Leif would thank her later for having the tact he lacked.

"Signy was right all along. You two were meant for one another." Lena looked between the two and observed how Leif hadn't yet let go of his pretty bride. She noticed how Sigrid leaned into Leif's side without even seeming to realize it. "You love each other."

Leif beamed as he leaned forward to kiss his mother's cheek. "We do. Very much."

"Before you crow about how you told me so, I should like a proper greeting, Wife. I'm growing very impatient." Ivar turned his wife as he took her into his arms.

"If you would simply accept that I am right, you old goat, we could save ourselves a great deal of time."

"The only thing you need to be right about is how you will kiss me," Ivar teased before claiming his wife's full attention.

"They are no better than my parents," Erik quipped as he and Freya came to stand with Leif and Sigrid. When Ivar released Lena, she almost pushed him over as she scrambled away.

"Freya, my love." Affection from their mother was the only kind Leif ever saw Freya accept in public. The women entwined themselves with each other as they whispered in one another's ear.

"How soon they forget us, Son." Ivar clapped Leif on the shoulder as the group ambled toward the village.

"Where are Tyra and Bjorn?" Lena asked.

"Mother, Tyra was injured while she and Bjorn fought together. He is with her as Lorna prepares for him to carry Tyra to her longhouse. He blames himself for what happened." Freya explained the rest of what happened during the battle as Strian and Rangvald joined them.

"Lorna will join us as soon as she and Bjorn see Tyra

settled. She woke just after Freya disembarked," Rangvald explained.

Freya turned back toward the boat, but Erik stepped next to her. "Tyra receives the best care. My mother's with her. Give her a few minutes to settle Tyra and to chase Bjorn away. He has been a bowstring ready to pop. Go in there now, and you may be on the receiving end of his frustrations. He won't unleash his temper on my mother, but he will on you." Erik looked down at Freya before checking over his shoulder. When he returned his gaze to hers, Freya saw something she didn't understand. "And I don't know how forgiving I can be."

Freya's brow crinkled, but she didn't ask any questions because they reached her parents' longhouse.

"We already have guest chambers prepared, so it should only be a few moments before they settle your belongings. I will send thralls to show you to the bathhouses," Lena explained.

"Mother, I would like the wedding to happen tonight. I know it's short notice, but I would have our people know Sigrid holds the place of distinction as my wife. I wouldn't want them to misunderstand how things stand."

Lena looked between the couple and then at her husband. The eagerness in the couple's face and the resignation in her husband's eyes made her smile.

"Then I shall have to arrange for us to prepare more food. When Lorna comes ashore, she can join Freya and me as we prepare Sigrid. Send her to the bathhouse when she's ready. Freya, Sigrid, let's gather what we shall need."

Lena took one hand as Freya took the other, leaving Sigrid to look back at Leif as they towed her away. His laughter made her scowl and stick out her tongue at him. She saw the laughter fade and the fire ignite as he marched forward. He caught her around the waist and spun her in the air as Freya and Lena gasped. His mouth crashed down on Sigrid's, and she welcomed the invasion, albeit short and swift. Leif tapped her on the backside.

"I shall remind you of that when we are alone, cheeky minx."

Sigrid stood on her toes and strained to whisper in his ear, "I should hope so." Leif growled and reached for her again, but Sigrid danced away. "Patience, my love. It's only a couple of hours. It's not like it's ten years."

Leif listened to Sigrid's laughter as it faded away when the women entered the longhouse. It tempted him to wait there for when they exited to go to the bathhouse.

"Leave them to their preparations. You have your own to perform." Ivar tilted his head to where Rangvald, Erik, Strian, and now Bjorn waited with silly grins on their faces. Leif shook his head.

"Oh no. We already pledged to one another. It's only the sacrifice that needs to take place to seal the marriage." None of the men were listening as they herded him toward the small graveyard where stacked catacombs created a final resting place for those who didn't go to Valhalla on a pyre. "Father, this is unnecessary. Besides, Erik, Bjorn, and Strian are unmarried. They're not part of this ritual. I doubt Rangvald will feel cheated if we don't do it. He's the only other married man who is now part of our family."

"But I would," chortled Rangvald. Leif glowered. "Afraid of becoming a man?"

Leif bit his tongue before he insulted the other jarl. "Which one?" Leif ground out between his teeth.

"Let me see if I remember. I set this tomb aside for you so long ago, but you welcomed none of my suggested brides. I suppose I can accept that now. I believe it's the second from the top right."

Leif looked at the tombs and felt a sense of dread slither through him. It was one thing to see a man die on the battlefield, to even be the cause, but it was something different to climb around the remains of those buried below his feet.

"You had better be remembering the right one, Father."

Leif made his way up to the tomb his father indicated and

rolled away the stones that sealed the entrance. He held his breath, anticipating a death stench, but no odor met his nostrils. The tomb was large enough for him to crawl inside. The lighting was next to none as his own body blocked any sunlight from entering. He felt around but his hands touched no cloth or bones. Instead, they brushed against the cold metal of a sword. He breathed a sigh of relief when he realized the only thing occupying the tomb was the ancestral sword. His father had spared him. He pulled the sword along with him as he backed out. He pushed most of the rocks back into place as he carefully maneuvered himself and the ancient sword back to the ground.

Ivar stood before Leif looking prouder than perhaps he had been after Leif's first battle. "Leif, you have proved yourself a man many times over. But taking a wife means beginning a family of your own, and with that comes responsibilities unlike any you have carried before. Leaving your bachelorhood behind means leaving the last remnants of your boyhood behind and emerging as a man, just as entering the grave and returning with the sword symbolizes. I don't say this often enough, or perhaps not enough people hear it, but I am proud of you, Son, and I am proud of the man you have become." Ivar placed his hands on the sides of Leif's shoulders and added, "I love you, Son."

"Thank you, Father. I love you, too."

"Then let us head to the bathhouse. You have quite the stench to wash off you."

The men walked together, joking about the upcoming ceremony, and spotted the women just as they entered their bathhouse. Leif's mind leaped to an image of Sigrid naked before him as they bathed together. *Tomorrow.*

He chanced a look around to see if anyone could read his thoughts, but the look of hunger on Erik's face shocked him. His eyebrows lowered as he considered for the first time that perhaps Erik thought he might marry Sigrid one day. They were close as both family and friends. It wouldn't be unheard of for cousins to marry, especially since it would have kept a talented seer in their village. Erik must have sensed Leif's gaze because he turned to him after clearing the emotions from his face.

"She's not the one I'm looking at."

Erik said nothing more as they entered the main chamber. Steam was already filling the room as the men found their tubs and climbed in after stripping down. Leif ran the soap over himself as he pictured Sigrid doing the same, or better yet, them doing it for one another. His cock twitched, and he forced himself to pay attention to the conversation around him. The last thing he needed was to stand up with a raging cockstand in front of his father, his bride's uncle and cousin, his own cousin, and his friend. He took deep breaths and settled, even though his attention was everywhere but the conversation flowing around him. He wondered what it would be like to live with Sigrid without the fear of battle or abduction looming over them. To leave in the morning to train and return to her in the evening for the meal. To share their tales of the day and prepare for bed together. He wondered whether she would agree to sail with him when he voyaged to Scotland. He daydreamed about waking up next to her in their chamber, their bed, with no worry of discovery or disturbance.

It seemed like only moments before the other men were standing and readying to move to the next chamber. They wrapped their hips in linens just long enough to pass through a door that led to an enclosed section of the fjord. Bjorn and Strian teased one another and included Erik as they jumped into the icy water. Leif laughed and joined them even though most of his mind was on what his bride might be doing on just the other side of the wall.

. . .

Sigrid could hear the men laughing through the wood partition. She knew they were enjoying the final cold dunk after relaxing in the steamy air and hot water. Freya, Lorna, and Lena all listened too, even though they could make out none of the men's words.

"Sounds like they're enjoying themselves," Lorna jutted her chin toward the noise.

"I imagine that is Bjorn and Strian more than the others." Lena cocked her head to one side as she remembered something. "Bjorn and Strian once dared Leif to stay in there for five minutes. They promised him their slingshots and desserts for a week if he could do it."

"And I'm the one who fished him out," Freya interjected. "After he practically froze to death. He refused to get out even when those two idiots realized he was in danger."

"What were you doing there?" Sigrid wondered.

"I wasn't. I was in here but heard them shouting at him. I got worried and rushed in. I'm glad I did. They stood on the side trying to convince him to come out while I jumped in and pulled him out."

"That sounds like Erik and his brothers. What is it about practically freezing to death that is both amusing and daring for our men?"

"I would say it's comparing the size of their cocks, but they shrivel in the cold."

"Freya." Her mother admonished, but her struggle to keep from smiling took the edge off her tone.

The noise on the other side of the wall ceased, and Sigrid assumed the men left to finish their preparations. Sigrid's bathing served the practical purpose of scrubbing away the filth from all she endured since leaving her hut rather than the ritual of scrubbing away her virginity. It had been nice to spend time with the other women. She wished Tyra could join them. She didn't know the other woman at all, but she sensed she would. She wished for Leif's sake that everyone who mattered to him could be there.

The women returned to Lena's longhouse and went to her chamber. They helped Sigrid dress in a gown Freya collected for her. After they brushed her hair until it shone like a white beacon, Lorna placed a crown on her head.

"This was your mother's. Signy wore it the day she married your father. She was the most resplendent bride I have ever seen, and you are the mirror image of her. She is so proud of you as is your father. I am sure they watch this day together."

"Thank you, Aunt Lorna." Sigrid choked out the words.

"It's time." Lena's hushed voice brought the women to their feet.

Leif was already waiting near the altar with his family and the rest of the village when the women arrived. Sigrid could see he wore his finest clothes and carried a sword she didn't recognize as his. She smiled to herself as she realized he must have been through the ritual and didn't envy him having to open a tomb. She saw a war hammer tucked into his belt to honor Thor and ensure a fruitful marriage.

As Sigrid neared Leif, she felt a wave of panic as she realized as an orphan, she had no one to pay the bride-price. She looked at Rangvald in a moment of worry, but his smile reassured her everything was settled. Sigrid met Leif in front of the altar and looked around. She spotted Tyra sitting in a chair with Bjorn and Strian on either side. Freya and Erik stood behind Tyra. She gave them a small wave before beaming up at Leif.

"Everyone you love is here."

"And the one I love most, my wife, is here before me."

The ceremony began as Leif's tribal holy man called for the gods' and goddesses' attention. It continued in a blur for Leif as he watched Rangvald step forward leading a goat for sacrifice along with a dowry he never expected. Leif presented Sigrid with the sword he had recovered earlier in the day. They would save it for their oldest son. Erik stepped forward next to offer Sigrid a sword she passed to Leif. The hilt of each sword held a ring that the shaman blessed. It was this exchange of rings that brought clarity back to Leif. He slid the ring onto Sigrid's finger and waited as she moved the ring meant for him over the notch of his knuckle.

"It's done." Leif's reverent voice enveloped her as he stroked Sigrid's cheek, a tiny tear dribbling from her eye. "Your mother's prophecy has come to be. I love you, Sigrid."

"I love you, too, Leif. I can feel my mother and father here with us. They are ready to feast with us."

The entire village congregated in the large hall of Ivar and Lena's longhouse. The celebrations began with Leif placing his Thor's hammer in Sigrid's lap just as he had placed his hammer necklace in her lap several days earlier. The crowd banged their mugs on the tables as thralls wove among the crowd to bring large serving platters of food to the tables. They reconfigured the head table to make room for their honored guests along with Strian and Tyra, who looked ashen and weak but happy to be a part of the merriment.

Someone placed a large pitcher of honeyed mead between Sigrid and Leif. People refilled their mugs throughout the feast to ensure they were both so inebriated they could hardly walk to their chamber, but it ensured their marriage was official. The celebrations continued into the early morning hours, even though Leif carried Sigrid to their bed. It was the first time she had been in his chamber. She saw where someone placed her belongings and noticed someone turned the bed down along with a plate of food laid out near the fire.

"Does this meet with your approval?" Leif drawled as he undressed his stunning bride.

"You've always met with my approval." Sigrid's saucy reply earned her a scorching kiss before Leif tapped her backside.

"That wasn't what I meant, and you know it, cheeky minx."

"It was what I meant." Sigrid assisted Leif in removing his clothes but paused to look around the room. She took in the shield hanging near the fireplace along with the sword she recognized as his. She saw the gold chalices and plates he must have captured while raiding. She looked at the furs that covered the floor and wiggled her toes in the one she stood on. Sigrid stepped away to examine the large bed that took up the center of the chamber. She recognized it from her visions, but she forced any thoughts of Leif's past from her mind.

Sigrid felt the backs of his hands brush along her shoulders before skimming down her arms. His warm hands spread across her middle as he pressed his chest against her back. She could feel his arousal and inhaled the scent she would recognize as his, even if she lost every other sense.

"This is where I intended to make love to you for the first time. I was so sure during that first time I kissed you in Freya's cabin."

"Do you regret it isn't?"

"Not in the least. I intend this to be the place where we create future members of our family." Leif nudged her hair aside as he kissed the sensitive skin on the crook of her neck. "This chamber felt lonely. I felt lonely. Now, with you here, I have a new sense of home. I am where I belong. It's not this chamber or this longhouse alone that makes it feel like home. It's being here with you. I am home when I am with you."

Sigrid turned in his arms and slid her hands over his bare chest until she could link her fingers against his hairline.

"It has been half my life since I felt like I belonged. You welcomed me without questions and have held faith in me despite how outlandish the future may have sounded to you. You've protected and loved me without reservation. My past and my future have melded into one. I am home because I am with you."

They spent the rest of the night in waves of ecstasy and sleep as the pleasure of lovemaking and the effects of the mead claimed them. It was well into the next afternoon before they emerged, and that was only once they ran out of food. They entered the main hall just as the thralls served the evening meal. Leif's people cheered their arrival, calling out blessings to the new couple. It relieved him to see the warm welcomes offered to Sigrid, who glowed with happiness. He noticed the light tinge of pink in her cheeks when some blessings were a little off color. They made their way to the jarl's table where his parents and in-laws welcomed him.

Freya wore a gown once again. She looked more at ease than she had in the past when she wore one. Leif made a note to himself to ask her about it later. Bjorn moved down a seat from where he had sat since they were children. Sigrid now sat to Leif's right while he remained at Ivar's right. Erik sat to Freya's left followed by his parents. Leif noticed that Strian sat with Tyra's family now that he had none of his own left. Tyra was noticeably absent, and when Leif looked down at Bjorn, he noticed he too was staring at the vacant seat. Bjorn lifted his mug and drained it in one gulp. Leif made another note to speak to his cousin. He would help his best friend assuage his guilt before it consumed him. Until then, he held Sigrid's hand as they rested on the table.

The night progressed with music and dancing along with copious amounts of food and drink. Ivar convinced Rangvald to stay on longer. Lorna worried their younger children, which rounded out their family to seven, would be too much of a burden. Lena promised they built the longhouse so large to not only accommodate but encourage guests. Sigrid looked at Leif when they both heard this. Sadness flashed in Sigrid's eyes as Leif offered her a weak smile. They both knew the truth was the home was made to accommodate more of the jarl's children, but only Freya and Leif had survived.

"Do you mind if we live here for a while before I build you a new home? I think my parents would enjoy having us here once the babe is born."

"My visions always involved us having two children before we moved to our longhouse."

Leif lifted Sigrid's hand and kissed each of her knuckles before whisking her into a dance. Leif twirled Sigrid and laughed along with her.

This woman has always been my destiny. The gods have blessed me, and I shall remember that every day for the rest of our lives.

EPILOGUE

Sigrid couldn't catch her breath as she reached behind her to shake Leif awake.

"Leif," she hissed, "Leif, wake up."

"Sigrid?" His groggy voice reached her ears, but she felt him reach for her.

"Get the midwife."

Leif snapped awake, and when he sat upright, he saw stars. "What's wrong? Has something happened to the babe? Did you envision the babe?"

"The only thing happening is this little one will be here before you come back with the midwife if you don't hurry."

Leif scrambled from the bed as he hopped about on one foot and then the other as he pulled his breeches on. He didn't bother with a shirt or boots as he bolted from their chamber. She winced as she heard him pounding on what must have been his parents' door.

Sigrid glanced over at the little boy sleeping on a small trundle bed close to her side of the bed. Their little redheaded son was almost two and the spitting image of his grandfather all the way down to his temper, which Sigrid attributed to the little boy's father as much as his grandfather. While they named their son Thorsen for the storm he was born during, it seemed worthy of his strong disposition. Affectionate with his parents and family, Thorsen was already a force to be reckoned with when frustrated. Sigrid smiled at the soft gurgling sounds the toddler made in his sleep.

It wasn't long before Lena glided into the chamber. She looked over at Sigrid before picking Thorsen up. She arranged him in her arms before coming to Sigrid. Lena bent low enough for Sigrid to kiss her son's cheek.

"Don't worry. I will keep him occupied once he wakes. He's in good hands."

"The best of hands. My thanks—" The rest of what Sigrid would have said was cut off by the sharp pain of a contraction.

"Where is that husband of yours?"

"I'm here." Leif rushed to Sigrid's side while Helga, the aged midwife, took her time as she set up her supplies. Leif helped ease Sigrid back onto the bed as Lorna, Freya, and Tyra entered.

"We heard the bull roaring and figured the babe was on the way." Freya grinned at her brother as she waddled toward them. She rubbed her hand over her own expanding belly.

"Don't be so hard on him. You know neither of our husbands will be any better," Tyra offered as she leaned against the bed post, her own rounded belly making it hard to stand for long.

"They will be far worse than I am. At least I know what to expect now." Leif kissed Sigrid on the forehead before straightening. "Well, then. Shall I leave you to it?"

Sigrid snatched his hand into her punishing grip, leaving Leif no chance to stifle his yelp. All the women, including the hard-of-hearing Helga, laughed. "Don't think for even a moment you are leaving me here."

Leif breathed easy. He had no desire to leave his wife, but he wouldn't have stayed if she wished for privacy from a man being present. "I wouldn't dream of it, my love, if that's not what you want."

"Such gallantry, Brother. You aren't fooling any of us. We know you don't want to leave. Just admit it. We might even think more of you for it." Leif marveled at how marriage had done little to curb his sister's sharp tongue and dry humor. "I know that look. Leave my husband out of it. He handles me just fine."

Freya winked as once again she rubbed her belly. Sigrid tried to laugh along with her sister-in-law and friend, but another contraction ripped across her abdomen as it tightened. Leif slid onto the bed and positioned himself behind her back. She wrapped an arm around each of his knees as the midwife examined her.

"This shall be over in a matter of minutes, my lady. It is a good thing you finally summoned me."

"Finally?" Leif twisted to look at Sigrid.

"Mmm. Yes. My contractions started early last evening. They were not very strong, and you distracted me from them for much of the night." Sigrid's cheeks burned as she admitted that in front of her husband's sister and their close friend. "They woke me a few hours ago, but they weren't close enough to disturb anyone."

"You mean you've been in pain for hours and didn't wake me, didn't say anything?" Leif sounded almost angry.

"My love, there's nothing you could have done but miss out on your sleep too."

"I could have kept you company. I could have held you and rubbed your back."

Sigrid rested her head against his shoulder. "I'll be sure to let you know next time. You can be at my side for all the tweaks and aches. You will find it quite boring."

"Next time?"

"Don't ask for what you aren't ready to know."

Leif sometimes became frustrated when he knew there were things his wife didn't feel comfortable sharing with him. He understood the reasoning and knew she didn't enjoy keeping secrets from him, but it rankled from time to time. He also knew she most likely shared more than she should. However, this was one time when she was right to hold back. He struggled with seeing his wife in this much pain again, let alone several more times. When they first arrived home, he joked he would keep her pregnant every year for the next thirty as he watched her body fill out and the happiness that settled over her. But it had taken only moments of being present for Thorsen's birth to make him consider never risking impregnating his wife again. That resolve lasted a mere minute the first time Sigrid initiated their lovemaking after her recovery.

Leif tried to find that resolve again as he felt her entire body bear down to push. It was only a matter of four pushes before their daughter entered the world. The smack and then wail echoed through the chamber as Helga placed the baby in Sigrid's arms. Leif helped support Sigrid as she brought the baby to her breast, and Leif accepted their family wasn't done growing. He also surmised he was where he should be. Husband and father, lover and teacher. Sigrid lifted her chin for a kiss that was tender and filled with devotion. Leif ran his finger along his daughter's downy cheek as she slept in her mother's arms, and Sigrid drifted to sleep in Leif's. Leif held his little family until his mother returned with Thorsen who had slept through it all. The four of them settled on the bed encircled by a fate filled with love and happiness.

THANK YOU FOR READING LEIF

Celeste Barclay, a nom de plume, lives near the Southern California coast with her husband and sons. Growing up in the Midwest, Celeste enjoyed spending as much time in and on the water as she could. Now she lives near the beach. She's an avid swimmer, a hopeful future surfer, and a former rower. When she's not writing, she's working or being a mom.

Subscribe to Celeste's bimonthly newsletter to receive exclusive insider perks.
Subscribe Now

www.celestebarclay.com

Join the fun and get exclusive insider giveaways, sneak peeks, and new release announcements in
Celeste Barclay's Facebook Ladies of Yore Group

VIKING GLORY

Leif **BOOK 1**

Freya **BOOK 2**

Tyra & Bjorn **BOOK 3**

Strian **BOOK 4**

Lena & Ivar **BOOK 5**

THE HIGHLAND LADIES

A Spinster at the Highland Court
BOOK 1 SNEAK PEEK

Elizabeth Fraser looked around the royal chapel within Stirling Castle. The ornate candlestick holders on the altar glistened and reflected the light from the ones in the wall sconces as the priest intoned the holy prayers of the Advent season. Elizabeth kept her head bowed as though in prayer, but her green eyes swept the congregation. She watched the other ladies-in-waiting, many of whom were doing the same thing. She caught the eye of Allyson Elliott. Elizabeth raised one eyebrow as Allyson's lips twitched. Both women had been there enough times to accept they'd be kneeling for at least the next hour as the Latin service carried on. Elizabeth understood the Mass thanks to her cousin Deirdre Fraser, or rather now Deirdre Sinclair. Elizabeth's mind flashed to the recent struggle her cousin faced as she reunited with her husband Magnus after a seven-year separation. Her aunt and uncle's choice to keep Deirdre hidden from her husband simply because they didn't think the Sinclairs were an advantageous enough match, and the resulting scandal, still humiliated the other Fraser clan members at court. She admired Deirdre's husband Magnus's pledge to remain faithful despite not knowing if he'd ever see Deirdre again.

Elizabeth suddenly snapped her attention; while everyone else intoned the twelfth—or was it thirteenth—amen of the Mass, the hairs on the back of her neck stood up. She had the strongest feeling that someone was watching her. Her eyes scanned to her right, where her parents sat further down the pew. Her mother and father had their heads bowed and eyes closed. While she was convinced her mother was in devout prayer, she wondered if her father had fallen asleep during the Mass. Again. With nothing seeming out of the ordinary and no one visibly paying attention to her, her eyes swung to the left. She took in the king and queen as they kneeled together at their prie-dieu. The queen's lips moved as she recited the liturgy in silence. The king was as still as a statue. Years of leading warriors showed, both in his stature and his ability to control his body into absolute stillness. Elizabeth peered past the royal couple and found herself looking into the astute hazel eyes of Edward Bruce, Lord of Badenoch and Lochaber. His gaze gave her the sense that he peered into her thoughts, as though he were assessing her. She tried to keep her face neutral as heat surged up her neck. She prayed her face didn't redden as much as her neck must have, but at a twenty-one, she still hadn't mastered how to control her blushing. Her nape burned like it was on fire. She canted her head slightly before looking up at the crucifix hanging over the altar. She closed her eyes and tried to invoke the image of the Lord that usually centered her when her mind wandered during Mass.

Elizabeth sensed Edward's gaze remained on her. She didn't understand how she was so sure that he was looking at her. She didn't have any special gifts of perception or sight, but her intuition screamed that he was still looking.

A Spy at the Highland Court **BOOK 2**

A Wallflower at the Highland Court **BOOK 3**

A Rogue at the Highland Court **BOOK 4**

A Rake at the Highland Court **BOOK 5**

An Enemy at the Highland Court **BOOK 6**

A Saint at the Highland Court **BOOK 7**

A Beauty at the Highland Court **BOOK 8**

A Sinner at the Highland Court **BOOK 9**

A Hellion at the Highland Court **BOOK 10**

An Angel at the Highland Court **BOOK 11**

A Harlot at the Highland Court **BOOK 12**

A Friend at the Highland Court **BOOK 13**

An Outsider at the Highland Court **BOOK 14**

A Devil at the Highland Court **BOOK 15**

THE CLAN SINCLAIR

His Highland Lass **BOOK 1 SNEAK PEEK**

She entered the great hall like a strong spring storm in the northern most Highlands. Tristan Mackay felt like he had been blown hither and yon. As the storm settled, she left him with the sweet scents of heather and lavender wafting towards him as she approached. She was not a classic beauty, tall and willowy like the women at court. Her face and form were not what legends were made of. But she held a unique appeal unlike any he had seen before. He could not take his eyes off of her long chestnut hair that had strands of fire and burnt copper running through them. Unlike the waves or curls he was used to, her hair was unusually straight and fine. It looked like a waterfall cascading down her back. While she was not tall, neither was she short. She had a figure that was meant for a man to grasp and hold onto, whether from the front or from behind. She had an aura of confidence and charm, but not arrogance or conceit like many good looking women he had met. She did not seem to know her own appeal. He could tell that she was many things, but one thing she was not was his.

His Bonnie Highland Temptation **BOOK 2**
His Highland Prize **BOOK 3**
His Highland Pledge **BOOK 4**
His Highland Surprise **BOOK 5**
Their Highland Beginning **BOOK 6**

PIRATES OF THE ISLES

The Blond Devil of the Sea **BOOK 1 SNEAK PEEK**

Caragh lifted her torch into the air as she made her way down the precarious Cornish cliffside. She made out the hulking shape of a ship, but the dead of night made it impossible to see who was there. She and the fishermen of Bedruthan Steps weren't expecting any shipments that night. But her younger brother Eddie, who stood watch at the entrance to their hiding place, had spotted the ship and signaled up to the village watchman, who alerted Caragh.

As her boot slid along the dirt and sand, she cursed having to carry the torch and wished she could have sunlight to guide her. She knew these cliffs well, and it was for that reason it was better that she moved slowly than stop moving once and for all. Caragh feared the light from her torch would carry out to the boat. Despite her efforts to keep the flame small, the solitary light would be a beacon.

When Caragh came to the final twist in the path before the sand, she snuffed out her torch and started to run to the cave where the main source of the village's income lay in hiding. She heard movement along the trail above her head and knew the local fishermen would soon join her on the beach. These men, both young and old, were strong from days spent pulling in the full trawling nets and hoisting the larger catches onto their boats. However, these men weren't well-trained swordsmen, and the fear of pirate raids was ever-present. Caragh feared that was who the villagers would face that night.

The Dark Heart of the Sea **BOOK 2**
The Red Drifter of the Sea **BOOK3**
The Scarlet Blade of the Sea **BOOK 4**